Praise for *Pleasantly Disturbe*

'Alive and kicking with big laug

'Effortlessly evoking its Eighties Midlands setting, *Pleasantly Disturbed* is a compulsive coming-of-age mystery that packs as many twists as a midnight burn-up across the Peaks with the humour of vintage *Smash Hits* and, at its core, a love story to rival *Gregory's Girl* – all set to a *Glittering Prize* of a soundtrack. I absolutely loved it.'

Cathi Unsworth – author of ***Season of the Witch: The Book of Goth*** and ***Weirdo***

'An upbeat love letter to the importance of popular music, *Pleasantly Disturbed* shows how it can educate and encourage the young to reject the restraints placed upon them by class prejudice and take control of their lives. While this novel shares the broader locations and sentiments of the great Alan Sillitoe, it delivers its story and message with Lee Stuart Evans's trademark humour and decency. This book will warm your heart. It will also make you chuckle.'

John King – best-selling author of ***The Football Factory*** and ***Human Punk***

'The world is complicated and cruel, but if I could switch on a button that allows me to come at it with all the guileless good faith that this book's teenage protagonist does, I'd be just fine. I laughed like a drain and my appreciation of Simple Minds was quadrupled. Magnificent.'

Pete Paphides – author of the smash hit memoir ***Broken Greek***

'My favourite funny writer.'

Harry Hill

Praise for *Words Best Sung*

'I very much enjoyed this debut novel. If you're a fan of *Billy Liar*, going down to London and the Kinks, so will you...' *#smashing*
Andy Miller – author of ***The Year of Reading Dangerously***

'Hilarious, touching, romantic... a really cracking read.'
Sally Lindsay

'Cracking debut... plenty of laugh-out-loud lines... will be loved by anyone with a fondness for the Swinging Sixties.'
John Baird – Nottingham UNESCO City of Literature

'A real understanding of the twists and turns of young love... Thoroughly enjoyable.'
Andy Smart – The Comedy Store Players

'A beautifully realised coming-of-age story...'
Clare Harvey – author of ***The Night Raid***

'A lovely, heartfelt story...'
Dave Johns – star of ***I, Daniel Blake***

***Words Best Sung** was Nottingham UNESCO City of Literature's Summer Read 2018 and named among The Best 100 Nottingham Novels.*

Pleasantly DISTURBED

Lee Stuart Evans was born in Chesterfield and grew up in north Nottinghamshire. A full-time comedy writer since 2002, he has written jokes and scripts for many brilliant and funny performers including Sean Lock, Harry Hill, Dawn French, Patrick Kielty, Frank Skinner, Jimmy Carr, Julie Walters, Jonathan Ross and many others. Some jokes Lee co-wrote for Ant & Dec about a former prime minister were mentioned in the Houses of Parliament and nominated for a BAFTA. His first novel, *Words Best Sung*, was published in 2017.

Pleasantly Disturbed

LEE STUART EVANS

Scratching Shed Publishing Ltd

Copyright © Lee Stuart Evans 2024
All rights reserved
The moral right of the author has been asserted
First published by Scratching Shed Publishing Ltd in 2024
Registered in England & Wales No. 6588772
Registered office: 47 Street Lane, Leeds, West Yorkshire. LS8 1AP
www.scratchingshedpublishing.co.uk
ISBN: 978-1068618925

No part of this book may be reproduced or transmitted in any form or by any other means without the written permission of the publisher, except by a reviewer who wishes to quote brief passages in connection with a review written for insertion in a magazine, newspaper or broadcast.

Every effort has been made to obtain the necessary permissions with reference to copyright material, both illustrative and quoted. We apologise for any omissions in this respect and will be pleased to make the appropriate acknowledgements in any future edition.

This is a work of fiction. All characters and events, other than those clearly in the public domain, are either the product of the author's imagination or are used fictitiously, and any resemblance to real persons, living or dead, is entirely coincidental.

A catalogue record for this book is available from the British Library.

Printed and bound in the UK
by TJ Books

Trecerus Industrial Estate, Padstow,
Cornwall PL28 8RW
www.tjbooks.co.uk

For Nina, Alfie and George

pleasantly *adv affably; good-humouredly; cheerfully.*

disturbed *adj worried; confused, esp emotionally.*

Prologue

Once Upon A Time

'You don't care?' said the careers adviser, sucking salad cream highlights from his moustache. 'That's the attitude you take towards your future, is it, Robin? *You don't care?*'

'I didn't say that, sir. I said –'

'Speak up, lad. You weren't shy of opening your mouth when you were carrying-on outside, were you? Yes, don't think I couldn't hear you. Now what did you say?'

He was not even a proper careers adviser, just a slack-time-tabled games teacher with a sideline in youth (un)employment propaganda. They could never fool me. I knew a whistle when I saw one. And a tracksuit. It was a waste of time, of course, his *and* mine. I'd long known who I wanted to be. Was *going* to be. And by the time the Fifth Year was summoned to room 12B, to hear how we might least destructively fritter away our sure to be inconsequential lives, my mind was made up.

'Jim Kerr, sir,' I said, raising my voice. 'You said what do I want to do when I leave school, sir. I want to be Jim Kerr, sir.'

'Jim Kerr?'

'From Simple Minds, sir. You must have heard of them, sir.'

'Must I?'

'Jim's the singer, sir – and lyricist – he formed the band with his friend Charlie Burchill – he's the guitarist – in Glasgow in nineteen-seventy-sev–'

'All right, all right, settle down. You don't need to tell *me* about simple minds, not this week.'

The careers adviser stood to remove his tracksuit top, draping it carefully round the scuffed shoulders of his grey plastic chair before, seated once more, he flicked open a cardboard file, sniffed at some indecipherable scrawl for about three seconds, then pushed it aside to lean forward with his elbows hard on the desk.

'Robin, have you thought about The Metal Box Company?'

'No, sir,' I answered truthfully. 'Why would I do that, sir?'

'They make biscuit tins, for Crawford's and Rowntree Mackintosh.'

'Right. Do they also make knickers and bras for Marks & Spencer, sir?'

'What? No, of course they don't. It's Morton Lendrex who make all the, um, ladies' underwear. And not just for Marks & Spencer.'

'Well, you'd know, sir.'

'*Hmm*? What do you mean by that, Robin?'

'You being a careers adviser, sir.' It was my turn to lean forward now. 'You were talking a lot about knickers and bras to that girl you had in here before me. Yes, I could hear you as well, sir. I thought it might all be the same place, one big factory full of knickers and biscuits. You could call it *Bums & Crumbs*, sir, if you like.'

'If I *like*?'

'Unless you can come up with something better, sir. Go on, sir, I bet you can't, sir.'

The careers adviser slumped back in his chair, whistling like a burst tyre as he turned to the window and gazed out at the frozen sports field as if through barbed wire. After a respectful silence I cleared my throat and said, 'Are you saying you'd like to see me in biscuit tins, then, sir?'

He scraped suddenly round as if surprised to find me still there, his tired eyes blinking with a newfound, watery enthusiasm. 'A proper apprenticeship, Robin. A career, with prospects.'

I nodded thoughtfully. 'And Helen, the girl in here before me, you'd like to see her in Marks & Spencer's knickers?'

'What?'

'And bras? Really, sir–'

'Now, Robin–'

'I'd be careful who you say that to, sir. Some folks might get the wrong idea, her father for one, sir, he's a right nutter.'

The rest of the interview didn't go quite so well as it had done up to that point, and by the time I left him with his forehead misting the window the poor sod seemed ready to strangle himself with a pair of those knickers he liked to go on about so much. Having not long turned sixteen my experience of life was, at that point, I'll admit, fairly limited. But I knew enough so that, before the door slammed behind me, I was helpfully able to inform the careers adviser that I thought he was in the wrong job.

Jim Kerr meanwhile was not in the wrong job. He had the best job going. The job of being Jim Kerr. And that, as you will no doubt remember, was no casual, part-time, cash-in-hand lark-about. To be Jim Kerr in 1986 meant holding down the twenty-four hours a day, seven days a week much envied role as the elfishly charismatic frontman of the biggest, most artfully sophisticated rock band in the world, a role requiring no less than total dedication to the exhaustive demands of constant touring and nightly performance, combined with the pressure to write the next wave of Simple Minds' ever bigger, ever bolder arsenal of stadium-busting songs, while at the same time ensuring his formidable co-legend and lady life partner Chrissie

Hynde had enough vintage Telecasters and meat-free ready meals to keep her rocking in his absence.

Yes, I suppose I do know a lot about Simple Minds, now that you mention it. But don't worry, I'm not one of these tedious superfans who boasts of having black-marketed a kidney to follow their idols around the globe since day one. In fact, I came to Simple Minds – or rather, as I see it, *they*, and Jim in particular, came to *me* – very late in the band's rise to Celtic-gods-like status. Already by the time I knowingly first heard them, Glasgow's finest had recorded *Don't You (Forget About Me)* for *The Breakfast Club*, John Hughes's big screen fry-up of eighties cool teen angst, bagging them a U.S. number 1 and international smash hit that built upon the success of *Sparkle in The Rain*, the album with which they'd toured the world in '84. Hughes then immortalised the band still further in his next and biggest film to date, *Ferris Bueller's Day Off*, via a huge poster prominently tacked to the bedroom wall of, as smarter writers might refer to him, the movie's titular high-school hero. And while I can't say precisely where Hughes, or Ferris B, first heard Simple Minds, I think it unlikely it was at an under-18s disco held every Wednesday at Nottinghamshire's – perhaps the world's – only fifteen-hole golf club.

It was here, on a raw February night in 1986, that I first heard *Alive and Kicking*. It was late, well after eight-fifteen, and fast approaching the climax of a solid two-hour set when the disco's 'DJ and Resident Golf Pro' would whip the kids into a final dizzying crescendo of sweat, hormones and Vimto hiccups with his rollicking Top Tune Chain featuring Duran Duran's *Girls on Film*, *Just Can't Get Enough* by Depeche Mode and *Wonderland* by Big Country, with Tears For Fears' *Head Over Heels* then neatly segueing into Bowie's *Let's Dance* and *Love is a Battlefield* by Pat Benatar, before Japan's *Quiet Life* and *Nowhere Girl* from local heroes B-Movie bookended Eurythmics' *Sweet Dreams*

(Are Made of This) ahead of the second or third airing of the night for Soft Cell's *Tainted Love*. Then, finally, the countdown to home-time big three: *Pride (In the Name of Love)* by U2, The Cult's *She Sells Sanctuary*, and, yes, Simple Minds, *Alive and Kicking*.

Stay until your love is...

It was a peak from which it took me all week to come down. For of all the singers adored by the fifty or sixty damp teenagers gathered in that thrillingly blacked-out, glitter-spun boiler room, there was not one who could even so much as daydream of being able to put across that final refrain like Jim Kerr did, not with such power, such deep and tender feeling.

Stay until your love is alive and kicking.

Hearts leapt as eyes were met, smiles returned. Framed in neon gestures, boys ached to hold girls who ached to hold boys. Several, I've since learned, harboured more ambitious achings. But rarely were they declared, for as always, at the stroke of nine, the fluorescent chill would sputter bright and out we would pour, blinking, steaming, across the gravel towards the bus stop.

So anyway, not fancying making biscuit tins for the rest of my life, I eschewed the wisdom of the dispiriting tracksuit and left Burns Green Comprehensive the following June with, or so it must have appeared, neither job nor hope. On the last day, after ceremoniously tearing every sleeve, vent flap, and pocket from each other's blazers in an improvised piece of wild street theatre, I exchanged last goodbyes with my fellow academic ejectees before we drifted away towards our scattered destinies, leaving behind a pavement strewn with dead ties and strips of black and blue cloth, the discarded skins of our childhoods, torn, shredded, and as useless as would be the handful of certificates that were to arrive in the post by the end of summer.

But like I said, he was not even a proper careers adviser.

One

1

Another thing I never wanted to be was a car mechanic, but Ricky dreamt of nothing else. At fifteen he'd sold his best BMX (an expensive American model) and, with money saved from his paper round, bought a shabby old Ford Escort van, from which he immediately removed the engine and stripped it down to the very last nut, bolt and valve-spring washer before teaching himself how to put it all back together, again and again and again, until eventually it started first time, every time, and ran smoother than it had ever done in the eighteen years since it was built. For his sixteenth birthday he'd asked for a set of welding tackle and got it. So it was no surprise he went to work at Stonebridge Motor Company.

'What's it like, then,' I asked him, 'being paid to get filthy?'

'It's not so bad,' Ricky shrugged, smudging a thick, treacle-black beard of sump oil back along his jaw. 'Should keep me out of trouble for a bit, anyway.'

Spotting Ricky coasting across the garage forecourt, heading home on his old paper round bike, I called from the bus shelter where I'd stopped to talk to this quiet girl I sometimes ran into. He couldn't have been at the garage above a couple of weeks, but already he'd acquired all the poise and self-assured air of a lifelong working man, qualities he'd apparently slipped on as easily as the grubby, and somehow impressive, Ford overalls he now wore with obvious beaming pride.

'What've you been up to?' Ricky said with a Fonz-like grin. 'Any idea what you're going to do yet?'

Perhaps because of the girl, or that Ricky was straddling his bike in the busy main road, I didn't feel this was quite the right time to announce that the only thing I'd ever wanted to do was to be Jim Kerr. Nor that I'd spent most of the last three months, in between thinking the unthinkable about Susanna Hoffs of The Bangles, staring up at my bedroom ceiling and listening to *New Gold Dream (81-82-83-84)* and *Live in The City of Light* on constant all-day rotation, although at the time I was wearing a Simple Minds T-shirt and had my hair cropped around a cool curtain of swishy fringe in homage to *Glittering Prize*-era Jim, so the clues were all there.

'I've applied for a couple of jobs. Hoping I'll hear back this week,' I said, though neither of these things was true.

Ricky had started to say something about a place going at the garage when a double-decker shuddered over the hill and honked him on his way. Smiling, the quiet girl took my hand and led me back to her house, which was much nicer than ours, where she made hot chocolate and played me her new favourite record by Prince.

Later, I danced home via the phonebox outside the Fox and Hounds, Ricky's number as I dialled familiar as if it were my own. Not that we ever had a phone to get familiar with. Mam said we couldn't afford one, which was true, but also, we didn't know anybody anyway, apart from mine and Cath's school friends and grandma and grandad who only lived three streets away. But I've always been good at remembering numbers. Stonebridge 474081, that was ours. Oh, we did *have* a telephone. It had come with the council house we moved into after Mam divorced my ex-dad and was to lay forever disconnected in the cupboard with the gas-meter, hidden away under a coal-singed hearth rug like some shameful family secret.

'Not as a mechanic,' Ricky scoffed. 'You'd be bloody useless. They want somebody in the parts and service department, booking customers cars in and sorting out spares for the workshop.'

Parts and service department trainee at Stonebridge Motor Company. I didn't fancy that. I fancied big stages and tour buses, being interviewed by *Sounds* and the *NME*. But I'd missed Ricky in the months since leaving school, and the garage was barely ten minutes' walk from home. Also, I didn't have a penny to my name, nor anything else in the way of alternatives.

'What would I have to wear, Ricky?' I asked carefully, catching my reflection in the phlegm-flecked glass of the phonebox. 'Overalls, like yours?'

'No, *you* don't get overalls. You get a little blue smock thing, like dinner ladies wear.'

'Dinner ladies?'

'With a Ford Parts badge on the pocket.'

'Jesus Christ.'

2

'Your *Smash Hits* came in today, Robin,' Mam would say, meaning the latest issue had been delivered to the newsagents where she worked mornings to top up what little she got off the Social.

'It's not my *Smash Hits*,' I'd remind her again. 'It's Cath's.'

'George Michael's on the cover.'

'Rubbish.'

'And there's a poster of her from The Bangles who you like.'

'Pass it here, then. I'll take it up to Cath. I bet she's waiting for it.'

It was Cath's *Smash Hits*. Yes, I'd bought it once or twice if

Simple Minds were featured. I may even have asked Mam to set up that standing order at the paper shop, but it was really for my sister's benefit. That said, I do remember reading, probably around the time of the golf club disco days, a Q&A in which, among Qs such as what car did he drive (a Saab 900 Turbo), and with which member of Bananarama would he most like to play Twister (all three), Jim Kerr revealed how, before the band hit the big time, he'd worked on a Glasgow building site, where he'd lived in constant petrified fear of being outed as a great big jessie if he'd ever, suicidally, forgotten to remove his eyeliner the morning after a gig.

And it was by recalling this fact, how it had been necessary for Jim Kerr to temporarily lower himself to the level of a mere mortal with a day job in order to achieve his true destiny, that I was able to slip into a pop-fastening dinner lady's smock and lower *my*self into a dusty, greasy world of oil-filters, spark plugs and wiper blades and be at the beck and call of car mechanics and other less exciting customers at Stonebridge Motor Company. It was only temporary, I reminded myself. In no time at all, just like Jim Kerr, I'd be transformed from but another snotty kid off the estate into an incomparable stage prowling presence whose every word and gesture captivated millions the world over.

'Youth *Training* Schemes!' Ken sneered. He hawked thickly and spat twice into the dustbin after the paper bag in which his sandwiches had been wrapped. 'Waste of fucking time, kidder. Never a job at the end of 'em.'

Ken was the van driver who shuttled parts between Stonebridge Motor Company and two dozen other garages and workshops within a roughly thirty-mile radius. He was very old and very frightening, and he'd neither seen nor heard of Simple Minds. But what Ken had seen and heard, and was very keen to tell me about, was his best pal during the war being launched twenty feet into the air by a German mortar and afterwards finding what little remained of him dangling in a thousand grisly baubles from the branches of a nearby tree.

'His innards hit me in the face like hot mince,' Ken said. 'And you know his knackers? His *ballocks*? Swingin' from the top branch until a magpie flew off wi' 'em. *Now then...*'

This was not what I'd anticipated of lunch in the garage canteen, yet neither Ricky or Vern, nor the two other mechanics whose names I'd yet to remember, seemed remotely surprised or even to pause behind their newspapers and Pot Noodles as Ken sprang this harrowing deviation from the day's spanner talk and gossip.

'Young lads today, you don't know you're fucking born.'

'No,' I agreed, thankful I wasn't wearing eyeliner.

'Do they, Vern? Don't know they're fucking born.'

'It's lad's first day, Ken,' Vern said, a quietly amused sigh in his voice as he shook his paper straight. 'You'll frighten him off.'

As Vern dug a pen from his overalls pocket and dived towards the crossword Ken broke wind loudly, spat twice more into the dustbin. 'What did you say yer name was again?'

'Robin.'

'Robin, aye. You want to join the Navy, Robin,' Ken nodded decisively. 'See the world. Not pissing away your best years stuck in there with Sheila, fine woman as she is.'

As if on cue, Sheila appeared at the door of the cramped canteen to say that she knew it was only five to one, but there was a queue at the front counter and would I be a love and cut short my lunch to open up and give her a hand.

'Take no notice of Ken,' Sheila said after we'd seen off four parts collections, three service bookings, and several phone calls between the pair of us. Sheila spoke very nicely, with a whisper of a Welsh accent she put to good use charming and teasing even the roughest customers. 'I've heard Ken's tales and Oh! he's enough to give you nightmares that one.'

'He is,' I agreed, and glancing through the window I winced as a magpie cast its hungry eye over me from the roof of the bus shelter opposite.

Sheila was, as Ken said, a fine woman. She smelt like Debenhams and dressed, beneath her smock, in the sort of posh old lady clothes Margaret Thatcher might have worn in her more frivolous moods. I couldn't imagine why she'd ever want to work in a garage. Her husband was somebody high up at a local engineering firm and she drove a nearly new Sierra Sapphire, so it can't have been for the money.

Me, though, I was there *only* for the money. All £27.50 a week of it. If I could fob Mam off with a tenner instead of fifteen quid for bed and board, that left me with seventeen-fifty to buy records and save up for a microphone and probably a guitar. I figured learning an instrument might not be such a bad idea. It'd help with my songwriting (which I'd be starting very soon), plus the guitar was easily the coolest looking thing to play, as well as being more practical to lug to rehearsals on the bus than a Mel Gaynor-size drum kit. Oh, and driving lessons. I'd also need money for driving lessons.

As ever, my spot of destiny shaping was soon interrupted, this time by the impatient rattle of empty oil jugs and a voice at the workshop counter shouting, 'Stores!'

'Shop!' cried another.

'See, I told Ken he'd frighten the lad off.'

'Robin's coming, Vern,' said Sheila.

'I'm coming,' I said.

3

The only pianos I'd ever seen before were on *Top of The Pops* and in the school hall, so for somebody I knew to have one of her own, in her house, seemed outrageous. It wasn't a snow-white Barbie's boudoir thing, like the one John Lennon took to heaven, nor the size of a cruise ship, the sort you hoped to see Elton John tossed into and the lid nailed down. This was both like a school piano in that it was compact and upright, but also different because it played in tune and didn't have a single pen-knife tattoo declaring such undeniable teenage truths as 'Jayne Luv's Scott 4 Eva' or 'Mr Robinson is a bell-end' carved into its lovingly polished mahogany.

'That's enough,' she said, closing the lid gently over the keyboard.

'Don't stop.'

'I feel silly.'

I'd run into the quiet girl again, the one who liked Prince. She liked me too, or so she said as we dawdled, earlier that evening, in the trickling shadows by the river, though not enough to let me do the unthinkable. I hadn't even asked (though I had been thinking about it), but she said she felt it was important to get these things out of the way before we wasted any time and got settled in the grass with incompatible motives.

Now we had settled at her piano, and my motives were purely musical.

'My mind's gone blank,' she said, drawing her baggy jumper sleeves over her hands to hug herself.

'No it hasn't,' I said. 'Play one more. Anything you like.' I rose from the stool to give her space. '*Please*?'

Before coming over all reluctant, the girl had played me Billy Joel's *Tell Her About It* followed by that sleepy, saxophoney one by Dire Straits, and both so wonderfully I struggled to see how such a sound could come from the neat pale hands that fluttered along the keys before me. But now as she began tinkling, smilingly, into *Bohemian Rhapsody*, I felt a turn had most definitely been taken for the worse, Queen having always struck me as overblown rock panto garbage that appealed only to children and the terminally misguided. And yet, the girl brought this usually nauseating nonsense to life so beautifully, so delicately, I found myself utterly captivated and wishing she might never, ever, stop playing – even *Queen*.

As she played on, making a hauntingly pretty job of Eurythmics' *Here Comes The Rain Again*, and beginning to sing now in a soft girlish voice so that I could just about hear her, I stood with my hands in my pockets before an expanse of floating timber shelves, absently studying silver-framed photographs and tall, glossy spines of books relating, mostly, to horses, hunting and antiques. There were also, among vases of twigs and ceramic nick-nacks, a large number of trophies, shields, and brightly ribboned medallions, some of which sprouted badly rendered likenesses of dogs, ponies or shotguns in gold and silver plastic.

I had just leaned in close, teetering on tiptoe to read the inscription engraved beneath a three-legged hound, when something between a loud growl and a roar sent me almost crashing face-first into the whole silly arrangement.

'Empty your pockets, son. Come on.' He must have blown in from the front room, or some other, beyond the light oak sliding doors, and now stood glaring at me with two large empty wine glasses dangling from his hands like a pair of cocked crystal pistols. 'I know your game, sunshine,' he said, 'don't think I don't.'

The quiet girl's father. The man who half an hour earlier, as I trailed his daughter round to the back of the house, had glared from the enormous front room window as if expecting me to run a key down the ice-blue Jaguar angled across the drive.

'Dad!' The music stopped and the girl half-rose from her stool as her father, settling the wine glasses on top of the piano, came pounding towards me. 'Dad, leave him alone.'

He was a big man, tall, thick-necked, and almost as sensible looking as the faun heavy knit jumper which he filled amply over mustard jumbo cords. Now, following his initial greeting, I prepared to be taken violently by the throat and launched across an acre of back garden. Instead, he reached out, inviting me to do the same, and then, taking my thin, limp hand, set about crushing it in his fat, hotly uncomfortable one.

'I know everything that's there,' her father said, breathing heavily. 'It's all been counted, many times. And before you look, there's no money hidden in those vases, either.'

To distract from the agony, I focused on his slippers, dainty little leather things that seemed at comical odds with the rest of his blustering bulk, and wondered if their florid shade of purplish pink had been chosen specially to match his nose. A question for later, perhaps.

'Dad!' the girl said again, before turning to me. 'Ignore him, Robin. He's teasing. He always does this when they've been drinking.'

Silencing his daughter with a wild eyebrow, the father at last released my numb hand and, stepping back, lifted his chins. 'This is Robin, is it?' he said, nodding thoughtfully. 'Well just make sure you don't go robbing *me*, young *Robin*.'

'Dad!'

'I won't,' I said, resisting a strange impulse to address him as sir, though I felt sure he'd have relished it.

He looked me up and down once more, this big man, and nodded quite affably. Then, turning to retrieve his wine glasses, strode away to the kitchen.

At the sound of an urgently pulled cork the girl mouthed a tight-smiled apology across the top of her piano before her father reappeared, lips moistened, large glasses darkly refilled.

'Do you drink, Robin?' he said, legs apart, the gunslinger again.

'Drink? I'm only–'

'She doesn't,' he said, nodding to his daughter. 'She doesn't drink any alcohol. I'll warn you to remember that.'

'Right. I will, er, Mr–'

'Oh, and another thing,' he interrupted. 'Upset her, just once, and I shall take hold of you and hammer you into the ground.'

'Dad!'

'Like a tent peg. Have you got that?'

The girl stormed after her father, sliding the wooden doors to behind her so that I could still hear their voices, though not what was said. By the time she reappeared I'd put my jacket on and was delicately walking my fingers over the piano keys, defying the urge to smash out an unhinged rendition of the Fuck You! Blues dedicated to the big guy in the next room. On the keyboard, the girl had marked what I later learned was Middle C with a gold glitter star.

'Please ignore all that, Robin,' she said, straddling the stool beside me. 'I'm so sorry. He was only messing about, but it comes out nasty when he's half-drunk. He's very nice, really.'

She took my hands and interwove them with hers, wriggling her fingers like pale hungry chicks. 'You've put your coat on.'

'Yes,' I said. 'I've got a pair of antique silver candlesticks down my trousers, so I thought I'd get off before your dad comes back with his camping mallet.'

'I'm sorry,' she said again. 'He didn't mean it, I promise. Please stay. We can go upstairs to my room and listen to some records.'

'Thanks, but I think I'll be off,' I said, knowing that listen to records is all we would do. 'It's getting late, anyway.'

After walking me through the large modern kitchen, across grey marbled tiles and into a sort of boot room that smelled of leather, fields and feet, the quiet girl pressed me hard up against the back door and surprised me with a long, slow and what seemed, having met her father, a highly dangerous but intensely enjoyable kiss. As my thoughts again turned towards the unthinkable, I felt her fingers on the zip of my jacket, her eyes smiling into mine as she unhurriedly drew it up before buttoning my collar. 'The security light's on,' she whispered with a peck for the tip of my nose. 'I'll buzz the gates to let you out.'

Two

1

In front of the big showroom window, David the sales manager knelt in shirtsleeves beside the open passenger door of a gleaming black Escort XR3i, carefully polishing, with a soft lint rag, at the tiniest tear of a dried water mark.

'Those cleaners, telling me this has been properly leathered-off. There were streaks all down both sides.' David's head shook in cool disbelief. 'So how many have you had now, then?'

'What?' I said, momentarily forgetting what we'd been talking about. 'Oh, driving lessons? Six. I can only afford one a week,' I explained, 'otherwise all my money's gone.'

David double-clicked his tongue. 'Need to get a move on and pass your test. You can come and give us a hand in here then. We can't keep up at the minute, all these miners spending their redundancy.'

'That's good. For you, I mean.'

'It's ridiculous, pal. We had another chap in yesterday, bought two. Orion Ghia for him and that red Fiesta there for his missus. I think a lot are thinking they should take the money now, while it's being offered, even if their pit's still got a few years left in it. So, you know, if they want to carry on like terminally ill pools winners and spend it on a nice car, I'll be very glad to sell them one.'

'Or two,' I said, pleased with myself.

'Or two, exactly.' David smiled, tossing the polishing rag onto the Escort's roof. 'Have a sit in, Robin - it's open.'

'So is this your new one?' I said, sliding into the velour hug of the sports seat and gripping the wheel. 'And you just get to drive it, and take it home, for free?'

'Perk of the job, pal.' David dropped into the passenger seat, fished a bottle of *Polo by Ralph Lauren* from the glovebox and fired two pungent blasts into each of his armpits. 'Like I say, get your test passed, and before long you could have one of these yourself, if you're any good.'

'I always wanted a Mini,' I said, eyeing the stereo. 'But this is nice. Very nice.'

2

Ricky, despite being a week younger than me, already had his licence, having been sent to one of those intensive quick pass driving schools for his 17th birthday present. And, of course, he had his beloved Escort van; which when it wasn't in a million pieces on the garage floor he'd raced more or less relentlessly round the field at the back of his parents' house for two years.

The van looked incredible. For a van. It had wide wheels and tinted windows and was painted a glossy post office red with a white stripe which showed Ricky's bodywork skills to be as accomplished as his mechanical. Inside, it sported tiger-stripe seat covers and a high spec stereo of dubious origin; a small furry Garfield swung on a noose from the rear-view mirror. But best of all, to Ricky's mind, it sounded and went like a bomb. It was fast. Much faster than my driving instructor's Metro. Which is probably why, when Ricky said, 'Go on, bud, give it a proper blast,' and let me take the wheel one drizzly Saturday afternoon, I immediately drove it sideways through a hedge, where it stayed until the farmer could come and drag it out with his tractor.

Knowing how Ricky loved his van more than life itself I was glad that, working in the parts department, I was able to not only supply the new bumper, headlight, and driver's side front wing he needed to get it back on the road, but also to give him a pretty generous staff discount.

'And,' I said, 'there's a door mirror, grille, and indicator lens upstairs that have been written-off as old stock, so I've asked Sheila and she says you can have them for nothing, as long as you don't tell anybody.'

'Oh, very generous of you,' Ricky said sarcastically. 'And what about the paintwork? And tyre? Who's going to sort that out?'

'Sorry, Ricky,' I said. 'I'm not used to driving in fields. I'll pay for the parts. I'll cancel some driving lessons.'

'Cancel? You need more, not less.'

'I know,' I agreed, pretending to tidy a shelf of spark plugs.

'It's alright, bud, don't worry about it,' Ricky said after an uncomfortable pause. 'I was thinking of respraying it again, anyway.'

It was that same Monday night we drove in Ricky's parents' Volvo to Matlock Bath for a bag of chips. It was a long way to go for chips, but for me these were always the highlight, whereas Ricky went to ogle the dozens of powerful motorbikes that lined up in heat-shimmering display along the roadside. I suspected this perverse interest was in some way linked to his criminal taste in music, which he advertised through nasty patches sewn all over his denim jacket, and by playing infernal rackets by the likes of AC/DC and Van Halen.

Even worse, it was to Motörhead that we set off, about nine o'clock, for home. Windows wound down, *Ace of Spades* turned up, I tuned out and decided that when I had a car the first tape I'd shove into the stereo would be Simple Minds' magisterial 1981 LP *Sons and Fascination*. Since skipping a driving lesson to buy the record a fortnight before I'd listened to it almost constantly when awake and then continued to hum it in my sleep. It had been a revelation. Life-changing, you might say. Flat out and full blast, hurtling along to the throbbing funk rumble of Derek Forbes's bass workouts on *Love Song* and *Sweat In Bullet*... I could think of no better sound to accompany a 30-mile drive for a bag of chips.

Suddenly the seatbelt jerked tight as my face rushed towards the windscreen.

'Nearly missed the turning,' Ricky laughed, flicking the indicator and skidding up to the white line. We waited as a red Fiesta XR2, braking just as sharply from the back road to Chesterfield, edged its impatient nose into the carriageway before us.

'Another madman,' I said as Ricky flashed to let him out. (He was coming either way). I sat up straight in my seat. 'Hey, isn't that Honeywell?'

'Can't look now, bud, I'm waiting for this clown.'

'It's this clown I mean. I'm sure that's Mr Honeywell.'

The driver of the red XR2, who, in the dazzle of headlights, did sort of resemble Giles Honeywell, our boss from the garage, appeared to look straight at us as he accelerated across the junction and away in the direction of Buxton and Manchester.

'He could've waved,' I said, snatching the opportunity to mute Lemmy's trapped-bollock howl.

'That wasn't Honeywell.'

'I know it's dark, but you can hardly miss Postman Rick's flying pillar-box.'

'Honeywell's wife has got an XR2. We serviced it about a month ago.' I gripped tight, unlike the rear tyres, as Ricky flung us squealing through a sea-sickening S-bend. 'And anyway,' he added, 'we're not in *Postman Rick's flying pillar-box*, are we?'

Even in the narrow blackness of the Derbyshire lanes the

smooth, comfortable ride, the quiet Scandinavian solidity, should have told me that. 'Course he wouldn't recognise us,' I said. 'We're in a bloody Volvo.'

'It wasn't Honeywell, Robin.'

'Why wasn't it? It looked like him.'

'Mrs Honeywell's car's blue.'

Three

1

A couple of weeks passed before I returned to the big house on Windmill Way, the quiet girl's reassurance and the unreliable privacy afforded by riverbanks and bus shelters having eventually won me round.

She was waiting at the gate. I don't remember now if it was a Wednesday or a Thursday, only that as I followed her into the dark boot room I tripped over those little pink slippers of her father's, which had been carelessly left by the back door. It appeared he was just as intent on breaking my neck when he was out of the house as he was when he was in it.

'Are you sure?' I said again before unzipping my coat.

'It's a fundraising dinner,' the girl said, pressing her lips softly to mine and sliding her hands underneath my shirt. 'Relax. They won't be home till late.'

Her name was Fliss, by the way. I know I've kept it from you far too long already, but even now I'm not sure. I've tried typing several alternatives, but none will do. I just can't see her as anybody other than Fliss. Fliss she was then and, to me, Fliss she will always be.

'How late?' I asked, attempting some under shirt exploration of my own.

'Late enough...we've got all night.' Fliss slowly untangled

herself from my arms and adjusted her clothing. 'Dad left you a note. It's through there, on the bureau.'

The *bureau*, it turned out, was an antique cupboard in the corner of the big front room they called the lounge. It had a drop-down front panel which when opened, as it now was, made a leather-topped desk. On its ink-stained surface, beside a tower of paperwork, lay a creamy envelope marked '*ROBIN*' in red biro.

Knowing how well my last meeting with her father had gone, I didn't expect this would be a thank you note. An apology, perhaps? Surely not. More likely, warming to his heat of the moment threat to drive me into the ground like a tent peg, he'd now had a solicitor put it in writing, so I should be in absolutely no doubt that he meant it.

I turned the envelope over in my hands, gave it a sniff. Then I slipped it into my jacket pocket and forgot about it.

'I learned this today,' Fliss said as I came through from the kitchen with two mugs of hot chocolate. And skipping over to the piano she began to play, with casual concentration and seemingly very little effort, *The Model* by Kraftwerk. She played the whole song perfectly, the sound of the instrument filling the room and transposing this iconic slice of synth-pop (another favourite from the golf club disco days) into a soaring classical rhapsody.

'That was so brilliant,' I said, open-mouthed against the piano. 'How do you make it sound like that?'

Fliss shrugged. 'It was a bit messy.'

'Play it again.'

She did and this time she began to sing, her girlish voice bringing a breathy, soulful warmth to the sparse lyric that was really quite moving. I joined in on the final verse, at first replicating the Teutonic android delivery of the original, before I found the confidence to switch to my proper Jim Kerr performing voice.

When we reached the end of the song again we waited, smiling across the piano while the last notes dissolved into silence. Then Fliss said, 'Oh, Robin, you are funny when you sing,' and she laughed so much her eyes still giggled when she silenced her mouth with both hands.

'How do you mean, funny?' I said. 'I was in tune, wasn't I? At the end, when I sang properly?'

Fliss took a sip of her now tepid chocolate and shook her head with a slow smirk of sympathy. 'Not really, Robin, no.'

Well, whatever she thought of my voice, there was no faulting my ears, and I skipped across the room to prise a small gap between the sliding doors.

'Robin, they won't be home till ten at the earliest.'

'I heard a car.'

'It'll be Grandma's television. It's her *Boon* night.'

I glanced across the garden to the little granny flat where Dot, Fliss's mum's mum, lived, in similar splendour I assumed, at the back of the house.

'Grandma won't bother us,' Fliss said. 'Do you want to go up and listen to some records?' And taking my hand she pulled me towards the stairs.

I had looked forward to spending the rest of the evening hotly entwined under the duvet, in Fliss's double bed, surrounded by textbooks and piled instrument cases and watched over by the dozens of pop heroes (Prince being by far the most prominent) that covered every inch of her bedroom walls and much of her furniture. But after an enthusiastic hour or so of "listening to some records" – a phrase which had become a euphemism for our soundtracked intimacies – my fingers as well as my thoughts must have strayed into still restricted territory and Fliss leapt up and out like a triggered mouse trap.

'Sorry,' I said. 'I got a bit...'

But rather than be annoyed, as I'd half expected, Fliss went over and stood before the full-length wardrobe mirror, her reflected upper half wearing only an amused smile before she slipped back into her bra and sweatshirt. 'There's nothing to be sorry for,' she said, turning and climbing back onto the bed. 'But I almost forgot – I made you dinner.'

2

She'd made lasagne and it was the best thing I'd ever tasted, despite being home-made rather than a proper, frozen one, out of a packet. Afterwards, at Fliss's suggestion, we each drank a bottle of her father's beer, cold from the boot room.

'Thank you. That was delicious,' I said as we sat round one corner of a large and very shiny table. 'You are,' Fliss smiled, and she swept back the fringe from my eyes so that I could see her better. 'No, *you* are.'

Through the french windows I could see about half the back garden and the end of the drive, where after hugging the side of the house it spread to form a gravel moat around a large double garage and parking for three or four horseboxes. That was the family business – horseboxes, trailers, saddles, reins, halters, helmets, bridles, jodhpurs, feed, blankets, bedding, the whole horsey lot. Or as the Markley Hall Equestrian catalogue (bundles of which I'd discovered stacked beside the chest freezer in the boot room) put it: 'For Your Every Equestrian Need'.

I knew the name, of course, from the quarter-page ads in the local paper. And since starting at the garage I'd personally supplied Markley Hall's workshop with parts on several occasions. Electrical items, mostly; bulbs, batteries, light units, but also wheels, mudflaps and number plates, the latter being nearly always just the yellow, rear, ones – for horseboxes. But I hadn't known of Fliss's connection before I properly got to know her. Why would I?

Naturally, being of keen equestrian stock, Fliss had her own animal. A piano *and* a horse. The very idea (and possibly the beer) caused me to rise from the table and come over all poetic.

> 'A horse? A horse?
> Of course Fliss has a horse!
> And she feeds her little horse
> On cold lasagne sauce
> Left over from dinner
> Of course!'

Fliss opened her eyes wide and, laughing, took my hand. 'Did you just make that up?'

'Don't sound so surprised,' I said coolly. 'When Michael Rosen visited our English class in Year 3 he said my poem about the milkman sitting on his eggs was "excellent".'

'*Really*? And was sitting on his eggs like a metaphor? For sitting on his testicles?'

'No, it was not,' I said, shaking my head in disgust. 'It was about sitting on his eggs.'

Fliss laughed at me again. It was becoming a habit. 'You're so funny,' she said. 'Though not half as clever as you think.'

I gave her a confused look.

'Because there never *are* any leftovers when I make lasagne – not even for Mungo.'

'Mungo?'

'My horse! Although he's not so little. I'll take you up to the stables to meet him one day, if you like?'

'That would be nice,' I said. 'I hope he's friendlier than your dad.'

When Fliss nipped upstairs I took the empty beer bottles out to the dustbin, their short fall reassuring me they were among friends and that of their theft – and his daughter's indulgence – Fliss's father would be forever none the wiser.

It was a clear night, the sky pinned high with bright and winking stars. Only the sound of gunfire ricocheting around Grandma Dot's sitting room ruffled the silence. I stood for a moment between the bins and horseboxes, looking up at the great dark outline of the house, with its wide, asymmetrical Swiss chalet roof and three thick-set chimneys bursting through the tiles like yellow-brick space rockets. I remember feeling how lucky I was to be there, to be invited into this house, a guest of these people. Or one of them. Filling my chest with kind autumnal air, I smiled up at the heavens, proud in some small, unclear way. But there was also a sadness, a quiet melancholy at knowing that I would never be able to take Fliss home to our house.

I found Fliss already back at the piano and breezing through the most incredible rendition of *The Way It Is* by Bruce Hornsby and The Range. Seriously. Suddenly the awful song no longer infuriated me as much as it always had done, as I knew it really should still. I was instantly won over by the dreamy, almost sultry, way she played it, but even more so by the fact that since her trip upstairs, instead of jeans and her 'New York City' sweatshirt, Fliss was now wearing (apparently) only a flimsy floral pyjama top that barely reached the cushion of the piano stool.

'Hello,' she said with the coolest of side-eye smiles as I settled beside her.

'Hello,' I said, curious as she arched her back, holding my gaze while continuing to play.

Did-ul-um, did-ul-um, did-ul-um

I glanced down at her outfit, doing my best to keep my thinking away from the unthinkable. 'Pyjamas?'

'Dessert,' she smiled, lifting an eyebrow. 'If you're still hungry?'

Did-ul-um–
Did-ul–
Did–

3

My head was still full of Fliss, so rather than picturing myself, as I usually did, as Jim Kerr, leaping up and off garden walls in lieu of a stage, I walked speedily home in a lust-fuzzy trance, grinning, with my hands bunched in the pockets of my jacket. It was only then I remembered the letter.

I stopped beneath the Lucozade glow of a streetlamp to read it. Fumes of her father's aftershave rose from the Markley Hall Equestrian headed notepaper, bringing down a magnificent moth, which crashed, providing some much-needed punctuation, among the five lines of upper-case text.

ROBIN
SIERRA XR4x4 WHITE BRAND-NEW
HAVE SALES MNGR TALK G HONEYWELL* RING ABOVE
BEST PRICE – CASH
LIONEL

**approximate site of moth crash*

At the foot of the page, where I balanced the moth hoping it might rise phoenix-like from the Chernobyl mists of *Paco Rabanne*, there was a P.S.; an order for three rear number plates. All newish registrations. But then people who could afford horseboxes could usually afford nice cars.

I laid the moth carefully on a garden wall, beneath the healing glow of the streetlamp. It'd been rather a night for the unexpected and I like to think the little fella made it.

Four

1

I had just turned off the oil pump and bolted the workshop hatch when there came an almighty thumping at the front counter. 'Who the fuck...?' I cursed, as was only decent after Sheila had left. Five-thirty fantasist, I thought, anticipating one of those delusional berks who always came in at closing time, had you trawl through a dozen catalogues, pricing-up every available accessory for their scabby old Capri and then said, '*I'll think about it*'.

He thumped again as I undid the padlock. 'We're closed, mate, I'm afraid,' I said, rattling up the shutters with politely frowning annoyance.

'Oh, ah, Mr Honeywell... Sorry, I thought it was a...'

'Not at all, Robin, *not at all*,' said Giles Honeywell, straightening the small silver pin he wore in his buttonhole. He looked up, unleashing an immaculate local dignitary smile. 'I'm the one who should be apologising to you. You must have been cursing me when I knocked, I'm sure. Lost track of the time, so much paperwork, you know – last quarter figures, stock to write-down, new Ford finance incentives and so on.'

'Yes, it's been busy, Mr Honeywell,' I agreed. 'David was saying what a good week they've had. He's just hung two more Sold signs in those out there.'

'Incredible, Robin,' beamed Honeywell, shaking his head as he turned to look out across the floodlit ranks of shiny saloons and hatchbacks angled with inviting precision towards the main road. 'Quite incredible. Terrific little team David's put together there, mind. Terrific sales team.'

With a startled tug at the sleeve of his grey double-breasted suit, Honeywell sighed into the face of a slim gold watch. 'The time,' he muttered, resettling his cuff.

'What can I do for you, Mr Honeywell?'

'Ah, yes.' Honeywell dipped into his trouser pocket and drew out a tight square of folded notepaper. 'I need a spare key for Pauline's – my wife's – car. You can cut them from just the code number now, can't you?'

'I can if we've got any blanks left, Mr Honeywell,' I said, flicking the overhead lights back on before diving among the rows of small parts bins under the counter. 'I ordered another thirty yesterday, but... Ah! you're in luck, still a few in there.'

I took the notepaper from Honeywell's fingers over to where the key-cutting machine sat, beside the till, on a bench ninety degrees and a couple of feet to the left side of the front counter, among a jumble of catalogues, invoice pads and a pair of greasy fingered telephones.

'Is it a Fiesta XR2 that Mrs Honeywell drives?'

'Yes, Robin, that's right. Smashing little car. "The Blue Meanie" she calls it – you know, The Beatles? *Yellow Submarine*? Pauline loves The Beatles.'

'Your wife's got very good taste, Mr Honeywell. In cars *and* music.'

'She does,' Honeywell nodded. 'She does indeed.'

'Key will take about five minutes, Mr Honeywell. Shall I bring it through to your office when it's ready?'

'Would you, Robin? That would be wonderful. Much obliged to you.'

On the wall calendar behind Honeywell's desk a mud-spattered blue-and-white rally car leaped high into the air from a humpback bridge. The month said January 1988, as indeed it was, despite the rest of the office – wood-effect panelling, caramel leather sofa with matching swivel chair, chocolate-orange-taupe geometric pattern carpet – being frozen round about the summer of '74. It was like wandering onto the set of *The Sweeney* but for the stink of cigars, the drifting blue fog of which was bang up to the minute.

'Yes... Thursday... No, *Thursday*... Goodbye,' said Honeywell, waving me in as he leaned across the desk to slam an end to his phone call. As he snapped shut his briefcase, whipped it across the desk, the little metal sign announcing 'Giles Honeywell, Dealer Principal' fell to the floor.

'Ah, excellent, Robin, thank you,' he said as I replaced it.

A brown mac from a browner stand was flung over his arm before he mumbled something I didn't fully catch involving awfully late petrol, a charity raffle and, I think, Susan with the dogs. I made helpful, comprehending faces as I handed him the freshly cut key and watched him drop it into his suit pocket.

'Thank you, Robin. Now if I can possibly impose still further on your leisure,' he said, indicating two boxes of what appeared to be wine beside a filing cabinet, 'would you do me the great favour of carrying one of those out to my car? *Would you?*'

I followed Honeywell along the rubber-floored corridor, past the shuttered front counter and into the showroom. His grey Granada Scorpio sat gleaming in front of the big window, the cleaners having valeted it inside and out, ready for the weekend.

'Quick word, boss?'

As David the sales manager clicked across the tiles, I carried the box of wine out to the car and then went back through the showroom for the other.

'It should be unlocked, Robin,' Honeywell called after me. 'If you wouldn't mind, erm, popping them in the boot?'

'Will do, Mr Honeywell.'

If you've never seen inside a Granada Scorpio boot, trust me, it's cavernous. Even with a set of golf clubs and one of those big wicker picnic baskets you only saw in afternoon films, strapped to the backs of roadsters driven by Kenneth More, there was still plenty of room for the wine. I packed both boxes safely between a tartan blanket and a waxed jacket, among various hats, flasks, socks, folding stools, a pair of spiked shoes with tassels and two pairs of green wellingtons. As I slid the spiked shoes into a gap I saw, on a muddy corner of newspaper with which they'd been stuffed, an advert for Markley Hall Equestrian. What are the chances? I thought. And picturing Fliss, I slammed the boot and walked away wearing a foolish smile.

2

I got home after six to find Mam, as I very often found her, kneeling before the open oven door with a knife in her hand. 'I was a bit late putting the meat in,' she apologised, rising through the steam of a carrot pan. 'Too busy gossiping. Go on in, we've got a visitor.'

Now, I've since learned that normal families, on being reunited with a close relative after weeks and months apart, often, and quite naturally, rush to embrace or even kiss one another on the face in greeting. Others shake hands or at least look like it's not the worst thing in the world to see them again. But not my uncle Alastair. I found him in the front room (the only room downstairs besides the kitchen and outside toilet), where he didn't so much as look up from his *Steam World* magazine as he said, 'Your mother says you didn't pass your driving test, Robin.' Alastair pronounced mother to rhyme with bother. Bookish in a casual, almost furtive way, this word was one of few concessions he made to his long-lost native dialect.

'No,' I said. 'Hesitation and driving too close to the white lines. I put in for it again, though, next morning.'

'No hesitation there, then,' Alastair said, now finally looking up with a grin. 'Never mind. You'll pass next time.'

'Catherine had hers earlier,' Mam said, excusing my sister's absence as the three of us squeezed round the kitchen table. 'She's gone across to Tracy's to do her homework. She had five puppies on Tuesday. Tracy's dog, I mean.'

Alastair poured himself a small glass of beer. 'I do miss the excitement of this place, Sarah,' he smiled. 'It's like Chicago in the twenties.'

'Get off with you. I was only making conversation. You always used to like dogs.'

'I still do like dogs. What kind are they, the puppies?'

'I don't know. Catherine didn't say.'

'Is that your car, Alastair?' I asked, meaning the new Golf I'd found parked at the front gate. He was always Alastair in person, never Uncle.

'It's hers, my good lady. Doesn't half shift. I was up here within a couple of hours this morning.'

'I wondered who it was when he knocked,' Mam said. 'Made me jump. I was reading.'

'I brought that telly over for your mother. I'd only had it a month or two before I moved down there, been up in Geoff's loft ever since. It'll need new batteries for the, er...' Alastair levelled his knife and made a squeezing gesture with his thumb.

'Remote control?' I said in disbelief. 'Really?'

'It's never bothered me, not having a colour television,' Mam said, contemplating a slice of packet beef.

'It has me,' I said, 'having to watch that museum piece. At school, Alastair, we were the only kids who had no idea what the *Multi-Coloured Swap Shop* was supposed to look like. We could've reported her to Esther Rantzen for child cruelty.'

'You do say some daft things.'

Alastair smiled across at Mam. 'Your world snooker finals must've been thrilling on a 12-inch black-and-white.'

'I only watch it for Alex Higgins,' Mam said, putting a hand to her mouth to stifle either a girlish giggle or a rogue carrot. 'But I shall enjoy him a lot more now, in colour.'

'How's Norfolk, Alastair?' I asked.

'Quiet after living above a pub for years. Nice spot, though, big garden, good walks. I drive her about a bit – she likes to go to the coast, with her paints and pencils.'

'He's got a little job,' Mam said with a warm glance at her brother. 'In a bookshop.'

Alastair shook his head. 'The odd hour here and there. It's her daughter's shop. I watch the till, dust a few shelves. Plenty to read, mind.' Pushing aside his empty plate, Alastair stood to reach for his coat. From an inside pocket he pulled out a set of keys and tossed them into my lap. 'If it's no good to you, Geoff can put it through the auction. But have a look at it, see what you think.'

I looked across at Mam, who gave a sheepishly conspiratorial smile before turning away to attack a tin of custard. My mouth full of potatoes, I stared transfixed by the keys in my hand; one large, two smaller, a worn leather fob bearing the blue-and-silver emblem of British Leyland.

'It's taxed and tested,' Alastair said. 'Insurance might be a bob or two, with your age, so have this towards it.' And before turning to look out across the back garden he handed me a brown envelope, unsealed and gaping thick with tenners.

'You can't, Alastair. A car, and all this – it's too much,' I said, tripping over my breath. 'Let me buy it off you, I can send you a bit every month.'

'Your mother's had my television and whatnot. You can have that. There's a bit in there for your sister as well. I don't know what they like at that age, girls.'

Alastair returned to his seat for treacle pudding and custard. 'I shouldn't get too excited, though, Robin,' he said. 'It's only that last runabout I had.'

I couldn't remember what Alastair had been driving the last time I saw him. For reasons that usually found him blowing into a bag for the police or retrieving his scattered belongings from a ditch the morning after, he'd rarely kept any car for long. But that, it seemed, was all behind him now, since moving away to be with his good lady. She was apparently somebody he'd known a long time ago, when he first left school, I think Mam said, and who, about a year or so before, had wandered back into his life a widow and invited him to go and live with her – and drive her new Volkswagen – in the Norfolk countryside.

'Which last runabout?' I could all but squeak.

'I always used to like them,' Mam said, blowing on her custard. 'It's dark blue, didn't you say, Alastair?'

'Darkish. Teal Blue, I think they called it. Good colour.' Alastair smiled with a nod towards Mam. 'Course, your mother would probably rather it was black-and-white.'

'What is it?'

3

'Oh no, do we have to?' I said, the first dispiriting notes of Genesis's *Watcher of The Skies* droning from the speakers.

'It's my turn,' Fliss smiled, flopping across her bed. 'You had last pick.'

'Yes, and I put Prince on – because you like him.'

'You like him too.'

It's true, in Prince I had begun to appreciate and to some extent share Fliss's fascination. Artistically speaking, I mean. Supremely gifted, and clearly bonkers, Prince's songs were fresh and exciting and totally unlike anything I'd ever heard before.

There was an urgent intensity to his music, always, even on the slower and sillier tunes. It was, Fliss had told me many times, "just all so flippin' sexy", and with this I found myself mostly in agreement, despite the poster on her wardrobe from which he glared in thrusting stripper knickers and a flasher's mac.

'I'd rather listen to Prince all night than this nonsense,' I said, frowning at the LP sleeve. 'Why's he dressed as a fox in a nightie?'

'That's Peter Gabriel. A lot of early Genesis is inspired by old English fairy tales, myths and legends,' Fliss said, drawing the duvet over our heads. 'And Tolkien.'

'What?'

'You know, *The Hobbit, Lord of The Rings*. I think it's cool.'

'I think it's stupid wizardy goblin nonsense. *Listen to it.*'

'I'd like to, if you'd shut up.' Fliss slid her hands under my T-shirt, pulled it over my head and threw it out onto the bedroom floor. 'And anyway, isn't your hero Jim Kerr a big fan of Peter Gabriel? *Hmm?*'

'Shush, Fliss,' I replied, feeling her heat as she nuzzled against my neck. 'I'm trying to listen.'

Five

1

'What was young David saying, Vern?' Ken the van driver asked through a mouthful of corned beef. 'About Belshaw from the miners' union? He hasn't bumped that new motor already, has he? They're too bloody fast for the roads, them things, if you ask me.'

'No, he hasn't bumped it,' Vern said, sweeping lunch crumbs from the lap of his overalls. 'He had it pinched on Wednesday afternoon, from outside the union offices.'

As I think I mentioned, the workshop had two other mechanics besides old Vern and trainee Ricky. 'That black Sierra Cosworth?' said Darren, who was one of them and aged about thirty.

'Hasn't he only had it a couple of weeks?' said Keith, who was the other and a bit older.

'It was in the *Evening Post* on Saturday,' I said, 'about that RS Turbo taken from Gordon Drive.'

Ricky nodded. 'There've been a few again, lately. All rapid stuff, mostly.'

'Gordon Drive? You mean Mrs Paling's motor?' Ken spat. 'I don't know what things's coming to. Folks should keep their hands off what don't belong to them. It's these unemployed hooligans,' he said, nodding towards me and Ricky. 'Your punk rockers. They want locking up.'

David the sales manager, who'd been hovering, jacketless and smiling patiently at the canteen door, took this cue to interrupt Ken's sermon. 'Sorry to, er–'

Keith leapt up. 'One step closer, Buster, and I'll ruin your nice clean shirt,' he said, his oily paws snapping, like black-hooded cobras, an inch from the sales manager's crisp white chest.

'Go on then, Keith, ruin it,' David said with an affable smirk. 'I can afford a couple of new ones now.'

'You sold another, David?' Ken said, voice proud as a father. 'Just now?'

'Brand-new Sierra XR4x4,' David said. 'White, full spec, mudflaps, floormats. Should be here end of the week. I might get you to deliver it for me, Ken, if that's OK?'

'I'll see if I can fit you in, David,' Ken winked. 'What is it, another miner spunking his redundancy?'

'No, not this one, Ken. Chap from up Windmill Way, owns the horse-riding centre at Oakerby.'

'Markley Hall? At the old station? I did a drop there yesterday.'

David turned to me, nodded, and said, 'Pop through and see me when you get a minute, Robin, will you?'

'Will do, David,' I said, the eyebrows of Ken and the mechanics lifting as one.

Vern clicked the lid on his empty sandwich box and slid it inside his rucksack. 'Is he still after you joining them in there, in the showroom?'

'Bet he takes home a decent pay packet,' said Darren. 'And a brand-new XR3i to swan about in.'

'You should see his missus,' Keith whistled. 'Proper goddess.'

'I don't know what it's about, Vern,' I said, only half truthfully.

'He does all right, does David,' Ken said approvingly. 'But if I were you lads, I'd get out of this trade and… See this young lass here, look. Says she's going on that programme on the television.'

Ken shook open the local paper, his stubby fingers framing the headline TUXFIELD GIRL MILLIE'S ONE TO WATCH above a picture of a striking young woman beaming beside the logo of a popular TV talent show.

'I love that programme,' said Keith. 'They never look anything like who they're supposed to be doing.'

'Remember Cliff Richard?' said Darren. 'He was the spitting image of my Auntie Eileen.'

Vern squinted across the canteen at Ken's newspaper. 'She's a lovely looking young woman,' he said, his voice taking on an unusually dreamy tone. 'Reminds me of somebody I once knew, when I was stationed abroad, about nineteen-fifty– ooh, I forget what year it'd be now, fifty-two, -three? A real lady she was.'

A wide smile, like spilled white paint, spread slowly across Vern's grubby features, settling there awhile as he gazed into the toecaps of his boots where the leather had begun to split, steel glinting beneath.

'You knew a woman, Vern?'

Vern carefully removed his cap before tossing it hard into Keith's smirking face. 'Cheeky sod. I could learn you a thing or two about women, I bet.'

It fell oddly silent as Vern replaced his cap before, smiling broadly again, he quietly surmised, 'I probably should have married her.'

Drawn into Vern's wistful reverie, I didn't mention how the pretty TV girl in the paper had also reminded me of somebody I'd once known, when I was much younger. Instead, I said, 'Why didn't you then, Vern?'

Another, longer, silence followed, and I felt suddenly very nervous of what might be said – of what Ken might say, especially – as all eyes turned again to the smiling face in the paper. But there was no need. Nobody said a word. And I can only put this down to the high regard in which they all held Vern.

'Why didn't I marry her?' Vern said. 'I suppose at the time I was too busy sowing my wild oats.' He smiled again shyly, shaking his head at the recollection. 'Army moved us on, I expect, you know how it is.'

I pictured a girl like the one in the paper, long past fifty now but still as beautiful, still as exotic, waiting for Vern by the fire, in a chair that had only ever been occupied by his mother.

'Ah, but you were only National Service, Vern,' Ken said after violently blowing both nostrils, one after the other, into the dustbin and wiping his hands on the front of his overalls. 'You were never proper army. Here, have I ever told you lads about that dust-up we had in Egypt – my poor pal, Eddie, what happened to him? By Christ!'

2

Leaving work on the dot of half-five, I made a leisurely detour to savour a bootlegged Simple Minds concert recorded in Holland during the spring of '84, and which, just three days after passing my test looked set to eclipse *New Gold Dream* as my number one favourite driving tape. A quid from a local record fair, it captured over two sides a truly spectacular performance by Jim Kerr and the boys that was let down only by a 32-second section covering the end of *Big Sleep* and the start of *Waterfront* where some evil, unthinking bastard had recorded over it with Duran Duran's *Hungry Like The Wolf*.

Through the new stereo, a high-spec item that Ricky had definitely not stolen from the garage, it sounded incredible, the thunder of the band, as I drove along, lifting me to a higher, barely short of magical plane, while also causing some of the more worrying noises the MG made to miraculously disappear.

A 1973 MGB GT, to be precise, that last runabout of Alastair's, which I'd found garaged, under an old eiderdown, behind the pub where he lived before moving to Norfolk. It probably wouldn't have been my first choice. And yes, it was a little bit scabby, with both rear wheel arches, a door bottom, and driver's-side front wing all bubbling with more tiny perforations than Britain's best-selling teabag. But it had wire wheels. It was a pretty cool colour – Teal Blue, as Alastair said – and it ran smooth as a sewing-machine once Ricky had been at it with his spanners and a screwdriver.

Much as I loved my car (nearly as much as I loved saying 'my car'), I knew better than to park it outside Fliss's house, aware its shabby presence on the swept liquorice drive would be guaranteed to send the value of her parents' property, and those of their immediate neighbours, plummeting. And also, from what I'd seen of him so far, I still very much felt that the less 'Lionel' was reminded of my existence the better.

'Are you going to Felicity's?' Mam smiled as I tied my shoes on.

'Maybe,' I answered off-handedly. Well, it's no good getting their hopes up.

'Do you love her, Robin?' Cath wheedled from where she sat flicking through *Smash Hits*.

'Shut up, spotty.'

'Susanna Hoffs is in here again. Shall I save it for you?'

'If you like.'

Fed, washed and changed, an hour or so later I made the ten-minute walk up to Windmill Way. So engrossed in visualising myself belting out *Promised You A Miracle* to a steaming Rotterdam crowd I even entertained a few deft centre stage moves in almost broad daylight. My grasp of these subtly emotive gestures, utilising the four key limbs, plus head and shoulders, was now so uncannily Jim Kerr-like – especially when combined with my fine singing – that at several points along the way I leapt up on to a garden wall, taking it for Mick MacNeil's keyboard-riser, from which I would then spring into an impressively ambitious scissor-kick before settling on the pavement in a low and sensuous feline crouch, pushing back a curtain of fringe as I held out my packet of Rolos microphone to the auditorium, inviting my spellbound thousands to sing along.

I'd just taken a final bow to the traffic and was waving myself from the stage when a lanky acne-spattered youth smacked suddenly, very hard and very deliberately, against my left shoulder.

'Wanker,' he said, pushing his fag-breath snarl so far into my face our heads cracked. 'I'll destroy you.' I recognised him immediately. During the single year our spells at Burns Green Comprehensive had overlapped he'd spat on my blazer, thumped me in the ear and twice nicked my dinner money. A notorious thug and Olympic standard glue-sniffer, he'd clearly chosen to pursue his boyhood hobbies as a full-time career.

I walked on, shaking my head in stunned sympathy, pitying him because I knew he'd never felt the love of the sweaty Dutch hordes, that morons like him would never be able to understand such moments. Because anyone that understood, even a tiny bit, wouldn't be laughing as he walked away eating my microphone.

I found Lionel and Ruth in front of the open garage doors, taking turns to slip behind the wheel of the new Sierra XR4x4 and press a few buttons.

'Thank you kindly for this, Robin,' said Lionel as he waved the yellow number plate under his wife's nose with a delighted smile. 'New number plate for your horsebox, darling. Hadn't even crossed my mind.'

'I thought you might want to try towing with the new car at the weekend,' I said, 'so I took down the number and had one made up.'

'I think I was wrong about this one, Ruth. Turns out he's a bloody good chap after all.'

Ruth's hand settled on my shoulder and gave it something

between a pat and a squeeze. 'That's very thoughtful of you, Robin, thank you,' she said. 'But for the record, can I just say that I always did think you were a bloody good chap, as well as being charming and handsome.'

'Now steady on, girl,' Lionel scoffed. 'I'm losing enough sleep worrying about what he's getting up to with my daughter without having to keep an eye on you as well.'

I wasn't sure if Lionel winked at me as he said this or if it was a spot of hay fever. I find with folks who make their living up to the elbows in horses and such creatures it can be hard to tell.

'Yes, steady on, Mum,' Fliss said, threading her arm through mine and leading me away from her parents, along the sweeping drive towards the street. 'He's *my* Robin and he's come to see *me*. Bye-bye.'

'Be good now,' Lionel called after us. 'And don't be late, Felicity, you've school in the morning.'

As the electric gates hummed shut behind us, Fliss pulled me close and planted a noisy kiss on my cheek. 'See, I told you Dad liked you,' she said. And I stopped and gave her a bigger, longer kiss on the lips.

Turning into the main road, we hadn't wandered five hundred yards when a figure I sighingly recognised came flailing round the corner towards us. I shoved Fliss into a cushioning topiary, for safety, and braced my shoulder against the oncoming loser.

'Little dancing wanker,' glue boy shouted into my eyes, the same ash-spittle sneer twisting his pale face into even sharper angles as he blundered past, knocking me sideways. As we walked on, I knew for certain he'd turned and was now walking slowly backwards while he repeated his three-word ditty I don't know how many more times.

'Why did he just do that?'

'Ignore him, Fliss,' I said. 'He's a moron.' And tightening my grip on her hand I made him fade away.

Six

1

You probably won't believe this, but between the ages of seven and seventeen I appear in maybe eight photographs. Ten at a push. From my Christening right up until the summer my dad became my ex-dad there are whole albums full of me. But after that, other than for a few buck-toothed school pictures and some faded snaps at an air museum with my uncle Alastair, I am for more than a decade invisible.

But among the very few pictures that I do have, though, there is one of me and a little girl standing in front of a semi-detached house, between a pair of open, white-painted gates. It is Jubilee Day, 1977. Union Jack bunting and tea-towels bearing the Queen's face hang from every door and windowsill, while red-white-and-blue-skirted trestle tables bow with the weight of fairy cakes, squash-filled jugs and white bread sandwiches with the crusts taken off.

In our matching red shirts, white shorts and blue socks, the little girl and I face towards each other, the palms of our hands pressed flat together, our fingers interlocked as we stretch our arms up to the sky. Our heads are thrown back, eyes scrunched tight in giggling summer ecstasy.

I am six years old. The little girl's name is Millie Smith, and she is my best friend.

For fourteen months when our family had still been a traditional four-piece we'd lived in a leafy cul-de-sac at Tuxfield, where, according to Mam, I liked to play at the Smiths' so much that when they went away on holiday to Trinidad I cried and knocked at their front door every day until they came back. I don't know about that, Mam often exaggerates these things, but what I do remember is that despite Millie's enormous older brothers, Garry and Winston, and her stern-looking father, a doctor at Tuxfield General, their house was always so peaceful compared to ours, even when the men were all out and Mrs Smith would play her records much louder than mums were really supposed to do. And that Mrs Smith always seemed to be cooking, filling the hallway, which doubled as both animal hospital and flightdeck of Thunderbird 2, with smells that never failed to make me feel hungry and warm and safe.

So when I said the TV girl in the paper, the one who'd sent Vern all flushed and aquiver, had also reminded me of somebody I once knew, what I meant was that I recognised her immediately.

She is seventeen years old. Her name is Millie Smith, and I hadn't seen her for eleven years.

2

Gillian came to Stonebridge Motor Company the first week in March. At twenty-three she was not only much older than me, but also Mr Honeywell's niece, and I remember being quite put out at this interloper to Sheila's and my little world, before I learned it was only for a week's work experience.

The mechanics, of course, all thought she was the best thing that ever happened to the place, with those who still had hair shaking the brake dust and oil-sludge from it before rattling for her attention at the parts hatch. While at the front counter, Gillian's arrival coincided exactly with the day the three salesmen, David, Graham and Andrew, suddenly became our most frequent and inquiring customers.

Unquestionably attractive in ways that suggested a girl from the mechanics' wall calendars come to life, Gillian was also sort of posh in the same way her uncle, Mr Honeywell, was sort of posh. By which I mean, while she was not exactly champagne and caviar, she was by no means spanners and Swarfega, either.

I barely noticed her.

'Can I give it a squeeze now, Robin?' Gillian said, throwing Vern a saucy wink he wasn't sure what to do with. 'What if it goes all in my hair?'

There was every possibility of that happening, too. I'd got the stuff in my own hair on more than one occasion, the tricky pneumatic oil pump having a tendency for roughly every twenty litres of engine oil dispensed to sneeze a further half litre all over the dispenser – or, in this case, squeezer.

'It won't go in your hair, Gillian,' I said. 'Just keep a tight grip and – Oh, hello, Sheila.'

'David on the phone for you, Robin love. Shall I do that, Gillian?' I heard Sheila say as I strode away between the racks to the front counter. 'It can be tricky in false nails.'

'Hello, David?'

'Do you fancy earning an extra tenner on Saturday, pal?' David said. 'It's our Spring Super Sale Event this weekend, so if you're still dead keen, how about putting a suit on and coming to give me and the lads a hand in the showroom?'

I wanted to clarify that I'd never been 'dead keen' on anything apart from my one true vocation of becoming Jim Kerr, about which David, naturally, wouldn't have the foggiest. I did however need every tenner I could get my hands on, so I said, 'Yes, please,' and thanked him kindly. 'Only problem, David – I haven't got a suit. Not even my old school uniform,' I said, recalling the blazer's violent last day sacrifice.

'Don't worry, pal,' David said. 'I can lend you one of mine. I'll bring it in for you in the morning.'

3

Beyond Fliss's house there was but one further property of similarly bespoke modern splendour before the town gave way to an undulating bedspread of patchwork fields that stretched, between scrappy hedgerows and a railway embankment, to the muddy hem of the main road where it climbed steadily in the distance towards the forest.

In her riding boots she'd marched me through the rubble of an old farmhouse, along a narrow sluice-side path and under a railway bridge that echoed with the hoots of smoking boys before we turned into an avenue of pine trees. 'Bloody hell, Fliss,' I said. 'Do you always come this way?'

'Yes, why?'

'It's a bit–'

'What? You're not scared, are you?' In the gloom I could barely make out Fliss's features, but her voice told me they were smiling, all of them. 'How can you call yourself Robin and be afraid of Sherwood Forest?'

'I don't call myself anything,' I said as she leapt onto my back, her arms tight under my chin. 'And no, I'm not scared–'

'Giddy-up, horsey, not far now.'

'I was thinking of you, actually, walking through here alone at night.'

'I'm not alone. And what are you worried about, a sex maniac jumping out and having his filthy way with me?'

'Course not. I know you'd tell him you're not that kind of girl, so not to bother getting his hopes up, let alone anything else.'

'You'll regret that later,' Fliss said, getting down just before we emerged from the trees. 'That's where Mungo lives, over there.'

At the end of a twisting narrow lane the low wooden buildings and toytown fences of the stables looked more like a medieval settlement, as pretty as a picture in its pine-bordered meadow. Barely a mile from home, it appeared as strange and unexpected as the bidet I'd discovered in Fliss's parents' bathroom, the one which, once its purpose had been explained to me, stopped being funny when an image popped into my mind of her father, Lionel, straddling it to make merry.

We scrambled down into a lane mined with the steaming evidence of well-fed horses. The evening was almost silent but for a distant coal train rattling along the embankment and the voice of Frank Sinatra warbling about strangers in the night.

But Frank was not alone. And as glances were exchanged, from behind a tall hedgerow there came a second singer's voice, one which easily overpowered Ol' Blue Eyes, in volume if not in harmony, between intermittent bursts of a whirring vacuum cleaner.

'Doo-bee-doo-bee-doo-oo'
(*whirr*)
'Doo-doo-bee-doo-bee-ee'
(*whirr*)
'Doo-bee-doo-bee-doo-oo-oo'

I dived after Fliss's jodhpur-clad bottom into the hedgerow, from where we peered out across the back garden of a dark and sleepy looking house that reminded me of the gatekeepers' lodges around Welbeck Abbey. Not twenty feet away a pristine silver Ford Escort Harrier dazzled in the dying sun, its doors wide open, stereo blaring. Beside it a figure in grubby trousers and an open-necked shirt carefully coiled the vacuum cable and folded a yellow duster into his back pocket before, placing one foot on an up-turned plastic bucket, he began to sing with all the love in his boots to a young border collie sitting, panting, in the driver's seat. Something about the dog's eyes being so inviting, something else about its smile. Once we'd finally stopped giggling, I poked my head through the hedge. 'Vern!'

'What are you creeping about at, up here?' Vern said, unhooking the gate and beckoning us into a garden as wild as it was ordered. 'Comes to something when a chap can't sing to his dog without being rudely interrupted.'

Vern studied Fliss for a moment from under the peak of his cap. 'Very nice to meet you, Fliss,' he said with a conspiratorial nod my way. 'I was beginning to think you were a figment of his imagination.'

Fliss laughed.

'You can talk,' I said. 'I thought you were serenading a lady.'

'I was,' Vern grinned, bending to ruffle the dog behind its ears. 'She's the only girl for me, aren't you, Betty? Eh?'

Fliss knelt to stroke Betty. 'She's gorgeous.'

Vern took a small biscuit from his pocket and held out his hand. 'And she loves a bit of Sinatra, don't you?'

'We were just going for a walk,' I said. 'Up to the stables.'

'I'm taking Robin to meet my horse.' I couldn't help but feel a double surge of pride and embarrassment at this. Pride at being with a beautiful girl who owned a horse, embarrassment at showing it in front of Vern. Neither seemed right, somehow.

'Well just make sure you keep him out of the saddle, won't you? I've seen how he drives.'

Vern locked the car, gathered up his Hoover and cleaning materials. 'If you hold on a minute,' he said, 'we'll walk with you. I'll just put this lot away and tell Mother.'

Betty ran ahead as we walked up the lane, Vern swinging her lead between his fingers. 'We're a bit early tonight,' he said. 'She likes to look for rabbits.'

'Does she eat them?' I asked.

'No, she just likes to run after them. A lot of rabbits in that field by the stables. We'll go through the woods tonight, I think, then back along the embankment from Oakerby. Expect you'll be having riding lessons next then, Robin.'

'No chance,' I said, shaking my head.

'I'm going to teach him,' Fliss smiled. 'As soon as my saddle's fixed. Dad can't do it at the shop, so Robin's off the hook for now.'

Vern looked quizically across at Fliss. 'Is he in that line, then, your dad? Horses and what have you?'

'Yes. Mum and Dad run Markley Hall Equestrian together. It's a riding equipment shop at Oakerby, near the railway bridge.'

'I know the place you mean,' Vern nodded. 'Doesn't Ken drop bits there from time to time?'

'That's right,' I said.

At the stables gates I looked back just as Vern threw a yellow tennis ball for Betty. A second later they'd stepped into the dark woods and were gone.

Seven

1

After bolting the showroom doors I carried the coat-hooked board hung with the keys of thirty or so used cars on the forecourt through to David's office.

'Eight used and five new today, pal,' the sales manager grinned, indicating a chair before vanishing himself in a cloud of aerosol musk.

'Is that good?' I said, and I handed over a sheaf of enquiry forms with names and telephone numbers of prospective buyers I'd shown around vehicles or taken for test drives, but who hadn't been able to wait around long enough to talk money with a proper salesman.

'It's bloody marvellous.'

'Sorry about your–,' I began to say before senior salesman Graham, a stern-faced Geordie, barged in, sucking air noisily through his teeth and tut-tutting in my explicit direction.

'You know how to make enemies fast, don't you? First day on the job and he goes and sells the boss's favourite motor.' Graham shook his head, tut-tutted again. 'I take it you've sacked him, David?'

'I could kick him across that forecourt,' David said. 'But what can I say? Of the half dozen folks he took out we've sold that XR3i of mine, you shifted that gold Fiesta to the old couple, and

Andrew's just taken five hundred quid deposit on the XR2 from his lady vicar.'

'Lady vicar?' Graham said, his short legs, double-chin and singsong Newcastle baritone lending him, despite the forbidding expression, the twinkle of a nightclub comedian. 'I suppose she'll get to heaven quicker now, in a hot hatchback.'

David waved my enquiry forms. 'And two more here say they'll be back in the morning to talk figures.'

'I'll let him off then,' Graham said, giving my shoulder a dig with his elbow. 'Go on then, Robin, who can I have for tomorrow? I only want customers who'll buy, though. Give Andrew the timewasters.'

David split the enquiry forms, passing half to Graham and asking him to put the rest on Andrew's desk. 'If they've not been in by lunchtime, ring and make an appointment.'

'He's here now, boss.'

Andrew, a bunch of keys swinging from his teeth and a plastic 'Sold' sign wedged under one arm, high-fived Graham before pulling a signed order from his blazer pocket and skimming it across the desk to David. '*And* another.'

'Good man. Get it marked up on the board.'

'Thanks for all your help today, Robin,' Andrew said, turning to me. 'Brilliant having you look after customers when we're all tied up.'

'He never made me that cup of tea he promised,' Graham said.

Andrew flicked through his enquiry forms. 'This a firm appointment, at eleven?'

'Yes,' I said. 'Is that all right?'

'Great. Are you with us again tomorrow?'

I looked at David. He arched his eyebrows. 'Fancy earning another tenner, Robin?'

2

Other than for a drive, or to the cinema now and then, Fliss and I rarely went out at weekends. With Ruth and Lionel away most Saturday nights at some do-gooding function or local business knees-up, it suited us far more to order a takeaway and make use of their video recorder and her bedroom and just enjoy being alone together. On the few occasions I had gone into town with Ricky and some of our old school pals I'd very soon found myself green with ale and wishing to be back at Windmill Way, listening to Fliss at the piano, or cosying up on the sofa in the big, low-lit lounge as we half-watched some old film from the rental shop.

Which is how we'd both looked forward to spending this particular Saturday evening. And we did, more or less.

To celebrate my first day in the showroom Fliss had made a huge and delicious mushroom omelette, which she served with various leaves and slices of crusty bread with butter. She showed me photographs of herself as a little girl, mostly, it seemed, taken on foreign holidays: holding Lionel's hand beside a whitewashed windmill; gazing nervously up at Mickey Mouse; a crouched teenage blur in a bright orange ski suit. Then afterwards we'd gone up to her room and got down to some pleasantly adventurous listening to some records, while remaining just the right side of proposing the unthinkable.

The hours slipped by and before we knew it Fliss was sitting on top of the chest freezer, her legs wrapped tight around me as we strung out our goodbyes in the boot room.

'I don't want you to go, Robin.'

'I don't want me to go, either,' I said, my hands lovely and warm inside her dungarees. 'But it's nearly eleven.'

'Will you think about me later, when you're in bed?'

'I never do anything else.'

A taxi was pulling away as I reached the electric gates and a shiny-faced Lionel came bounding up the drive like a St Bernard wrapped in salmon cashmere.

'Robin!' he beamed, clapping me manfully on the shoulder. 'You're not leaving, I hope? So soon? Come in and have a drink. Felicity's still up, I take it?'

'Let Robin go, Lionel, he has work in the morning. Have you both had a nice evening, Robin?'

'Yes, thank you, Ruth, lovely. We had mushroom omelette.'

'Any left? Ruth, go and get Felicity. And Robin, you come with me and I'll get us all a little nightcap.'

I thought of reminding Lionel that his daughter didn't drink alcohol, as he'd once so kindly warned me, but Ruth moved swiftly, squeezing my shoulder goodnight before she spun her husband on his heels and led him away towards the house.

As Ruth said, I did indeed have to work on Sunday. And yet, tired as I was, when I got home and saw the MG waiting in the moonlight I had a sudden and desperate need to be in holy deafening communion with my Scottish idols, and instead of going in, and straight to bed, I jumped in the car and raced to Chesterfield, *New Gold Dream* once more providing the soundtrack to a film only I would ever see.

The post-pub evacuation to the nightclubs and chip shops was in full staggering flow by now, but I found Ricky where I knew he'd be at this time, laughing with two pale, underdressed girls outside The Spire Bar. He whistled as I drew up against the kerb.

'All right, bud.' Ricky flopped heavily into the passenger seat, smelling like he'd been boil-washed in Newcastle Brown and then garnished with a full ashtray. 'Thought you were seeing Fliss tonight?'

'I was,' I said. 'Where are the lads?'

'The Fleece, I think.'

'Have you struck lucky, or are you ready to make a getaway?'

'Didn't you see who that is? It's Gillian – Honeywell's niece. Her mate's gorgeous. Park your skip and come to The Spire. You can keep Gillian company while I tell Mandy how brilliant I am.'

'I'm hardly dressed for a disco,' I said, disappointed that for Ricky the night had obviously only just begun and he'd be unlikely to want a lift home. 'And I'm working in the showroom again tomorrow.'

'I'm not getting anywhere with two of them,' Ricky said. 'But if I got Mandy on her own, I reckon I'd be in.'

I was about to say that he'd soon be out, if he didn't get back to her, when Gillian, who must have been thinking along similar lines, appeared at Ricky's window.

'Robin!'

'Hi, Gillian.'

'*Ro-bi-ii-ii-in?*' Gillian wheedled, smiling from ear to ear. 'I don't suppose you'd be a honey and give me a lift home in your supercool sports car, would you?'

'Er,'

'It's not far.'

I glanced at Ricky.

'Does your friend need a lift as well?'

'No, she wants to go to The Spire with Ricky – if he's interested.'

Ricky gave my elbow a nudge before climbing out to hold the door for Gillian, his eyes widening as she lowered herself into the passenger seat and swung her bare legs under the dashboard.

'Drive safely, young man,' Ricky said with his Fonz-like grin.

I watched in the rear-view mirror as Ricky crossed the road to take the skipping, freezing-looking Mandy by the hand and join the weaving queue for The Spire.

'I wouldn't wait up for him tonight,' Gillian said as we pulled away and drove steadily out of town.

'Do you live out this way as well?' I said, careful to let just one eye linger over Gillian's goose-pimpled thighs while keeping the other for the road. 'Like Mr Honeywell, I mean?'

'Yes,' she said. 'We're quite near to Uncle Giles. I'm not in any hurry to get home, though, if you're not. Robin, what *are* you listening to?'

Before I could answer, Gillian had ejected the cassette, quickly read the label without comment, and pushed it back into the stereo with a forceful snap. '*Hmm*. Mind if I smoke?' she said, nodding indifferently along to *Big Sleep* as she flipped open ten Silk Cut.

'Yes, I do, actually,' I said, sounding like I was being amusing. 'You're not stinking my lovely car out.'

Gillian laughed, then, realising this hadn't been a joke after all, dropped the cigarettes back into her handbag and turned to look sulkily out of the window.

As we took the turning for Bakewell I felt her hand settle a good way up my left thigh, so far up, in fact, I was soon glad I had my wallet in my pocket. She appeared to be in about as much hurry to remove it as she was to get home. With a glance at the fuel gauge, I floored the accelerator and turned up the volume.

When I drew up outside our house some time later, I sat awhile as the engine cooled to hear the final fade-out of *Somebody Up There Likes You*. No Jim Kerr, of course, it being an instrumental track, but sheer SM magnificence all the same.

I had promised Fliss that I would think about her when I was in bed. And I did.

For what was left of the night, I could do nothing else.

3

The first customer I sold a car to committed suicide, right in the middle of the showroom. There was nothing I could do to stop him.

I'd instinctively looked to Graham for help, but he was already deeply embedded, fluffing an expectant young couple at his desk with tales of his loveable and entirely imaginary grandkids. David was in the back yard, carrying out a part-ex appraisal on a Vauxhall three sizes too small for the rowdy family and assorted animals who'd evacuated from it. And not two minutes since, I'd waved Andrew off on a test drive with the red-hot prospect I'd given him the day before. So, there I was, twenty-five past eleven Sunday morning, my second day in the showroom, faced with a suicide, alone.

His name was Oliver Dilks, he worked as an accountant at Sheffield University and arrived in a sleek Opel Manta driven by an even sleeker male friend. On the outside he'd seemed a happy and balanced enough chap, but after only the briefest tiptoe round a three-month-old red Escort RS Turbo on the front pitch he'd practically run towards me and said, 'Could I have that one please, my friend? I'll leave a thousand deposit now and pay the balance on collection, if that's all right?'

No sit in. No test drive. No negotiation. I'd barely mumbled good morning. That, in the lexicon of the showroom, is what's known as a suicide.

'Bloke walked in with both hands up and threw himself on young Robin's sword,' Graham winked over coffee and sandwiches during a brief lunchtime lull. 'I spent an hour and a half signing those bloody teachers of mine, while laddo here's taken a grand deposit and made himself a pot of tea by half-eleven.'

'Nice one, Robin,' belched Andrew over a can of Tizer. 'Jammy sod.'

'Ignore these two,' David said, squeaking Mr Dilks up on the monthly sales whiteboard along with Graham's pregnant teachers, Andrew's (my) red-hot prospect, and three more deals already that day. 'Doesn't matter how we sell them, a sale's a sale. You keep 'em coming, pal. Tasty deal as well, that Turbo. You two won't be complaining when I split the commission between you.'

I'd no idea how much commission Andrew and Graham could expect to receive from Mr Dilks's or the several other sales I'd in varying degrees contributed towards. Nor did I much care. Besides the tenner a day David had promised to pay me, he'd also said, as I left on Sunday, to fill up the MG at the pumps and charge it to sales. On top of my £27.50 YTS money, I felt like a rich man.

When Oliver Dilks came to collect his red RS Turbo the following Thursday, David phoned the front counter and invited me through to his office, where he hovered, making polite conversation, as he oversaw me with the uncomplicated paperwork. What Mr Dilks made of me being in a grubby dinner lady's smock rather than David's suit, I can't imagine, but he never mentioned it.

'Have you bought cars from us before, Mr Dilks?' David said, oozing polite confidence. 'You look ever so familiar.'

'No, I haven't. But my last one, an Escort Cabriolet, I had serviced here two or three times. I've always been very well looked after by that nice lady–'

'Sheila?'

'*Sheila*. I'd spotted that red one on the forecourt, so when the insurance money came through, I came straight to see you.'

I looked up from writing out a receipt for, to me at least, an eye-watering balance. 'Was your cabriolet written-off then, Mr Dilks?'

'You weren't injured, I hope?' David oozed in.

'Oh no – thank you. I wasn't involved in an accident. The car was stolen from the university car park, eight weeks ago.'

Eight

1

'Fifteen years ago we started, me and Felicity's mother, selling animal feed and straw through the classifieds in the *Evening Post*,' Lionel said, rasping his fat hands together as he went about turning keys and switching off lights and cash registers. 'We expanded to a market stall, at Newark, then to a trailer we'd take along to horse trials, gymkhanas, country shows – Chatsworth, Bramham, Burghley...'

'Wow.' I took my time to look about, wide-eyed. 'And now here you are, with all this,' I said, thinking that was just the sort of thing somebody like him would want me to say.

'That's right,' Lionel agreed, coiling a proud arm around his daughter's shoulder. 'Remarkable, really, when you think about it... I suppose we haven't done too badly, Felicity, have we? Not too badly at all.'

Indeed they hadn't.

The headquarters of Markley Hall Equestrian, beneath whose rafters Lionel's words now echoed, was an impressive and spacious neo-rustic showroom of glass, timber and steel, constructed within the tall arch-windowed stone walls of the former railway goods shed at Oakerby station, two miles east of Stonebridge, on the edge of Sherwood Forest. The small staff had gone home by the time we arrived, just before six, leaving

Lionel free to lead us, as he went about his locking-up, on a brief, self-inflating tour of the premises.

It was a bit like a car showroom inside, with its polished tiled floor and overbright illumination, only with a lot more shelves and clutter, and apparently nothing whatsoever to excite a seventeen-year-old whose entire equestrian career amounted to a few Skeggy beach tantrums on the backs of itchy beasts named Posie, Molly and Bob. But as Lionel paused to tidy a display of upset brochures my eye was drawn to the far corner, where three shiny new horseboxes formed an unconvincing diorama of country life. The first 'box had been positioned, tailboard down, to reveal within a table and benches-shaped arrangement of straw bales upon which a fake picnic had been laid beside a large silver trophy flowing with blue and yellow ribbons. Another, at right angles to the first, had been fitted out with racks displaying a selection of highly buffed saddles and various bits of towing equipment. While over the raised tailboard of the third 'box there bulged the most enormous pair of grey plastic horse's buttocks, complete with electric fly-swishing tail.

'It's only the horsebox that's for sale,' Lionel chuckled, cutting the tail's power once I'd fully appreciated the spectacle. 'But the bottom's great fun, don't you think?'

'Oh yes,' I nodded. 'Great fun.'

Not far away, in the window at the front of the shop, were displayed not only more enormous horses' buttocks, but two entire life-size animals, which stood on an oblong of fake turf staring gormlessly at one another while wearing every conceivable piece of kit and accessory no horse ever dreamed it needed – in some instances several of each – their plastic legs visibly buckling with the weight of saddles, bridles, reins, blankets, muzzles and stirrups, not to mention blinkers for eyes and guards for flies, or the innumerable brushes, hoods, girths, boots, and other bits and pieces whose names offered zero clue as to their purpose.

'If I tickle both their noses at the same time,' I said, standing between the two dummy horses, 'will the whole lot go up, like *Buckaroo*?'

For a second Lionel's face froze, his bottom lip sagging with deep thought as if this might actually be a real possibility he'd overlooked. But then, rocking back, and cradling his beachball belly, he began to laugh like he'd never heard anything so funny. 'You know, Robin, I really wouldn't be surprised if it did. Just as long as I'm not the one who has to put it all back together again in the morning.'

'Thanks for getting it fixed, Dad,' Fliss said, giving Lionel's arm a little pat as he carried Mungo's refurbished saddle out to the Jaguar.

'Anything for my girl,' Lionel said. 'Katy's made a fine job of it. Good as new.'

I'd been wondering, as we stepped out into the car park, whether Fliss would be expected to ride home with her father now, rather than with me, and how I might feel about it, but I needn't have worried. As Lionel went back to set the alarm, he turned in the doorway and blew his daughter a kiss and, with a very matey nod, reminded me I was to drive carefully.

2

Perfume clouds swirled thickly above Sheila's desk, the antiquated electric fire glowing volcanic, as always, by her feet, on full three-bar power.

'Did you want me, Sheila?' I said, hovering on the threshold, my face averted as if I'd opened a Chanel-powered blast furnace.

'Sorry, lovey, I hadn't realised you were on the phone,' Sheila smiled, rubbing cream into her hands as she swivelled round on her chair. 'Would you be able to cut me a key when you've a moment? I'm rushing to do these invoices before they come to collect their cars, and there's that big insurance estimate for Kevin at the body shop. Have you time?'

'Course, I'll do it now. I've got another one to do for sales, while I'm at it.'

'The mechanics say these new security locks are no good. The keys, or is it the barrels, wear out much quicker than the old kind.'

'We definitely get through them. I ordered twenty more blanks yesterday. Which car's this for, Sheila?'

'Oh, it's not here, Robin, it's for a phone customer.' Sheila peeled off a Post-It on which she'd written a name and a bold five-digit number. 'You know Mr McGargle, from Norton? There's the key number.'

'Shop!' Keith rapped at the workshop hatch. 'Stores!'

'Where's that lad got to?' I heard Vern say. 'Service!'

'Coming!' I bawled along the aisles, sending dust motes dancing in the beams beneath the skylight.

Sheila sighed. 'Noisy lot. It's time I learned to use that key machine myself. You'll have to give me a crash course, Robin.' These last words came out especially Welsh, which for some reason I always found very comforting.

'Any time, Sheila. It's dead easy.'

'Thanks, lovey. I don't know how I managed before you came. Oh, Robin? Some number plates arrived for your friend at Markley Hall. I put them under the front counter.'

'Shop!'

'Has Robin gone home?'

'Ken's going that way this afternoon, Sheila,' I said. 'I'll get him to drop them off.'

After I'd served Keith and we were alone at the hatch, Vern said, as I dished out his order, 'I say, do you know much about that building opposite your young woman's father's place at Oakerby?'

'The old station?'

'That's it. Is that her father's concern as well as the horse-riding shop?'

'No, the station's nothing to do with Lionel,' I said. 'He looked into it once, Fliss said, but British Rail wouldn't sell it him. It's unsafe, full of asbestos.'

'Asbestos? Is it? Ah. Only, I were up that way last night, walking with Betty, and just as we turned in towards the embankment – you know, past the bridge – two of these here XR2s come racing out of the station yard and shot off, I'm not kidding, like what's-his-name bloody Mansell.'

'Everybody's like what's-his-name bloody Mansell beside you, Vern. It's wasted on you, that lovely Harrier.'

'You leave my driving alone. Anyway, what I was going to say is, it made me wonder if those cars hadn't just been pinched, you know, like these others.'

'They're the right sort,' I agreed. 'Newish?'

'Aye, one black and one that metallic blue. Either way, I thought you might want to warn her father to keep an eye out. If there are wrong 'uns carrying-on they might have a go at breaking into his place, or that little workshop. He's a bit tucked away up there.'

'Thanks, Vern,' I said. 'I'll pass the message on to Lionel later. Did you by any chance get the reg. numbers of the XR2s? You could see if they match any of those that've been stolen.'

'I can barely see your spotty face in front of me, never mind a speeding number plate. Now look sharp and get me these bits, I'm on the clock for this job and you're holding me up with all your chatterboxing.'

As soon as I'd finished with Vern, Ricky and then Darren appeared. I speedily sorted them out with oil, filters, spark plugs, a set of brake pads and a headlight bulb, nothing out of the ordinary or which demanded thrilling consultation with the microfiche. Afterwards I boiled the kettle, dropped two bags in

Sheila's private teapot, and let it brew while I cut a couple of keys, one for sales, and one for Mr McGargle from Norton.

3

One evening as we lay curled beneath Fliss's duvet, listening to some records, the most incredible thing happened, the thing I'd been longing to happen more than anything else in the world. If Lionel and Ruth, sitting downstairs, had heard their daughter's headboard suddenly banging like a shed door in a hurricane, I'm sure they'd have both not only understood my youthful exuberance, but actively rushed upstairs to applaud it.

'Yes!' I shouted as Fliss tightened her arms around my neck.

'Oh, Robin, that's amazing!' she said with a little squeak.

With things between the sheets hotting up nicely we'd switched over to the radio, to save having to change records, just in time to hear a DJ announce that Simple Minds had been confirmed to play at a special concert for Nelson Mandela's 70th birthday. The event was to take place at Wembley Stadium in June and would be broadcast live on television and radio.

Simple Minds. Live. That summer.

'Yes! Yes! Yes!'

Cool as it would be to say it was John Peel, I can't believe I would've been in Fliss's bedroom after ten o'clock on a school night. But whoever it was made the announcement, the news, combined with the bed-bouncing, left me breathless. When Simple Minds had last toured the UK I'd been fifteen, and far too young, according to Mam, to go to pop concerts by myself (or indeed with anyone else, had I known such a likeminded soul). Well, I was old enough now. I had a job (temporary), and a sports car (kind of). And I wouldn't be going by myself, either, I'd be going with Fliss, my girlfriend. The two of us off to Wembley Stadium, in London, to see Simple Minds.

'They don't take bookings at night,' Fliss said when the local coach firm failed to pick up the phone. 'Even for Simple Minds.'

'Worth a try,' I said, carefully replacing the receiver so as not to disturb her parents. 'I'll ring as soon as they open in the morning.'

I ran home with barely enough room in my head to contain all the excitement of the evening. Before leaving, Fliss and I, excited at the prospect of our adventure to London, had had just enough time to get carried away on her bedroom desk to the point where we very badly crumpled a brand-new copy of York's Notes for *Jude The Obscure*.

I was about halfway up the hill to our street when I turned to give a final wave to the ocean of ecstatic faces chanting my name and singing the ba-ba baaa-ba bit of *Alive and Kicking* from the shadows of thirty council house gardens. Another blinding show over, I thrust my hands, with a satisfied smile, into my jacket pockets and found in one of them a cassette tape I'd no recollection of ever having put there. A handy streetlamp showed that although the cellophane had been removed, the labels on both box and cassette remained blank, which was not at all the way I operated. Nor was it my preferred brand of blank tape, either.

I threw off my clothes and climbed into bed untangling my Woolworths headphones. I pressed play on the hi-fi and two seconds later the tape began to hiss. I clicked off the bedside light. It didn't improve the hiss, but I now heard a sniff and a scrape before the sound of a throat being gently cleared. Then a piano, a trickle of notes in a minor key played quietly, lightly, and very beautifully. No further accompaniment, just this solo piano, tinkling in a distant, echoing space somewhere out in the darkness. I closed my eyes, the tune soon growing familiar, unmistakeably so, though I had never heard it played quite like this, so sparse and hauntingly reimagined.

But what, and *who*, was it? I couldn't think. Until I heard her voice. *It doesn't hurt me*, she sang, sounding as fragile as a dandelion clock in a stiff summer breeze. *Do you want to feel how it feels?*

It was a brave performer who took on Kate Bush without being found woefully wanting. But taken it on she had and it sounded like nothing on earth. It wasn't Kate Bush, of course, nothing ever could be, except Kate herself. But it was magical and wonderful all the same and captured more than enough of the passion and poetry, the innate feminine intensity of the original to make clear that here was a musician who understood, from somewhere deep within herself, the sensations and emotions with which she was dealing, and which she had now chosen to put across on tape to her rapt, smitten, audience of one.

I listened to the song over and over until I fell asleep, her voice whispering in my ears, her eyes smiling in the dark in the way they only ever did beneath a duvet when her parents were out.

It's you and me, Fliss sang. *It's you and me.*

4

'Sheila, is it OK if I make a quick phone call, before they start bawling?'

'Of course, Robin love. You've no need to ask.'

A minute before nine, receiver jammed between ear and shoulder, I flicked, trembling, through the grease-fingered pages of my notepad and dialled the number.

'Saturday the eleventh of June... Yes, that's right, Wembley Stadium... Two please... No, two... Pick up from Stonebridge Bingo Hall.'

'Shop!'

'Come on, Robin, chop-chop!'

'Sorry, Sheila,' I said, finding her in rubber gloves and decanting anti-freeze for Vern at the hatch. I filled Vern's and Darren's oil jugs and swiftly doled out spark plugs, filters, a couple of gaskets and a mirror glass.

'I think they wait, deliberately, until we pick up the phone,' Sheila tutted, ungloving her hands when we'd got rid of them.

'Sorry,' I said again. 'I had to ring Bailey's Coaches first thing or my life would not be worth living.'

'Oh? Are you going on holiday with your girlfriend, is it?'

'No,' I said. 'We're going to London, to Nelson Mandela's 70th birthday party.'

Sheila laughed and put a freshly creamed hand on my arm. 'Oh, Robin, you are funny. Doesn't he live in South Africa?'

5

'You've gone and lost your earring, Robin,' Graham said, the third weekend I put on David the sales manager's spare suit to work in the showroom.

I squeezed the gristly hole in my left lobe. 'Thought it was probably time to get rid of it. I've had it since I was fourteen.'

It was no big deal. A tiny silver sleeper, barely even noticeable. But you needed to look smart in sales. The slightest things scared customers off. I should have taken it out long before, really, soon after I won the playground dare to get my ear pierced by the following morning. I did it myself, with a sewing needle and a couple of ice cubes. It hurt like hell, and yet there was hardly any blood on my school shirt, not like the time when I was seven and my ex-dad had torn Mam's big gold hoops from her ears. The shoulders of her yellow blouse had bloomed with crimson epaulettes and she hadn't even noticed, she hadn't felt a thing, she said, after he'd marched her into the hall and smashed her head repeatedly against the bottom stairs. It was a nice blouse, too. It had really suited her.

The other thing, of course, was that Jim Kerr didn't even wear an earring, so it was not like by removing mine I was in any way selling out or letting myself down as an artist.

'You pierced your own ear with your mother's sewing needle?' Graham said, knocking back half a mug of tea. 'You mad young bugger. Come on, then, there's two lots of customers wandering about on the bottom pitch.'

Nine

1

'You were right to not be a mechanic,' Ricky noted pityingly as I wrestled with an evil air-hose designed, apparently, to suck more air out of a car's tyres than it put into them. 'What're you playing at, man?'

'You're a great help.'

Ricky leaned against the car, filling his mouth with beef flavour Monster Munch, stuffing the empty packet inside his overalls, and bursting open a second. 'I'm eating my tea.'

'This thing's knackered.'

'It isn't. It's just you that's useless.'

The click of loafer on forecourt brought Mr Honeywell whistling out of the showroom and swinging his briefcase towards his grey Granada Scorpio, where it had been polished and parked on the far side of the petrol kiosk.

'Is she running well, boys?' Honeywell said, swerving to a halt beside the MG.

'She is now Ricky's had a look, Mr Honeywell,' I smiled.

'The points were shot and it was running a bit rich, that's all,' Ricky said. 'The cleaners left your keys on the pumps, Mr Honeywell. I'll nip in and fetch them.'

'That's all right, thank you, Ricky. I've to pick up some milk on my way past.' Honeywell stooped to peer in through the MG's open window. 'I ran one or two of these myself when we were a BMC franchise, many years ago. Wonderful motors. *Hmm*. Well, enjoy your evenings.'

I'd got on well with Honeywell since that time I cut a key for his wife's car and loaded his boot with wine. Although he spent much of his day behind frosted glass, in that time warp office of his, he'd often be seen making urgent dashes through to sales, or out on the forecourt inspecting the used car displays. Now and then he'd appear at the front counter, fussing over one of his cronies or a silk-scarfed wife from the Rotary Club, Round Table, or whatever it was they all belonged to, bantering about Tudor Barns and Parish Hall beanfeasts as he personally booked their cars in for service. What I liked about Honeywell from the off was that no matter who you were, he always had that exact same way of talking to you, like you were the very best of old friends.

'Actually, gentlemen, there's something you could perhaps both help me with,' he said, clicking back over a minute or two later with a carton of milk and evening paper. 'I've a couple of vehicles need delivering, tomorrow evening, to one of our big business customers over in Sheffield.'

'British Steel, Mr Honeywell?' Ricky said. 'They have a lot of cars from us, don't they?'

Honeywell gave a sure-faced nod, setting his briefcase, milk and paper between his shoes while he straightened the knot of his tie. 'They do, Ricky, they do indeed. Yes, two more to go over, an Orion and – I forget now what the other one is, but both nearly new, ex-demonstrators, you know. They're not here yet actually. Arriving tomorrow, I hope. *Hmm*. Now I know you're both considered excellent drivers and, er,' Honeywell frowned at one of the less picturesque areas of the MG's bodywork, 'I thought perhaps you might appreciate some extra funds to help maintain your classic motors.'

'Can do,' Ricky nodded. 'I wouldn't mind a run to Sheffield.'

'What time would it be, Mr Honeywell?' I asked, wondering how much some extra funds amounted to.

'As I say, it wouldn't be till early evening, I'm afraid. After hours. Say leave here at eight o'clock?'

'Should Robin wear his salesman's suit, Mr Honeywell?' Ricky smirked. I stuffed the air-hose down the neck of his overalls and gave him a good blast.

'Oh no, a suit won't be necessary,' Honeywell said, chuckling awkwardly as if he feared he might be next. 'The paperwork's all done and been faxed on ahead. It'll just be a very simple handover.'

'Great,' I said. 'Thanks, Mr Honeywell.'

'Well, gentlemen, if I don't see you before, we'll say tomorrow evening then, eight o'clock sharp.'

We waved as Honeywell purred across the forecourt and away into the early evening traffic. Ricky made a face. 'Why's he asking us to deliver these cars instead of the salesmen?'

'Who cares? Like he said, we've got classic motors to maintain. Now will you please come and do these bloody tyres for me?'

2

I wasn't due to see Fliss on Wednesday, she was supposed to be revising for her A-Levels. But having arranged to go to Sheffield the following evening, on this job for Honeywell, I thought I'd swing by the phonebox and ring her up on the off chance.

'Of course I'd like to see you, silly!' she said with an excited delight in her voice I don't think was entirely due to me rescuing her from Thomas Hardy. 'Hurry up and get changed, I'm making risotto for dinner.'

'Delicious,' I said, sure it would be, whatever risotto was. 'Hey Fliss, I was just listen–'

There came a sudden heavy iron squeal behind me, of the

phonebox door being pulled open. I reached back, not bothering to turn round, and yanked it closed again.

'What was that?'

'I said I was just listening to your tape, in the car... No it's *not*, and you know it isn't... Fliss, it's fantastic, it's... it's beautiful, it's really, really beautiful.'

I've no idea how Fliss replied to that, or even if she replied at all. For just as that second 'beautiful' left my lips, my entire body left the phonebox, yanked out by the collar of my dinner lady's smock to be punched twice in the ear with such sharp, numbing force my whole head seemed to inflate as whatever had become detached inside it began to whistle like an angry kettle.

I hadn't completely gone over when I landed in the High Street, but in the dazed attempt to free myself from whichever bastard's grip had so impolitely severed me from the receiver I'd spun through several wild pirouettes and into a drunken sideways stumble before smashing down on my right kneecap against a knobbly iron manhole cover.

'*It's really beautiful,*' a familiar sticky voice sneered as I got to my feet in a tangle of navy-blue. As if wearing a smock like a dinner lady wasn't already enough, now, with it hanging provocatively off one shoulder, I resembled a very slutty one. '*It's really really beautiful.* Ahh, kiss-kiss. Teach you to slam the door on me, you little wanker.'

Somebody seemed to find this highly amusing, and I turned, rubbing my ear to shush the whistling, to where another youth, a smaller, yellow-spiked version of my lanky dark assailant, slouched like a shot-blasted Billy Idol across the concrete steps that led to the allotments. This giggling goon sucked with scab-cracked lips at a bent roll-up, puffing the smoke out almost immediately so he could resume dangling thick greenish ropes of phlegm into the expanding pool between his battered boots.

'Brought your little sister to help?' I said, slipping out of my smock and wringing it murderously, nervously, between my hands. 'Strong family resemblance – same runny nose, dead dog eyes.'

'Think you're funny, don't you?' lanky glue boy said, his Adam's apple jutting through his skin like a broken bone. 'I don't need any help to destroy you, you little wanker.'

'You like saying wanker, don't you? What's your problem? What have I done to you?'

'You're my problem. Singing and dancing about on walls in your fucking ballet shoes.'

Billy Eyesore laughed and coughed up another thick rope.

'They're actually kung fu slippers,' I corrected, grateful I wasn't wearing them now.

'You get right up my nose.'

'Really? I'm surprised there's room with all that glue you shove up it. Is that why you two stick together? Ha ha!'

I'm not sure Lanky got the joke, but either way he'd obviously had enough chit-chat and he suddenly sprang at me swinging his fists and kicking and clawing at my throat. I leapt back, tossing aside my smock and bobbing and weaving about enough, and so nimbly, that as he came at me again, leather limbs flailing, he'd only time to stick a heavy, stinging boot into my shin and glance a lucky, numbing punch off my shoulder before I saw my chance and, catching him off balance, I pounced and smashed a mighty blind fist up and under his bony jaw. There was no crack, smack or ker-thwack, like in films, disappointingly. The tight sallow skin just felt sharp and greasy against my knuckles, like punching the cold carcass of a roast chicken left over from Sunday dinner, and I'm sure it hurt me far more than it hurt him, three-parts-anaesthetised on craft adhesive as I expect he might have been.

Lanky staggered back clutching his throat and making strange gargling noises, like he'd sprung a fatal leak. Even so, he was perfectly positioned for a work boot in the knackers and, the fight gods being in my corner, I was about to give it to him when his pal Billy Eyesore rose from the steps, tossed away his roll-up, and moved towards me looking dangerously unpredictable with his fists bunched. I checked Lanky would be staying put for the time being and turned back thinking how clever I was about to sound when I told Billy it was a nice day for a right kicking, only to find him being lifted by the lapels and thrown against the side of the phonebox by a wild-eyed Ricky, the squeal of whose van tyres I now half-recalled hearing amid all the violent drama of a few moments before.

'Come on, girls, let's make it a fair fight now, two-on-two,' Ricky said, pushing his nose hazardously close, I thought, to little Billy's and stamping on his toes.

'No trouble, mate,' Billy said. 'No trouble. Come on, Clay, leave it.'

'Clay?' I shouted after them, as they scuttled away up the allotment steps. '*Clay*? That's beautiful mate, that is, really, really beautiful!' Ricky handed me my smock as a couple of stones chimed heavily off the side of the phonebox. 'Where were you five minutes ago, when I needed you?' I said, cupping the throbbing fire of my ear.

'I wish I'd driven past now and let them murder you. What happened?'

I shook my head. 'They wanted to use the phone. I was on it.'

'Arseholes.'

Ricky tilted his head and slowly curled his lip in disgust.

'What?' I said. 'What's that face for?'

'You've got a massive load of green gob in your hair.'

3

'Your hair's all sticking up at the back,' Fliss said after we'd dried and put away our dinner plates. 'What have you been doing?'

'Nothing.' I splashed my fingers under the cold tap, a few

droplets falling like heaven onto my still throbbing ear as I smoothed my gob-matted locks. 'I mean it, though, Fliss,' I said, returning to the conversation we'd started over our mushroom risotto. 'Your singing and playing on that tape is brilliant.'

I carried two mugs of hot chocolate through to the back room where, with easy, horsey habit, she swung a wide leg and sat astride the piano stool. I did the same, though far less elegantly, almost spilling the HCs before I got settled, facing her. 'The tape's brilliant and you are brilliant,' I said. 'Why shouldn't you send it in?'

Fliss gave me a weak smile before leaning close and resting her forehead against mine. 'Oh, I don't know,' she sighed as she took my hands and held them against her hips. 'That's not why I made it, though.'

I kissed the top of her head. 'You play so beautifully. And your voice... I've heard you sing, lots of times, but not like you do on that tape. Where did that come from?'

Fliss shrugged. 'But that's just it. I do love singing, and playing, but only to myself, here, on my own. Why do I need some complete strangers to listen and decide whether I'm good enough? I don't care what anybody else thinks. My music is... mine, it's kind of... I don't know, *private*.' She looked up at me with questioning eyebrows. 'Is that a really stupid thing to say?'

'No, of course it isn't,' I said. 'As long as you'll still play for me, I don't mind what you do.'

'I made that tape for you, Robin, not to get on a stupid television show.'

It had been her mum's idea. Some weeks before, Ruth had seen the article in the *Evening Post* inviting applications for the new series of the TV talent contest *Show Me The Stars* and encouraged Fliss to send a tape to the studios. She hadn't by then heard her daughter's breathtaking version of *Running Up That Hill* that she'd recorded for me only a few days before, but Ruth, like Lionel, was very proud of Fliss's incredible talent and achievements and I suppose, in that way of parents and folks without a clue about these things, she thought the chance to appear on a big show like that was just what Fliss had been working towards all these years, that this was what she wanted.

'You don't have to send in a tape, you know, if that's not what you want to do.'

'No...'

'But if you're not going to apply,' I said, grinning as an image involving silk shirts and dry ice popped into my head, 'I think I might.'

'What? You wouldn't dare.'

'I would.'

'Really?' Fliss leaned back squeezing my cheeks between her fingers till my lips formed a fishy pout. 'Who would you be?'

'*Ing urr.*'

'Jim Kerr!' she laughed, releasing my face.

'Why not?'

Fliss planted a kiss on my brow and reached for a hot chocolate from where I'd left them to cool on top of the piano (coasters, naturally). She studied me as she blew and took a long, thoughtful sip. 'You'd make a better Limahl.'

'*Limahl?*'

'Or the blonde girl from The Human League.'

'Susanne?'

'You'd make a fabulous Susanne.'

'I'd make a fabulous Jim Kerr. I know all the words, I've got the haircut, and I've definitely got the moves.'

'You mean these moves?' Fliss rose, placed her foot on the edge of the piano stool and began to make some really quite ridiculous hippy-like waving gestures with her arms before pushing the splayed fingers of one hand back, in the most idiotic poseur-like way, through her mop of dark curls.

'What's that supposed to be?' I asked. 'You look like you're drowning.'

'That's how you used to dance at the golf club disco. To every song.'

'I did not.'

'*In Between Days.*' Fliss was drowning again. '*The Killing Moon.*' More drowning. '*Pretty In Pink.*' Still drowning. '*Love Will Tear Us Apart.*' Before she went under, I reached out my arms and pulled her to safety, tight against my chest.

'I hate you,' I said, giving her lips a gentle nibble. 'I did not ever dance like that.'

'Did. Oh, Robin.'

We sat awhile in each other's arms on the piano stool, neither of us saying a word, hearing Grandma Dot chatting away to the birds on her patio as she pottered about, topping up their feeders.

I wasn't used to seeing Fliss upset, and I didn't like it. I could see that she was torn between the deep but very personal joy she got from her music and the performer's natural curiosity to experience, perhaps just once, the thrill of playing on a real stage in front of a big audience, to taste what it might feel like to be a star. (Something I'd soon be experiencing myself, of course.) There was no doubt about her being good enough. She was too good. I mean, how many folks who go on these shows can play even one instrument, let alone four or five, and certainly not to the standard Fliss had already achieved at just eighteen, grade seven or eight or whatever she was in jazz, classical, blues and the rest. She seemed to be able to play any pop song you could name, from Nina Simone to The Smiths, and had a drawerful of little hardback notebooks filled with lyrics and poems and ideas for tunes she had written herself or was in the process of writing. I was never allowed to look at them very closely, though occasionally she might share a lyric she was especially pleased with or play some unfamiliar but fantastically catchy piece and afterwards, if pressed, shyly admit to it being her own composition. Yes, if I ever felt Fliss lacked one thing as a budding musical genius, it was that she didn't seem to be at all the kind of person who craved the spotlight. Quite the opposite. And I worried that if she did suddenly find herself thrust into its bright, unforgiving glare she might very easily get hurt.

I lifted her face and kissed her lips gently. 'Don't get upset. Why don't you think about it for a few days? There's no real rush, is there?'

'For Mum there's always a rush,' Fliss said, her mouth twisting sideways.

'What do you mean?'

'The tape – the stupid thing's already gone.'

'What tape? *Running Up That Hill*?'

Fliss nodded. 'I made a copy. Mum posted it at teatime. She talked me into it. Robin, let's not talk about it anymore. What shall we do?'

'Play me something,' I said, gathering our mugs to take through to the kitchen. 'Anything you like. And just try to pretend I'm not here.'

She played *Little Red Corvette* and *The Look of Love*, her singing just loud enough that I could recognise hints of the same magical voice I had heard on the tape as I lay in my bed, open-mouthed, in the darkness. Afterwards she shuffled along the piano stool, slid her legs over mine and wrapped her arms around my neck. 'I don't ever want to pretend you're not here,' she said. 'I want you here always.'

Keeping an ear alert for Lionel, we kissed until there was no other choice but to go up to her room to listen to some records.

Ten

1

We joined the M1 at junction 30, Honeywell already touching ninety as he hit the fast lane so that Ricky and I, excellent drivers that we apparently were, had a job to keep up with the weaving black Saab.

We'd expected to be following Honeywell's Granada Scorpio. But then we'd also expected the two cars to be delivered to British Steel, a metallic grey Orion Ghia and a bright red Sierra XR4x4, would be waiting ready for us at Stonebridge Motor Company. Instead, bang on eight o'clock, this Saab had pulled up at the bus stop opposite the showroom with Honeywell, wearing a nasty tweed cap he must have found on a golf course, waving from the driver's seat for us to get in.

'A terrible accident,' Honeywell informed us as we sped towards Worksop. '*Terrible*. Our poor drivers were stuck in the tailback on the A1 for close to three hours, so when eventually they did extricate themselves, they were forced to leave the vehicles in a safe spot for us and, er, head back. It's not ideal, gentlemen,' Honeywell said, 'but I promised Peter these cars tonight and I'm assured they're both equally tip top.'

'This is nice, Mr Honeywell,' I said, from the passenger seat.

'This? It's Adrian, my son's, car. He likes me to give it a run when he's away.'

'They bloody shift, these high-pressure turbos,' Ricky noted helpfully from the rear.

'They do indeed, Ricky,' Honeywell smiled. 'They do indeed.'

We found the two cars to be delivered parked in a quiet corner of an industrial estate near Manton colliery. They were, as promised, equally tip top, a fact I found less surprising than, having been left with their keys tucked behind the sun-visors, that either of them was still there.

'Bags the Sierra,' Ricky said after we'd given them the once-over with a duster. I couldn't have cared less, but knowing how excited he got about big engines, I jumped into the Orion.

The tape chosen to accompany our evening hurtle northwards was a compilation of Simple Minds B-sides I'd recently put together, in thrillingly random order, my favourite being a blistering live version of *Up On The Catwalk* recorded at Barrowland in the band's home city of Glasgow. It's difficult to leap about very much behind an unfamiliar steering wheel, but I did what I could. I was in fine voice and all set to rewind the track for a third singalong when Honeywell, some way ahead of me and Ricky, indicated at the very last minute and swung across three lanes of coaches towards the exit.

We plunged, braking, through a tangle of flyovers before emerging into a night of silhouette foundries and shadow factory warehouses where chimneys rose by the dozen, reaching, like mismatched skittles, towards a dim bowling-ball moon. Demolition cranes loomed heavy over stubborn walls as we threaded close along a mile or more of sawn-off viaducts and drab swathes of waste ground. At regular intervals the spare rib of a cobblestone road would branch off only to terminate, after a few hundred yards, in a heap of dead rubble. I'd never been to British Steel before, but I knew it couldn't be long now until we turned into some vast industrial complex, a real-life James Bond set, all floodlights and flags flapping from the rooftops as we drew up in the nightglow of a raging furnace.

It was not a raging furnace, however, but the angry glow of Ricky's brake lights that snapped my mind suddenly back from its wandering. In fact, I almost ploughed into the back of him doing sixty, my wheels locking as I slammed the brake pedal before slowing to follow the red Sierra to where Honeywell's black Saab had pulled over onto a patch of waste ground opposite the tall, closed, gates of what appeared to be a brewery.

A couple of streetlamps wilting either side the gates made a weak pool of light for Honeywell as he got out of the Saab and clipped over to Ricky's Sierra. He spoke a few words then made his way towards me. Honeywell's lost, I thought, hiding a smile as I buzzed down my window.

'Pop the keys behind the visor, Robin, and leave this on the passenger seat, if you'd be so good and, er...' Honeywell said, handing me a sealed manilla envelope he'd magicked from somewhere on his person. 'The paperwork to transfer the warranty, radio codes, and so on.'

'Aren't we taking them to British Steel, Mr Honeywell?' I said as he made a swift circuit of the Orion. He must've heard the skid and was making sure I hadn't crunched it.

'*Hmm*? It's rather after hours now, Robin, for the transport division. But as Peter's promised these cars to two of his managers tomorrow morning, I agreed to do him the favour of delivering them this evening. They'll no doubt run them home now and hand them over first thing. Bit of a ball-ache for us, but just the sort of gesture our fleet customers appreciate – going that little bit out of our way, you see?'

Finding Ricky installed in the Saab's front seat, I climbed into the back just as a dark blue Granada drew up. Two men got out, middle-aged and smartly overalled. After some crouching and hands-on-hip inspecting of the Orion and Sierra, each gave a thumbs-up to the driver of the Granada before setting off, at a very leisurely pace, towards Sheffield city centre. As Honeywell started the Saab the Granada flashed its lights twice, made a wide turn in the road, and purred away, almost as leisurely, after them.

'Are either of you gentlemen music lovers?' Honeywell said as he floored the Saab back down the M1. And he bunged in a cassette of the most awful opera bollocks you've ever heard, a riot of rusty violins and booming lardy voices, the properly painful stuff they used in adverts and to torture suspected terrorists. Thankfully, after a while, he turned it down a bit and started on at us about his big plans for the garage, of designs for a new showroom and a bigger workshop.

'That would be mint,' Ricky said. 'I could have my own bay.'

As I wouldn't be sticking around to see Ricky and the boss's dreams come true – I'd far bigger ones of my own to chase – I tuned out. I slumped in the back seat, watching Honeywell's hands play fiddler on the wheel and remembering that this was the same model Saab that Jim Kerr had talked of owning in my sister's *Smash Hits* – a 900 Turbo. Jim would never drive a black one, of course, I mused confidently. It would be blue, for Scotland, metallic, probably, with black leather seats.

But even as these thoughts percolated there was, to my mind, something not quite right about the idea of Jim Kerr driving a car. Any car. Or for that matter doing anything that ordinary, boring people did to get through their empty and purposeless days. (My eye was drawn to Honeywell's nasty cap as I thought this and caused my lip to curl.) You see, the way I always liked to picture Jim, off stage, was ensconced behind the blacked-out windows of the band's tour bus, reclining on his bunk decorated with thistles and the claddagh symbol, his pixie-booted feet curled on a good, heavy tartan as he sketched lyrical ideas for the next big tune, or read up on the latest developments in South African politics and the lost songs of The Velvet Underground.

'Much obliged to you both,' Honeywell said, pulling up again at the bus stop opposite the showroom and handing us each a ten-pound note. Not bad for a couple of hours bombing up the motorway in fast cars.

'Thanks very much,' I said, folding the money into my pocket.

'Cheers, Mr H,' said Ricky.

'No, no, thank *you*, gentlemen. You've both been an immense help. But if I could ask that we perhaps keep this trip between ourselves for now? I know one or two of our colleagues who do a bit of driving for us now and then (he meant Ken and the cleaners) might feel put out at my having taken you two this evening instead of them, but... it's important we present the right image with these big customers and, er, well, when it comes to things, you two have a bit more about you, if you know what I mean. Good evening.'

2

About six weeks after Fliss's mum, Ruth, had taken delivery of her brand-new Sierra XR4x4 I found an internal envelope, addressed to me, among the morning's post. And once I'd switched on the lights, dropped the workshop hatch, and rattled up the front counter shutters, I made a pot of tea and opened it with Sheila looking interestedly on as she counted the cash float into the till.

Inside I found a cheque for £30 and a Ford-logoed notelet with the pen-written message '*Robin. Commission for sale of white Sierra XR4x4 reg no. E--- --- to customer Markley Hall Equestrian. With thanks. David.*'

There were a couple of big jobs first thing, one requiring much *hmm*-ing at the microfiche and another four trips upstairs to fetch a windscreen and complete exhaust system for an old

Transit. So it was about an hour before I tapped on the thin glass of the sales manager's door.

'Thanks, David,' I said, taking out the envelope, 'but I don't think this is my commission.'

'Course it's yours, pal,' David said, returning a tin of shoe polish and a duster to the bottom drawer of his filing cabinet. 'You brought us the customer, chap did a deal, car's been delivered. That's your share.'

'But I didn't do anything. I only gave you that note from –'

'That's what I told him,' Graham said, ambushing me from behind in a bear-like death-squeeze. 'I said young Robin's got pots of money now, working all week with Sheila then weekends in here with us. He doesn't need commission. Not like I do. The missus and nippers spend all mine before I've earned it.'

'Put it in your pocket, Robin,' David said once Graham had let go. 'You weren't being paid to work in the showroom then. We didn't make a fortune out of it – the chap's a friend of Giles, Mr Honeywell's, isn't he? – but it's a decent deal.'

'Thanks very much.'

'When did you say you turn eighteen?'

'September.'

David sucked his lips. 'I was going to talk to Giles about you joining us full time. Get you off that poxy YTS and earning some proper money. I'd have you tomorrow but... You might not be able to have a car, though. It's eighteen, I think, for the insurance.'

'I'm not having him in here, nicking any more of my bloody commission,' Graham winked. 'Where's Andrew? The two of us'll be out on strike if you bring this young upstart in, David, I'm warning you.'

'It wouldn't matter about a car,' I said, the words tumbling out before I knew what I was saying. 'I've got my MG for now.'

'A woman looking round that gold Escort, Graham.'

'Seen her, boss.'

David sat back in his chair. 'Well, have a think, then, pal. I'll talk to Giles. And to Sheila – I don't want her getting on at me if I poach you. Her family have had three cars off me and I'm hoping they'll be having another in August.'

3

Most Saturdays Fliss worked till about three behind the counter at Markley Hall Equestrian before spending the rest of the afternoon at the stables or out riding with her friends. So my first weekend off from the showroom, feeling unaccustomedly flush with cash and petrol, I drove to Nottingham thinking I might treat myself to a record or two, as well as *Parade* on LP to replace Fliss's cassette copy which she'd literally played to death, it having the evening before strangled itself around the tape-heads, seconds into *Mountains*, just as we were hitting our stride beneath the duvet.

'How disappointing,' Fliss said, looking up at me and meaning, I'm almost sure, what had happened to the tape.

Never the keenest shopper, I didn't hang about in town. After buying the Prince album in the Vic Centre I headed straight to the Lace Market, where I found a 12-inch single of Simple Minds' *Sweat in Bullet*, and the 7-inch of *Ghostdancing* with that cool photo of Jim Kerr holding an unusually camera-confident white dove. I also picked up a new stylus and, while browsing among the dingy boutiques, a few choice items of attire I'd long felt were lacking from the wardrobe of one destined, like I was, for stadium superstardom.

A black velvet waiters' waistcoat, a size too small, would look just the part worn over the voluminous white shirt with billowing loose-cuffed sleeves, especially when gathered in at the waist with a glossy black belt. (Plastic, of course – buckled leather reminding me too much of my ex-dad.) Add to this some slim black Levi's cords and a pair of matching suede pixie boots and I had, but for a thistle-brooched Tam o' Shanter, practically the complete late-'85 tour outfit, the full Jim Kerr Alive in Rotterdam ensemble.

I knew, of course, just like Jim Kerr had known about his eyeliner on that Glasgow building site, that I'd never in a million years be able to parade through the streets of Stonebridge in my new outfit. Not in its entirety. Such majesty would only cause the mortals to frown and have uncomprehending headaches. That's why, when I got back, I took my record bags in first, making sure Mam and Cath were both safely out of the way, before dashing back to the MG for the rest.

Unlike at Fliss's there was little hope of privacy in our house, the locks of all the upstairs rooms having long ago petrified beneath decades of white gloss. So after I'd fitted the new stylus and set *Sweat In Bullet* going on the turntable, I quickly pushed the chest of drawers up against my bedroom door and threw off all my clothes except my underpants. Then, having laid the Rotterdam ensemble across my bed, I began excitedly to slip my pale, insubstantial person into each of the magical, transforming garments in turn.

I started with the cords. Hmm. Flattering though they were, I noted, admiring my outline in the wardrobe mirror, for the challenge ahead they weren't quite right. They lacked a certain give about the gusset and buttocks, which I felt was crucial if total freedom of movement in these key areas was to be achieved satisfactorily. The things Jim Kerr wore on stage looked both flexible and snugly supportive, as well as being *sheer*, if that's the word, a bit like...

Swiftly pulling off the cords, I pushed aside my chest of drawers and ran into Cath's room to riffle through hers.

Bingo!

A minute or two later I was panting resplendent in my new

(if a little fusty) outfit. I whacked up the volume and, with the eyes of twenty-seven various era Jim Kerrs looking down from the wood-chip walls, I leapt up on to my bed. There was a click and a faint crackle as the arm swung across and the needle settled on the disc. I, too, settled, crouched down on the duvet with my arms spread wide, my sleeves billowing, and eyes half-closed as I waited, poised, still as an owl.

I cleared my throat. 'This next song is called... *Ghostdancing*.'

Charlie Burchill's opening guitar riff echoed through the house as Jim Kerr began to sing of cities, buildings falling down, of satellites come crashing down. Then, as the bass and drums came crashing in, I launched myself into a high and mighty leopard pounce, smashing my head against the ceiling light before landing textbook legs akimbo on the threadbare carpet. With a shuffle and a dip, and a side-to-side hop, I bobbed briskly, buoyantly, my left arm carving through plumes of dry ice as I delivered the line about falling out the sky like eagles to the grinning, speckled, face in the wardrobe mirror. Only it was no longer a wardrobe mirror at all. It was the packed auditorium of the Universal Amphitheatre, Los Angeles. The Entertainment Centre, Sydney. The Ahoy, Rotterdam. I was where I longed to be. I was live. I was *alive*. And barely half a song in I had each and every one of them, ten, twenty, fifty thousand fans, right there in the palm of my hand.

I was by now lost in my own brilliant performance, stripped of all inhibition, twirling and leaping about as though my life depended on it – which, in a way, it did. Keen to push my ensemble's performance durability to its limits, I made another spring from my duvet, landing so that I could stretch my right leg up high and place the heel of my pixie boot on top of the chest of drawers. I remained like this awhile, rocking back and forth to the thumping beat, and stretching as far as my elastic young anatomy would allow as I heartfeltly bellowed, '*Tell me about the dawn in Eden!*' into my deodorant spray microphone.

It was unfortunate that this was the moment the bedroom door had to suddenly swing open and Mam and Cath barge in, the pair of them immediately raising both hands to their mouths and gasping like they'd happened upon a gentlemen only late-night sauna party.

'Robin, you can hear your music halfway down the street,' Mam shouted, as if this were now really her first concern. 'Why d'you have to have it on so loud?'

'That's my Brownies beret!' Cath screeched. And I followed her eyes and mouth as they moved slowly, ever-wideningly down from her beret to my chest to my feet and then back up again to my gymnastically splayed private portions upon which they seemed to become uncomfortably snagged. Cath gasped. Then gulped. 'And they're my best tights! Mam, why's our Robin wearing my best tights?'

'It's not what–' I began, cursing myself as I swung my foot down off the chest of drawers, the drawers I'd been clever enough to use as a stage prop but had stupidly forgotten to push back against the door after I'd dashed through to Cath's room to borrow her beret and very snug Pretty Pollys.

'He's made a great big ladder in them, by the looks of it,' Mam said, placing a sympathetic hand on my sister's shoulder. I tugged down my shirt front, shrinking into my pixie boots as I considered my glossy belt. '*Take me away-ay*' Jim Kerr sang now as the track began to fade. I shared his feelings entirely.

Mam gave a little cough into her handkerchief and turned to the door. 'I think we'll go and put the kettle on, Catherine, shall we?' The two of them were silent until about halfway down the stairs, when Cath suddenly spluttered and said, '*Oh my flipping sodding God!*'

'We shouldn't laugh,' I heard Mam say in a grave voice, 'catching him like that. I expect he would rather have told us in his own time.'

Eleven

1

Ken buttoned up his overalls. He'd lowered them, with much lip-smacking palaver, to get his hand inside the front of his trousers and scratch whatever it was that troubled him down there.

'As I were saying,' he said, sniffing his fingers before taking a corned-beef sandwich from his snap tin. 'We were in Belgium, and there were these three nuns...'

'This a dirty joke, Ken?' said Darren, hopefully.

Keith laughed. 'Were they in a bath?'

'I'm glad y'all think it's summat to laugh about. They were only young lasses, young nuns – Catholics, mind, but by Christ, the things them Gestapo bastards'd done to them.'

Across the table Vern's eyebrows rose cautiously over the top of his newspaper. I peered inside my packet of crisps in search of an exit.

'Anyroad,' Ken continued, snapping at his sandwich. 'Bleeders got what were coming to them when the Yanks got there. Shot a couple of the ringleaders in both legs so they couldn't get away, then they let nuns take turns at driving back'ards and for'ards over 'em in a Sherman tank. *They* weren't bloody laughing.'

I never knew how the canteen found itself so often under attack by Ken's gruesome tales. You never saw them coming. One minute the talk would be of camshafts and cup finals, the next we'd all be suddenly ambushed among the Normandy hedgerows, Ken pulling the pin of a grenade with his false teeth while the rest of us braced ready to be showered with the scrotal remains of a Panzer division. As I always understood it from my grandad, old soldiers didn't like to talk about the war, it being a hell best forgotten and all that.

But it was having survived such hells, and shared them so frequently, with such relish, that in the event of a corpse car being delivered to the garage Ken and his unsentimental iron stomach would always be first called upon to deal with it. A corpse car, by the way, if you're unfamiliar with the term, is a vehicle which has been involved in a fatal accident, one so horrific that much of what little had remained of its occupants following impact was still to be found either in, on, or about its mangled bodywork. 'Like you'd stamped on egg-box full o' tomatoes,' as Ken never tired of describing one particular Escort struck head-on by a milk tanker.

'Robin, are you there?' I finished scribbling down a phone order and went to the workshop hatch.

'What's up, Vern?'

'Ask Sheila if I can borrow you for half an hour, will you? Corpse car in the yard and my lad's gone and let me down.'

It was my first and only brush with a corpse car. Most recovery drivers knew to take them directly to the body shop, or if not, having come to us first, were happy to drive the gruesome tarpaulined wrecks the extra mile across town. Now and then, though, like that afternoon, you'd get a bolshy bugger who, either claiming he didn't know the area, or to be in a desperate hurry, would have none of it and unhelpfully dump his load in the middle of the yard. That's where Ken would come in. And he would have done now if, shortly after lunchtime, his appendix hadn't burst like a couple of nazis beneath the wheels of a three-nun tank.

'He'd have enjoyed this one,' Darren said, careful to step around Ricky's lunch which, the smell of death not mixing with Sweet & Sour Pot Noodle, he'd thrown up, colourfully, beside the breakdown lorry.

Keith, gagging, slipped a sanding mask over his face. 'It stinks like a butcher's dustbin.'

'Bet it looks like one an' all.'

'Shut up and push,' Vern said.

It was a particularly nasty wreck, by all accounts. And with one wheel smashed and another missing completely it had been a hell of a job to drag it up the ramps, using a couple of trolley jacks, onto the back of the breakdown wagon, the four of us heaving (in every sense) with shoulders, boots and backsides while avoiding the various dark stains which mapped the tarpaulin.

After unloading the corpse car at the body shop (unfortunate name in the circumstances) and locking it away in a garage reserved, at the farthest edge of the yard, for these macabre motors, Vern and I were glad of the cup of tea offered by the body shop's manager, Kevin. And seated on a trio of old Cortina seats, we drank the strong brew, with its subtle top notes of spray paint and filler, overlooking the battlefield of automotive carnage that was the compound. It looked like a bank holiday car park in which a well-fed herd of elephants had been learning to pogo.

'You've got plenty of work to go at, Kevin,' Vern said, scanning the rows of variously bashed and battered cars and a few small vans.

'Not as much as there looks. Not for us. One or two nice big jobs, but a lot of them have been written-off by the insurance. A couple might go for damaged repairables.'

'Does that mean you won't get to fix them?' I said as Kevin held out a packet of Hobnobs.

Kevin's head, as he shook it, looked like it was wearing a poodle rolled in chalk dust. 'Nope,' he said. 'Three or four over there, those two XR3s, that cabrio, black Granada... an Orion as well... they've all been written off. Not that bad either, a couple of them. They've had a good wallop, but you could put them right. They'll just go to the breakers, for scrap. What's that one like you just brought over? Nasty?'

'I didn't look, Kevin,' Vern said. 'From what I hear, though, it's one to keep covered up. Another XR-RS-whatnot. If they're not being pinched or broken into they're wrapped round trees.'

'When're you going to sell me that old Harrier of yours, Vern?' Kevin said, giving me a wink. 'I hear there's a queue now, waiting for it.'

'Too bad. I'll be taking it with me, that one. Not that I'm planning on going anywhere for a good while yet, mind.' Vern smiled and slurped the last of his tea.

'There's a breaker's wagon here now, look,' Kevin's poodle nodded as a large yellow-and-white flatbed growled into the yard and made a wide gravel-crunching turn before hissing to a standstill. 'What's he come for? I bet it's one of them right at the back.'

'We'll leave you to it, then, Kevin,' Vern said, waving his arms for me to haul him up from his burst car seat.

'Thanks for the tea and biscuits,' I added, pocketing a Hobnob for the drive back.

'Now then,' Vern said a minute or two later, as we slowed near the church for a set of temporary traffic lights. 'That's got me wondering, that has...'

'What has?'

Vern rubbed noisily at the sandpaper underside of his jaw, rumpling his nose. He *hmm*-ed. Took a deep breath. *Hmm*-ed again. 'Are you supposed to be seeing your young woman tonight, Robin?'

'Yes,' I said, extending half a Hobnob. 'Why?'

Vern licked his lips and took the biscuit. Then he turned to me, crunching, with a sly, quizzical expression. 'What time do you reckon to put her to bed usually?'

2

With Ken wounded in action, his manoeuvres were covered by Johnny, an equally ancient, but far less terrifying old boy who for as long as anybody could remember had gone about the garage, a few hours a week, whistling at his pot plants and changing lightbulbs on a ladder so precarious it was on commission from the grim reaper.

This was a relief, because for a brief moment I feared I might be about to add delivery driver to my ever-expanding set of professional bow strings, when what I needed to be getting to grips with, and sharpish, were guitar strings. Or bass strings. Actual bow strings even, on a violin, like Charlie Burchill had played on *Pleasantly Disturbed*, the very first song he and Jim Kerr had written for Simple Minds. Anything that would take me another step closer...

The singer's moves, as you know, I had mastered fully. Of my stage prowling presence, the uncanny ability to interpret through my lean physicality and blessed grace of movement the rocking heart and Celtic soul of Simple Minds' music as self-assured and hypnotically as Jim Kerr himself, there was no doubt. If the world's most captivating frontman needed a double to save him having to leap and twirl about quite so much in his band's next big-budget video, I could with absolute confidence say that I was that man, and I'd defy even the most ardently pedantic of observers to spot the difference. I'd even go so far as to say that, if instead of Mam and Cath it had been Chrissie Hynde who'd barged into my bedroom that Saturday afternoon, and discovered me projecting resplendent in my sister's tights, I think she'd have been so breathlessly convinced I was the real Jim Kerr she'd have gone down on her faux-leather knees and begged me to marry her all over again.

As for the singing, well, just as I had all the moves, so I had all the words. What's more, I had a mouth that could say all those words in the right order and in the right spaces within the music where the band had intended. And yet, when I recorded myself into Cath's radio-cassette, singing along to the instrumental version of *Sanctify Yourself*, what was captured on tape was not Jim Kerr's vocal doppelganger, or even a distant relative, but something that sounded akin to a laryngitic crow crash-landing, highly sensitive feet first, into a chip-pan fire.

Of course, Cath was never properly into music like I was. And her radio-cassette player, with its crappy microphone – from Boots, the chemist! – was just some horrible red, cheap-looking affair aimed squarely at little sisters whose tastes were dictated entirely by *Smash Hits* (the magazine I only ever read because my sister left it lying around all the time).

What I'm saying is, hampered with such inferior, unprofessional equipment, Jim Kerr himself would have struggled to sound amazing – and that's not a claim I would ever make lightly.

3

'You smell delicious,' Fliss smiled, gathering me in her arms before I'd barely crossed the threshold of the boot room. In light of her welcome, and where I hoped it might lead, I decided against sharing how it had taken an especially vigorous scrub in Mam's lily of the valley bubble-bath to shift the whiff of dead motorists from my nostrils. Instead, I dropped the parcel of three sets of number plates I'd brought from the garage for Lionel on top of the chest freezer and got my lips working around hers.

'Dad's not home yet,' Fliss said, pushing her hands deep into the back pockets of my jeans. 'And Mum... [KISS]... has gone to her committee meeting.'

'Oh, that's a shame. I was... hoping to give your dad... those... number plates. I think he's... in... a hurry... for them.'

'He'll be at the shop late tonight... stock... taking... We can... drive up after... if you like.'

'After what?' I asked.

Fliss slid her hands from my pockets and, taking a couple of steps back, pulled the hem of her baggy sweatshirt up to her chin and held it there. As on the occasion with her pyjama top, she'd forgotten to put anything else on underneath it, and before I could award prizes (it would have been a dead heat), in a jiggling blink she turned and dashed away towards the lounge and upstairs.

When Sheila had taken down the order for the plates, she'd drawn a box and underlined, beside 'Markley Hall' and the three registration numbers, *Reqd. THURSDAY a.m.* It was only Tuesday, yet something Vern said as we drove back from the body shop that afternoon had made me keen to pay another visit to the equestrian centre to see if he wasn't getting himself all worked-up about nothing, like old folks often tend to do. Because ever since that night he'd seen, on his walk with Betty, those Fiesta XR2s racing from Oakerby station yard, Vern had become a little bit obsessed with thoughts of hooligans stealing cars and robbing other people's property. In recent weeks he'd spotted similar cars tearing about the area, so he told me, all newish sporty and high-spec models, which he felt sure can't have been up to much good. It didn't seem to occur to Vern (whose own much-coveted sports car was rumoured never to have been in top gear) that people who bought fast cars should actually want to drive them fast.

'I think we've missed him,' Fliss said as I screeched the MG up to the shuttered doors of the Markley Hall Equestrian workshop. This was a small, newish building at right angles to the showroom which, as well as supplying and fitting towbars to customers' cars, was kept very busy servicing and repairing their horseboxes and trailers. 'His car's not here.'

The reserved space where the Jag usually dozed between thick icing-sugar lines was indeed empty. And, like the workshop, the green-painted steel shutters over the showroom windows and side door had been lowered and severally padlocked.

'He's definitely not inside,' I said, rattling the heavy corrugated steel. If Vern thinks anybody will be breaking into this place, he must be out of his mind, I thought. You'd more chance of getting over the Berlin Wall in broad daylight dressed as Ronald McDonald.

'He must've had enough of stocktaking,' Fliss said as the tarmac began to rumble beneath our feet. 'Train!'

The rumble grew and became a deep throbbing hum. Fliss grabbed my hand and pulled me, running, round to the back of the showroom, where, pressed against the high wire-mesh fence we watched as a loaded coal train, clouding the air with spent diesel, powered up the incline from Oakerby Colliery. The last wagon had just about trundled past when Fliss suddenly turned, looked up, and shouted, 'Dad!'

'Eh?' I said, following her eyes.

I knew the Markley Hall showroom was an old goods shed and that the railway still ran merrily alongside it, back and forth to the pit. But I had never on any of my previous visits noticed that fifty yards along the line, still connecting the weed-strewn platforms, was a flaking rust-grey iron footbridge. Nor had I known that Lionel was such a keen trainspotter. But there he was, giving it the full Jenny Agutter and waving excitedly (though thankfully not his red knickers) twenty feet above the still tingling line.

'Hello, darling!'

'What are you doing up there?'

'I'm coming down, darling.'

This would be no easy task. The footbridge had been closed off on both sides of the line with a tangled barricade of wooden stakes and barbed wire strewn across its lower steps, and I smiled to myself wondering how Lionel hoped to negotiate his way around this tricky little nest without losing his trousers as well as his dignity. But no. Stopping just short of the anti-trespass defences, and with surprising agility for a man of his age and hog-like shape, Fliss's father clambered up the iron trellis and over the handrail and dropped down heavily but surely among the weeds and nettles. He now crunched the twenty yards or so along the platform before slipping through a snip-cut section of the fence to join us behind his Markley Hall showroom.

'What're you doing up on that bridge, Dad, it's not safe,' Fliss said as her father carefully secured the wire mesh back in place behind him.

'You're probably absolutely right, Felicity darling. But I've been very concerned about the information Robin's friend from the garage kindly passed on to me about those young hotheads racing about up here, late at night, thieving and getting up to heaven knows what sort of no good and troublemaking.'

I resisted asking if it had been the same young troublemakers who'd cut a big hole in the railway's anti-trespass fence, feeling Lionel might not take it in the spirit intended, like I knew his daughter would, later on.

'I don't think anybody's going to steal a footbridge, Dad,' Fliss said.

'You'd be surprised, darling. If a thing isn't nailed down these days, it's as good as gone. Robin's colleague says he's seen these joyriders tearing about the station yard on several occasions, so I thought while there's nobody around I'd have a quick wander across and see if there are any signs of damage or vandalism.'

'Did you find anything, Lionel?' I asked, wincing slightly as his eyes smiled damply at my using his name. Perhaps, even after our bumpy start, I thought, he cherished ideas of one day becoming my Lionel-in-law, though I couldn't see it, not with my lack of pedigree.

'Nothing at all, Robin, I'm glad to say. Station's as secure as Fort Knox. But do please thank your friend for his concern, and for taking the trouble to let me know. I'm very grateful. No,' Lionel said, turning to look across the railway line, 'there's no fear of anybody getting in there. And even if they did, they'd likely end up in hospital, if not dead.'

I glanced at Fliss thinking that even for Lionel, a man never shy of promising physical violence, this seemed severe. 'Place is riddled with asbestos, Robin. Riddled.'

'Oh, yes,' I said, nodding. 'I remember you saying, now.'

'Will the shop be okay, Dad? We've got an alarm and everything, haven't we?'

'Yes, darling,' Lionel said, clapping his hands assuredly together. 'Alarm, shutters, security locks. We're as secure as we can be. It's always good to keep a close eye on things, though. I've noticed cars over there myself, recently, when I've been here late.' He curled a little smile, shared a wink between the two of us. 'Probably just courting couples, wanting a quiet spot to be alone together.'

Lionel shook some keys from his trousers and turned towards the blue Jaguar, which I only now noticed was parked behind the workshop, beside the piles of old tyres and a skip for scrap metal. 'Will I see you both back at home?'

'Yes. We might go for a drive,' Fliss said, her eyebrows making the suggestion at me. 'But we shan't be long. Oh, Dad – Robin brought you these number plates.'

I'd been holding them all this time, like a fool. 'Our van driver was rushed to hospital this afternoon with a burst appendix,' I said as Fliss handed Lionel the parcel. 'So I thought I'd bring them up.'

'That's very good of you, Robin. Thank you.' Lionel turned once again towards the Jag, saluting us with the number plates. 'I can see why Giles Honeywell considers you such an asset, Robin,' he said. 'See you both later.'

After a few steps he turned back. 'I hope your driver makes a speedy recovery – Ken, isn't it?'

'Yes,' I said. 'That's right.'

'Could we go to your house, Robin?' Fliss said as, after waving her father off, we fell into an embrace against the side of the MG. 'I really want to meet your mum. Properly, I mean, not just in the paper shop on my way to school.'

'It's a bit late for her now, tonight,' I said. 'She has a bath and gets into bed with Catherine about nine.'

'Catherine? Do your mum and sister share a–'

'Catherine Cookson. She's one of her writers.'

Fliss nodded slowly, made a thwarted little girl face. 'Another night,' I said. 'Soon.'

I ran my finger slowly, softly, down the slope of her delightful nose and drew a curlicued moustache over her delicious mouth. Nothing Freudian, before you leap to repressed Poirot-fixated conclusions. It was simply while I made a small calculation based on those two ingredients crucial to many a furtive nocturnal activity, motivation and opportunity, both of which I now had in brimming abundance.

'Those courting couples your dad mentioned,' I said. 'What do you reckon they get up to alone in their cars together?'

'I've no idea,' Fliss said. 'Maybe if we got inside the car we could find out...'

I won't share the details of what happened next because it's really none of your business. What I will say, though, is that the soundtrack was, as usual, first class, and that it was probably a good thing that the shutters at Markley Hall Equestrian were drawn over the windows and that gormless pair of plastic horses were each wearing three sets of blinkers.

Twelve

1

The house stood back in neat wild seclusion near the top of Three Millers Hill. With its pitched zigzag gables and dark leaded windows, it looked even spookier from the front than it had done from the back. And as the door slowly opened with a creak worthy of the best Hammer horror, it struck me that not a soul knew where I was that night and, now that I came to think about it, I really knew very little about Vern Priestley. Who was to say that in his spare time the mild-mannered car mechanic wasn't a knife-wielding psychopath, or some dodgy old perv who invited young lads up to his lair in the hope of–

'S'all right, Mother, it's for me,' Vern called back over his shoulder. 'I'll lock up on my way out. Yes, will do. Goodnight, Mother.'

It wasn't quite ten o'clock as, trailing Betty, we stepped between miniature greenhouses and various cane-sprouting plots and through the back gate into the lane from where Fliss and I had spied Vern treating his beloved sheepdog to the full Sinatra. 'How old is she, Vern?' I asked as the kitchen light went out.

'She's, what now... fifteen months, or thereabouts.'

'Not Betty – your mum.'

'Oh, now then, Mother, she'll be eighty-four next. And fitter than I am. Go on then, girl, off you go.' Vern coiled Betty's lead into a pocket of his donkey jacket, pulled a small, marbled notebook from another. 'I brought this. But you watch, there'll be nobody there tonight.'

'How many times have you seen this stuff going on then?'

'Up at the station yard, two or three times. But then a couple of other nights I've seen them, like I said, tearing through Oakerby from the direction of the railway bridge, so...'

After crossing the lane that led to the stables we turned into the woods, the dot-dash flicker of Betty's coat guiding us, rustling, through the blackout.

'You don't think it might just be boy racers, do you?' I suggested, the darkness making me whisper.

'Ah, could be. But they're never the same cars, Robin - unless it's the same lot in different cars, and they're just pinching them for a tear-up. Did you have a word with your young woman's father?'

'Yes. But they won't have much luck breaking into his place,' I said. 'It's got more locks than Fort Knox. We were up there tonight, me and Fliss. Lionel had been over to the station, after what you said, to have a look round.'

'Had he? And what does he say? Anything for concern?'

'No, no signs of breaking in or anything, just the usual graffiti and fires and stuff. It's all boarded up, by the looks of it.'

'That's right, steel plates. I don't know, there's something niggling me about it. Anyroad, we'd better look sharp, on Sunday I reckon we were about five minutes too late. A black Sierra, one of them with the silly great wing on the back, Cosworth, came thundering under the bridge just as Betty and I got there, about half past ten. I'd have sworn it was the one pinched from the miners' union.'

'On its own?'

'Looked that way – unless I'd already missed something else.'

'Did you get the reg. number?'

'Shut yer face. Why d'you think I've brought my notebook? We shall have to rely on your eyes, though, for taking down any numbers.'

'That Cossie, though, Vern. It was taken weeks ago. If you nick a car like that for joyriding, you'd have to be an idiot to still be tearing about in it so near to where you took it from, wouldn't you?'

'Well, yes, you'd think so, Robin. You'd think so.'

Exiting the woods we tramped a further half mile or so along a narrow cinder path beside the railway embankment, the ground steadily rising until the line plunged between muddy fields and began to curve towards the headstocks of Oakerby Colliery. Here the cinders gave way and the path opened out suddenly onto a wild and derelict sprawl of weed-sprouting rubble, with variously neat and tumbled stacks of wooden sleepers dotted among the remains of several small brick-built structures, the purpose of which mattered now only to the sort of characters who liked to plague stations in their duffle coats.

I knew where we'd been headed. But it was only now as I recognised the security lighted gables of the converted goods shed, the skeleton of the footbridge linking the two extinct platforms, that I saw we were on the other side of the railway line from Markley Hall Equestrian, some several hundred yards along from the condemned Oakerby station, in the overgrown wilderness of what had once been a sidings and goods yard.

'In here,' Vern said, slipping into a bombed-out public toilet at the edge of the wasteland. The below-stairs portion of a signal box, he corrected me, though somebody had definitely used it as a toilet, and quite recently, too.

'It stinks, Vern.'

'Sorry, it's my age. If I need one again tonight, I'd watch your shoes. Time is it? Ten twenty-six. Now keep your voice down.'

At ten to eleven, two Betty-sized rats scuttled past beneath the jagged window-frame of our lookout, causing the real, canine Betty great excitement, though she remained where she was told, swishing her tail and growling from the doorway.

'Don't want her being spotted.'

'Spotted by who, Vern?'

'By *whom*, Robin. Now shush.'

It was not Vern but me who needed the toilet. I went round the back. At a quarter past eleven, and with still no sign of joyriders bent on late-night grands prix in stolen hatchbacks, or masked raiders drilling into Markley Hall to pull off the biggest saddle-wax heist of all time, Vern suggested we make our way cautiously across the ballast, between treacherous islands of half-buried metals and masonry, up to the station.

'If you see or hear a car, Robin, try to get back to the signal box. Don't lie down in the grass, whatever you do. The buggers are likely to come up here and you'll be run over.'

'Nice.'

The station had been closed since the early sixties and had lain empty ever since, its stone and brick walls slowly crumbling within a tight girdle of ivy, its windows steel blinded and mascara-licked by the angry fires of delinquents. It was a big old pile and even now, stripped of its canopies and extensive collection of outbuildings, seemed far too grand for a little town like Oakerby, some Victorian beard no doubt having over-estimated the touristic appeal of the big geriatric tree up the road.

'It'd have made a nice house, if you knew what you were on with,' Vern whispered, gazing up at half a dozen cold chimneys. 'Bit far gone now, though.'

'I'll say. "Warning: Asbestos! No Unauthorised Persons Beyond This Point. Danger! Unsafe Building! Keep Out!"' I read. 'The next train to arrive at this station will have a bulldozer on it.'

'Probably won't be long.'

I stuck close to Vern as we crept a dark circuit of the building, following his lead as he pulled and probed at the heavy gauge steel panels drilled and bolted over the dozen or more tall arched windows and doors, looking for weaknesses and points of forced entry.

'Your young woman's father were right about Fort Knox,' he said, rapping his knuckles against a vast steel plate beneath the lavishly carved inscription BOOKING HALL. 'Nobody'll be getting in here in a hurry.'

'There are quite a few tyre marks, Vern,' I said, indicating where several trails ran up from the gravel of the station yard and round into the mossy shadows along the platform. 'But loads of people must come up here at night.'

'*Hmm.*' Vern followed the criss-cross braid of tyre tracks along the platform until he was beyond the far side of the building where, after making sure the station yard was still free of unwanted visitors, he'd begun to retrace his steps before he halted and knelt down to run his fingers over the soil and gravel. After a second or two, and with a glance across the railway line, then back towards the yard, he got up again and resettled his cap with a '*Hmm*' that sounded heavy with disappointment.

By now, Betty had lost interest in our dead-end games, and after dipping her hindquarters in the platform weeds she trotted away to resume her own private investigations into the local (oversized) rodent population.

'I can't see anything, Vern.'

'No. And no boy racers either. You're probably right, lad,' Vern said, squinting into the palm of his hand. 'Whoever comes up here's more likely after getting into brassieres than old stations.'

'What is it?' I asked as Vern held a tiny object up to his nose, turning it slowly between his fingers so that it sparkled in the moonlight.

'Looks like some lass's lost her earring. Now, where's that dog got to? Home, Betty! Come on, girl! There are no rats up here.'

2

Thursday was three quarters gone and without a hint of momentousness. Not a whiff that it was to become perhaps the most pivotal late mid-weekday in March of both mine and Fliss's musical careers. But then I got in from work to find waiting for me not only an envelope on the mantelpiece from Bailey's Coaches containing two tickets to the Nelson Mandela 70th Birthday Tribute concert in London, but also, in the back garden, a homing pigeon which, according to Mam, had spent all afternoon nibbling cheese & onion crisps and bits of bread she'd thrown it while trying to ward off a steadily multiplying audience of cats.

'I didn't dare leave it for long,' Mam said. 'I brought my book into the porch, but I've only managed to read three pages. I've been shooing since two o'clock. I don't know where they've all come from. I think it's lame in one of its wings, Robin.'

'Can a pigeon be lame in a wing?' I asked, distracted as my fingers reverently traced the sacred text of the £25 tickets:

Wembley Stadium. Saturday 11th June 1988

'Course it can,' Mam said, scattering satsuma sized lumps of white Sunblest. 'Why shouldn't it be?'

Turnstile B. Doors Open 11 a.m.

'Not something you hear about, is it, lame pigeons?'
'You hear about lame ducks all the time.'
'Yes, but lame ducks are usually politicians, or failing industries. Never actual ducks. Or pigeons.'
For that I got a whack on the elbow with *The Mallen Streak*.

'I think you just say these things to make me sound stupid,' Mam said. 'Well, it can't fly, whatever you want to call it. It'll be one of Jack Kettley's. When you've had your tea, Robin, you can take it round to him, he'll be missing it.'

Slipping the tickets inside my pocket, I tiptoed across the lawn to kneel within touching distance of the bird grabbing all the attention. It barely skipped a peck at the piece of crust between its toes, just fixed me, and the envious, salivating cats, with one of those glassy sideways stares pigeons always do so well. (They get no praise, pigeons, but for my money, in the glassy sideways stare category, they deserve every award going.) 'It won't be missing Jack Kettley if you've fed it three packets of crisps and a whole loaf,' I said. 'No wonder it can't fly.'

When Mam put down her book and made for the outside toilet, I realised immediately that a once in a lifetime opportunity had just landed right in my lap – or rather, garden – one that must be acted upon without a second's delay. As it dived for another crust I seized the moment and grabbed the pigeon, and, leaping several hungrily vibrating cats, rushed it through the house and up to my bedroom.

The first time I drove to Fliss's in the MG Ruth had told me to park it round the back, beside the dustbins. I hadn't bothered since, preferring to walk anyway, especially on nice evenings, when I'd stuff to read and muse upon. Inside the envelope with the concert tickets had been a brief itinerary and a four-page leaflet about the event in which I'd become so engrossed, reading and rereading it as I lingered along the pavement, I couldn't say for sure if the figure who lolloped into the estate at the corner of my eye had been my old pal Sniffy Glue Boy or not. I hadn't seen him since that incident at the phonebox and, to be honest, had almost forgotten he existed. But now as I read the words 'Artists Against Apartheid', 'Amnesty International' and 'This historic event', I felt another blow had been struck against the thug Clay Clements, knowing how he would likely never be part of anything like this, that he could never begin to understand what I felt at the gut-fizzing prospect of very soon becoming one with an elated crowd of eighty thousand, beamed around the world as united we punched the air and sang along to Simple Minds live at Wembley Stadium.

I wondered whether Clay Clements had ever felt anything, including the (accidental) knock-out right I'd landed him smack under the jaw. I doubted he'd heard of Simple Minds, let alone studied every last letter, full stop and comma on almost every LP, EP and single the band had released since their debut in '79. And I'd bet my life that neither he or his greenie gobbling pal had ever stood before a speckled full-length wardrobe mirror, resplendent once more in billowing white shirt and his sister's best tights, to present a trembling, wing-wounded homing pigeon to his own moodily earnest reflection in homage to the back sleeve image of *Ghostdancing*.

When I eventually got to Fliss's I found her sitting outside, drinking lemon barley water on Grandma Dot's wooden bench overlooking an immaculate field of back garden.

'Evening, girls,' I said, sneaking Dot a cheeky wink before settling on the arm nearest the younger of the two ladies. 'Lovely out here.'

'It was till you came,' Fliss said with a gentle squeeze for my knee as I lowered my lips towards hers.

'Ugh, Robin, what's that?'

'Eh? Oh, pigeon shit,' I said, not thinking. 'Sorry, Dot, I mean...'

Dot rocked back on her bum cushion, hugging herself in a warm old lady chuckle. 'It must have been a big one,' she said, and pulling a cricket ball of tissue from her cardigan sleeve, dabbing it against her tongue, she leaned across to set about my thigh like Joseph sanding a windowsill.

Pleasantly Disturbed • 109

Fliss wrinkled her nose, and not in a cute way. 'How did you get *that* all over your jeans?'

'Thank you, Dot, that's smashing, thank you,' I said as the old woman began to ferret in her sleeve for more Kleenex. 'We had an injured pigeon in the garden. I took it round to its owner on my way up. Every cat in the street was after it, it must've been terrified, poor thing.' (I didn't think it worth mentioning the bedroom/mirror/'dove' scene, as a result of which I'd had to smuggle another pair of Cath's tights out to the dustbin.)

'You are a good lad,' Dot said, her tongue flicking as if she were contemplating having a second crack at my bird-caked thigh. 'Felicity, are you going to tell Robin your news?'

I'd noticed Fliss had been warming something under her own bum cushion. Without a word she pulled out an envelope, looking up at me as she handed over the enclosed letter with great big eyes and the sort of smile you keep for hospital waiting rooms.

'They want you to audition!' I said, leaping up to face the anticipating bench. 'I told you they would, didn't I? That's fantastic!' I pulled Fliss up into my arms, kissing her noisily on the lips. 'Ah, Fliss, *you. are. brilliant.*' And I kissed her again.

'Have you got one left for me, duck?'

'Always got one left for you, Dot,' I said, and I bent down to plant a peck on the old woman's powdery cheek.

'I've been telling her not to be silly, Robin,' Grandma Dot said. 'She's good enough to be on that television programme, isn't she?'

'Too good. They won't know what's hit them. Especially with her going on as a man.'

'What do you mean,' Dot said, shuffling forward with a sudden confused look. 'Going on as a man?'

'Hasn't she told you? She's going to sing as Johnny Rotten from The Sex Pistols. That's why I'm here. I've come to give her swearing lessons.'

Dot looked up at Fliss. 'You're not, are you, Felicity? Going on as a man and... and *swearing*?'

'No, of course not, Grandma,' Fliss smiled, shaking her head as she sat to drape an arm around Dot's shoulder.

Dot tutted and gave me a mischievous look. 'He's a card, isn't he, Felicity, eh? He's a card.'

'No, Grandma,' Fliss said, jabbing her baseball boot into my shin. 'He's an idiot.'

3

'No hanky panky in the back seat, though, please, Robin,' David warned as he tossed me the keys to a nearly new Fiesta. 'I'm hoping to sell it to my sister-in-law on Sunday.'

Although I'd had only six or seven weekends in the showroom, and wasn't yet eighteen, David had arranged for me to have a company car overnight and to take the Saturday off when I was due to work. I realised such kindness and generosity must (though not entirely) be part of his plan to win me over to the sales team before the summer rush, the big bonanza months when customers stormed the showroom to order their cars in time for the new registration letter on 1st August. But I could live with that. For now, all that mattered was that Fliss got to her audition sixty miles away on the other side of the Pennines, the chances of which, as David pointed out when I filled him in, in confidence, would be far better in a boring new Fiesta than my cool but flagging MG.

'Your mum was looking forward to taking you, on Thursday,' I said as we buzzed, yawning, towards Chesterfield shortly after dawn. 'She must be disappointed.'

'She is, though I can't say that I am very much. She'd only make me more nervous than I already am.'

'And won't I make you nervous?'

'You'd better not. I told Mum I'd ring her at the shop when it's all over. For now, though, let's just think nice things all the way to Manchester, shall we?'

'Good idea,' I nodded. 'How's the dog, then? Is it all right?'

'No, it had to be put down.'

'*Hmm.*'

The plan had been for Ruth to drive the three of us, herself, Fliss and me, to the TV studios in Manchester, while Lionel took up the reins at Markley Hall. But then the day before some high-ranking, high blood pressure type from one of his committees or dodgy handshake brigades had fallen from a tractor and landed on his Jack Russell, in turn landing Lionel with supervising a barn dance which he simply couldn't get out of, darling, not even for his most wonderful and talented daughter. I realised that while never wildly vocal about Fliss's musical ambitions, it was Lionel and Ruth who'd given her the initial push, as well as the means to explore them through a decade plus of school bands, private tutors, and several instruments besides a piano that were worth more than my car. Yet I couldn't help feeling Fliss had been let down, that from parents like hers she deserved better.

Despite the two of us thinking only nice things (squashed dog aside), the sky rumbled with dark thunder as we neared Buxton and rain began lashing the car like chucked rice. For the journey I'd packed *The Hounds of Love* and *Never Forever*, the two Kate Bush tapes I owned, thinking they might help get Fliss into a suitably kooky-loopy frame of mind ready for her performance. 'Which one?' I said, rattling them cheerfully under her nose.

But Fliss just shook her head, continued smiling dreamily out at the galloping storm. 'Nothing can help me now, dear Robin,' she said in a soft, ghostly voice. 'Just hold on tight and drive us safely through the rain.' I doubted there could be a more perfect Kate Bush-like response, and I knew right away that however the audition might go Fliss's frame of mind would not be a problem. We drove the rest of the way without a word, Fliss reclined and dozing in her seat while I marvelled at driving a car with wipers that arced across the windscreen without sounding like a dustbin dragged across a schoolyard.

We found the studios huddled, steaming, beneath a rainbow. And although we'd arrived almost two hours early, it seemed hardly any time at all before the same clipboard-wielding young man who'd greeted us at reception knocked and poked his head round the dressing room door.

'Hi, Felicity. They're ready for you if you'd like to come this way?'

'Wish me luck,' Fliss whispered, giving me a tight side-saddle hug from where she'd been curled, brooding, since our arrival, across my lap.

'Just pretend nobody's there,' I whispered back, the young man tilting with a silent '*Ahhh*' as I kissed the end of her nose. 'You're brilliant.'

Before he'd taken her away, young master clipboard had apologised that I wouldn't be able to sit in on Fliss's audition, handing me a small yellow ticket as he waved me off with limp directions to the canteen. I took an apple from the fruit bowl and went in search of a cup of tea and a window.

The corridors were buzzing with anxious faces. Some, either seated or leaning against the walls, pored anxiously over scraps of hand-written lyrics, while others, mostly younger, wore headphones and gurned and strutted about like they'd been had by a Butlin's hypnotist. Every way you turned signs and posters shouted '*Show Me The Stars*'. Which was just what I was thinking. I mean, it might not have been a full dress audition, but honestly, with the exception of a dead spit for Buster Bloodvessel (who turned out to be a studio security guard), and of course myself, not one of this lot looked remotely like a pop star.

I blew my lunch voucher on a ham sandwich, two four-fingered Kit Kats and a mug of tea and carried them over to an empty table overlooking the magnificently miserable skyline. Nothing can help her now, dear Robin, I paraphrased quietly to myself. Just hold on tight and drive her safely through the –

'Robin Manvers!' I swung round, hamster-cheeked with processed meat. I nearly choked. 'Chuff me!' the girl squealed.

Adjacent diners and the two tabarded women behind the counter, no doubt expecting such exuberance would be sure to have a celebrity attached to it, paused to gawp as the very tall and incredibly striking young woman seemed to step over the tables towards me.

'Millie Smith!'

'I knew straight away that it was you,' Millie said, laughing as she skimmed her clipboard across the table, upsetting my mug of tea. Before I was out of my seat, Millie had thrown her arms around me and was making me part of her jumper. 'Oh my gosh, Robin! I can't believe it. So are you here with – *Felicity*? Is she your girlfriend? She's gorgeous.'

'Yes,' I said, confirming all three points and sitting back down. 'She's just gone through with–'

'Laurence,' Millie smiled. 'I saw him taking you to the dressing room and I knew straight away it was you. Oh wow!'

'I knew you straight away as well,' I said, feeling my face start to flush. 'I can't believe it, Millie. What are you doing here?'

'I work here!' Millie said, and with a quick glance at her watch scraped back her chair. 'Stay right there. I'll get us some tea and then I want to hear everything you've been up to, Robin Manvers.'

It was a coincidence worthy of a lightweight comic novel. Millie Smith working on the same television show for which Fliss had been invited to audition. Millie was, of course, the TV girl Ken had pointed out as doing well in the local paper that day. But I hadn't realised that the piece about my old friend, and the other, on the facing page, seeking talent for *Show Me The Stars* were related, and by the time Fliss came to send in her tape, and with all the hoo-ha there was over that, I'd forgotten all about Millie.

I unwrapped one of my Kit Kats and offered Millie Smith a finger. 'But you never wrote to me, either,' I said, laughing.

'I didn't know your address. But you had mine, and I didn't move, so you've no excuse!'

'I was only seven, Millie, and not much of a letter-writer,' I said, smiling as she took another finger. 'I'm still not now. Everybody I know, I see.'

We traded brushstroke life stories, Millie telling how, much against her father's wishes, she'd left school for a production apprenticeship at the studios, me explaining that Mam had divorced my ex-dad after we left the Tuxfield close where we'd been best friends, less than six months after the Queen's Silver Jubilee.

Millie covered my hand with hers. It was hot, from her tea. 'That must have been miserable for your poor mum.'

'It was more miserable for her with him.'

'I had to promise Dad I'll still take two A-levels at night-school,' Millie groaned, burying her face in her hands. 'Did you stay on in the sixth form?'

'No, I'm a sales executive,' I lied, coolly waffling some rubbish about a small but prestigious motor dealership in Stonebridge. '*Trainee*. But the money's all right, and you get a company car.'

'That's great, Robin!'

'It's only temporary,' I was quick to point out. 'I'm studying myself, actually.'

'Yeah? To do what?' Millie said, leaning forward on her elbows as she sipped her tea. 'Afterwards, I mean?'

'I haven't settled on a specific role yet,' I said breezily. 'But I'm working towards a career in the music industry. Yeah, I'm up in my room most evenings working on assignments.' And with these words up sprang my horrified reflection as Jack Kettley's pigeon flushed its frightened bowels through my fingers and all over my sister's best tights.

Millie Smith gave me a sly smile. 'They say music's the food of love.'

'How d'you mean?'

'You and your girlfriend. You share a passion for music. Robin, she has such a wonderful voice.'

'I know,' I said, shaking my head. 'She writes songs as well, but she's funny about people watching her. I didn't think we'd make it here today.'

I offered Millie my last finger.

'Thanks. I shouldn't really, but I've not had any lunch again.'

'How are your mum and dad?' I asked. 'Are they still at Tuxfield?'

'No, they moved to Nottingham, six years ago now. Dad and Winston are both at Queen's Medical Centre. Garry works for a bank in Chicago. And Mum's a primary school teacher, *loves* it.'

'I bet she does,' I nodded. 'Does she still bake delicious cakes?'

'Oh yeah! I make her send them to me through the post. Costs her a fortune, they're so heavy.'

Millie sat up to wave across the canteen to Laurence. As he lingered beside the sausage rolls and pasties I saw that the underside of his blue clipboard had been decorated with a sparkly gold star set at a jaunty angle. 'Looks like I've got to go.' Millie rose from her chair, pausing a moment to put a hand over her mouth. 'I can't believe it's you, Robin. It's so lovely to see you.'

'It's lovely to see you too, Millie. Ten years...'

'Almost eleven. I love your T-shirt, by the way.'

I looked down to check which one I had on. White, with the

Once Upon A Time LP cover on the front. Nice. 'Do you like Simple Minds?'

'Of course! That's such a great album. Coming, Laurence!'

I smiled as Millie turned to go. 'See you later, Millie.'

'You will.'

A short while after, Fliss flung her arms round my middle and buried her face in my shoulder. 'How did it go?' I ventured.

'Rubbish,' she said, letting go a long, defeated sigh.

'She was *wonderful*,' Laurence said, twinkling Mancunian enthusiasm from the dressing room door. 'It was like a religious experience for all those present, honestly. It really was.'

Thirteen

1

At the garage on Monday morning the big story was the three-month-old Escort RS Turbo belonging to the town's solicitor, Edwyn Matthews, that had been stolen from outside Stonebridge village hall as he enjoyed his daughter's wedding reception.

'He parked it up after the ceremony, about half past two, then when he went to nip it home, sometime between the speeches and the disco, it had vanished.'

'Sheila was at the wedding, Vern,' Ricky said, leaping up to sit cross-legged on the workshop counter. 'Weren't you, Sheila?'

'Our Craig was at school with Sheryl,' said Sheila, cooing up the Welsh notes. 'Looked absolutely gorgeous, she did. Poor Edwyn's car aside, it was a smashing day.'

'Expensive day,' Vern smiled. 'What's that saying, lose a daughter, gain a son, is it? Poor chap lost his car and his no claims bonus.'

Darren leaned over to crack me across the knuckles with a spark plug wrench. 'You want to get on the phone, quick, Robin, and sell Mr Matthews another car before Graham or Andrew hear about it.'

'Never mind sales,' Vern said, elbowing a space to rattle his oil jug. 'I was here first and Robin's going to hurry up and get me these bits before I clip his earhole.'

After lunch I rattled up the shutters to find Gillian sitting among the rubber plants and cacti, in the low windowsill opposite the front counter, her knees nakedly raised to make a suntanned plinth for her chin.

'Hello, Robin.'

'Gillian,' I smiled. 'And what can I do for you this fine afternoon?'

'I've come for a lift,' Gillian said, stretching out her arms and mini-skirted legs at the same time, so that in not knowing where to look first I missed everything all at once. Her immaculate, blatant womanliness made me shrink and feel ashamed in my grubby smock, my skin, my hair tight with that hanging film of grease-dipped dust which passes for air in mechanical workshops.

'But I'm at work,' I said, checking my watch. 'I don't finish till half-five.'

Gillian pushed herself up and came over to lean against the front counter, primarily, I think, to give me a better look at her vest, which flashed white for danger beneath a sort of off-the-shoulder lumberjack number. 'A lift from Uncle Giles. I've been into Tuxfield, shopping, with a friend. He just dropped me off. Is Ricky about?'

'Ricky? I think I just saw him go up the road in a customer's car.'

'Only, Mandy hasn't heard from him for nearly a month, and she really likes him.'

'Mandy?'

'My friend who you met at Chesterfield. The night you gave me a ride home.'

'I didn't meet her,' I said, suddenly noticing a display of catalogues that needed straightening. 'I was in the car.'

'It's surprisingly comfortable your little MG, isn't it?' Gillian said, peering along the aisles of shelves behind me before catching my eye. 'Robin, has anyone ever come in here and asked you for a screw?'

'Oh yes,' I said, completely matter-of-factly. 'Vern asked for one over the workshop counter this morning. For a headlamp - they often fall out.'

The door from the showroom groaned as Mr Honeywell swung through rubbing his palms together and smiling like he'd just slipped a banger into a cardiac's back pocket.

'Ah Gillian, Gillian, lovely to see you. I think we may have just closed a rather nice deal with the East Midlands Electricity Board,' Honeywell said, nodding this last snippet to me as he carefully realigned his tie. 'Three new vehicles for May and, all being well, the same again in September. Come through to my office, Gillian, when you've finished with young Robin here. I've to leave early this afternoon.'

'Could I have a lift please, Uncle Giles?'

'Yes, of course,' Honeywell said, tugging back his sleeve to squint at his watch. 'All smooth and shipshape in there, I take it, Robin?'

'It is, Mr Honeywell,' I said, gently booting a pallet of oil- and air-filters which had been delivered at lunchtime. 'Or will be, when I've got this lot put away.'

'Smart young chap this one, Gillian,' Honeywell said, skating away towards his trilling phone. 'Doesn't miss a trick.'

'Tell Ricky to ring Mandy, okay?' Gillian said, bending into the windowsill for her shopping. 'We could go out in Chesterfield together, all four of us. See ya!'

'Robin love, did you see that big requisition from the council depot?' Sheila called as the boss's Scorpio accelerated off the forecourt.

'Just doing it now, Sheila.'

The council order was lengthy but straightforward. Service items for Transit vans, mostly, but enough to work up a sweat between the aisles and running up and down stairs for mirrors and exhaust pipes. There was also an alloy wheel needed urgently at the body shop, a set of number plates to be made up for the morning, and a key that needed cutting from code to be left with sales for collection after five-thirty. With Johnny, the old boy wearing Ken's driving trousers, anxious to be away with the afternoon run – pensioners leading such busy and exciting lives – I knocked off the council order first, gave him the wheel, then phoned the number plate people. Afterwards, in between half a dozen shouts to the workshop counter, I made a pot of tea for six, letting mine cool while I stuck a blank in the key machine ready for cutting. We were getting low on blanks again. I made a note in the book to order some more.

2

I don't know what I thought would happen if Fliss were ever to see our house. Inside, I mean. She knew the outside well enough, having to walk by it on her way to and from school on days when neither Ruth nor Lionel were able to drive her. But I was worried. Embarrassed. Ashamed for being ashamed of the bruises of mould among the woodchip and the balding patches of the carpet for which we no longer had enough cheap furniture and Skeggy market prints to hide. I think I assumed Fliss would only be able to see our shabby little council house from the detached and comfortable heights of her own spacious family home, with its stylish this and latest that, its fragrantly tasteful everything else.

But I needn't have worried. What you don't realise at seventeen is that your parents, though becoming increasingly invisible in your own expanding universe, remain fully visible to everyone else, including your girlfriend. And I should have known that if Fliss spent just two minutes with Mam she'd see straight away that she was all the warmth and comfort any home could ever need, even if we couldn't run to three matching sandwich plates or a colour licence for Alastair's old television.

'Oh, isn't that lovely?' Mam said before Fliss was even halfway through the kitchen door. 'All those knitted flowers and tassels. I've never seen anything like that before. Is it from abroad?'

'No, my grandma made it for me, for my birthday. It's meant to be a poncho. My grandma loves knitting.'

'I do, but I've never made anything as nice as that.' Mam touched the hem of Fliss's cloak of granny colours, as I'd rubbishly named it. 'Yes, that's what it is, isn't it, it's a poncho. Go on through, Felicity, I'll put the kettle on.'

My bedroom was a different matter altogether. For that I felt nothing but pride. And I couldn't wait to get Fliss upstairs to show off my veritable shrine to Simple Minds in all their Blu Tacked poster, postcard and knitted-scarf glory. There were also two other pictures, one each of Belinda Carlisle and Susanna Hoffs, torn from Cath's *Smash Hits* (not mine) and precision mounted at optimum pillow-eye level on the wall beside my bed.

'She's so lovely,' Fliss said, her fingers dancing melodies across my chest as we lay on top of the single duvet. 'You can see she thinks the world of you.'

'Who? Belinda or Susanna?'

'Your mum. And your house is really nice, saying it was – what did you call it?'

'A squalid dump fit only for unfussy rodents?'

'What an awful thing to say. Your bedroom's way cooler than mine. And you've got a much better stereo, mine's rubbish.'

'So's my bed. It's like an ironing-board.'

Fliss slid her hand underneath my T-shirt. 'I bet it's cosy, though, for two.'

'Probably,' I said, patting her roving hand. 'Sadly, though, I think we're about to be three.'

The door creaked open and Mam shuffled in carrying a tray with two mugs of tea and a saucer of assorted biscuits. She set them down carefully on the chest of drawers, a perm-muffled ear turned towards the speakers. 'Is it Prince you've got on?' she said in the crisp and oddly refined voice she usually left, with her pale-blue tabard, at the paper shop. 'I thought Felicity might like another drink.'

'Thank you, Mrs Manvers. Yes, it's Prince – *Purple Rain*.'

'I thought it was. Call me Sarah. Hate that name, Manvers. Mind you, I never liked Sarah, either. But I think your name's lovely. Catherine's got a record called *Felicity*, hasn't she, Robin?'

'No, Mam. I have. Cath steals it.' I swallowed a fig roll, holding the saucer while Fliss took a chocolate wafer.

'I don't think anybody likes their own name,' Fliss said, smiling. 'Maybe we should swap, Sarah.'

'Please don't,' I choked. 'Bye, Mam. Thanks for the tea.'

'That's so kind,' Fliss whispered over the rim of her mug as the door clicked. 'My mum would never do that.'

'Barge in unannounced? Mine can't seem to resist,' I said, my mind flooding again with appalled sisters and laddered hosiery.

'I mean bring me tea and biscuits in my room.'

'Mine's never taken me skiing or bought me a horse,' I said, the words sounding more churlish than I'd intended. It was Fliss having seen the house that did it. I took another fig roll, sideways.

'I know I'm very lucky,' Fliss said, settling her mug on the carpet before sliding under the duvet. 'But sometimes all a girl wants is tea and biscuits… and a cuddle.'

Walking home two hours later, my lips still tingling from a surfeit of kisses, I thought how stupid it'd been to worry about what Fliss would think of our house. But what most surprised me, though, was how soon Mam had suggested Fliss might like to go up to my bedroom to listen to some records. Mam wasn't party to our euphemism. But she probably thought that any mischief I might get up to with a girl like Fliss would always be preferable, based on recent events, to what I might otherwise get up to by myself, left, as it were, to my own ends.

As we held each other beneath the duvet Fliss had tilted her head to study the two soft focus beauties watching over my pillow. 'If you had to choose between Belinda and Susanna,' she said, 'who would you choose?'

'Susanna,' I answered without too much thought.

'Why, because she's dark and petite, like me?'

'She's got very nice lips and is probably the coolest woman ever to swing an electric guitar.'

Fliss thought for a second then pushed out her lower lip in a sort of puppyish, theatrical sorrow. 'I'm sorry I don't swing an electric guitar.'

'Not yet,' I said, hoping Susanna wouldn't take what I was about to do too badly. 'But you are gorgeous... and have got the... best... lips... ever.'

3

'Me mum around, mate?' Craig said, tapping his keys and whistling aggressively at the front counter. 'Robin, is it?'

'That's right,' I said. 'I'll just fetch her.'

Craig, being five years older than me, had left Burns Green Comprehensive the summer I started, but I recognised him even before he spoke. He had his mother's bright, long-lashed eyes and his father's easy sideways smile, and as I looked up from composing a cabinet display of thermostats, gaskets, and fan-belts worthy of the Turner Prize I calculated he must've been about the same height as both his parents would be if one were standing on the other's shoulders.

'Hello, Craig love...'

As mother and giant nattered over the counter a cold panic began to trickle through me as though an egg had been cracked inside my skull. Flattered as I was by David's invitation to join his team full time, and much as I liked working in the showroom at weekends, I'd avoided making any definite commitment, hoping to quietly ignore the situation for as long as I could without appearing ungrateful. But what if I'd now missed my chance, or David had changed his mind, and Craig here, with his rugger-bugger chin and clinging Next checked suit, had come about a job – *my job* – in sales?

'Would you like a cup of tea, Craig?' I asked, thinking I might delay his passage through to the showroom. Damn, he looked the part. Far more the sort of bloke you'd want to buy a car from than I did. 'I was about to put the kettle on.'

'Thanks, mate, but I only called in for petrol. I'm running late. Derby this afternoon, soon as I've been to your body shop.'

'Have you had a bump?' I said feeling uncharitably pleased at the prospect.

'Craig's a Vehicle Damage Assessor,' said Sheila, her voice going all proud and Welsh over the syllables. 'For Royal Falcon Insurance.'

'Brilliant,' I said, meaning brilliant he wouldn't be nicking my salesman's job. Well, that was a relief. 'Keeping you busy, then?'

Craig licked his lips and sucked air into his lungs until his jacket squeaked. 'Never stops at the minute. Still, there are worse jobs. Right, I'd better be off.'

Once Craig had kissed his mother and strode on his bull-necked way, I put the finishing touches to my still life masterpiece – a rocketing ignition coil and two headlight bulbs amid a constellation of wheel nuts – then went to make that tea. There was a short delay while I served Keith and Ricky with parts for a couple of biggish jobs and another as I went out to replace a wheel trim for a heavenly-scented travel agent, but at the first quiet moment I got I leapt across the front counter and through the swing doors into the showroom.

4

Working three weekends out of every four had given me the perfect excuse to avoid it. But as the days grew longer, the evenings lighter, it was clear I wouldn't be able to put it off for much longer. The pressure had been steadily growing since that saddle went away for repair. But now that it was fixed, and with the riding school which operated from the stables up and running with its spring programme of evening horse care classes and riding lessons, the moment had unavoidably arrived and there was no way out.

'Shit, they're a lot bigger in real life,' I said, narrowly dodging a butting by the long bristly nose. 'I think I'll just watch you, Fliss.'

'You can't be frightened of horses. Look, we'll just go five minutes round the paddock.' I must have looked confused at this. 'Over there.'

It appeared innocent enough. 'Have many people been killed there?'

'Don't be silly, Robin, it's just like riding a bike,' Fliss assured me, which is another way of saying she lied to me. It was nothing like riding a bike. I'd ridden lots of bikes, even raced BMX a couple of seasons, and not one of them had ever fixed me with a look of such pity and contempt as I tried unsuccessfully to swing up into their saddles as the one I now got from this horse, Bertie.

'Nope. You're wrong, Fliss. I can be frightened of horses. Forget it.'

'Bertie's not frightening, *are you, Bertie*?'

'He bloody well is. He was eating his stable.'

That said, though, once my 20-minute staring contest with the enormous dark animal was over, and I managed to remain seated long enough to slide my feet into the stirrups and be trotted gently round the stable yard on a lead held by a very patient Fliss, it wasn't half as bad as I'd expected. I wouldn't say it was fun exactly, or even enjoyable, but nor was it completely awful, either. In fact, when it was all over I quietly congratulated myself, thinking I might even ask Fliss to give me a second lesson, if she and Bertie were available in, say, eighteen months' time.

'Thanks, Bertie,' I said, limping for the toilet as Fliss led my new pal away.

When I returned, expecting we'd be heading home, I found Fliss where I'd left her a few moments before. Only now she wasn't leading big bad Bertie, but sitting high in the saddle of her own horse, the friendlier looking, though not much smaller, chestnut-coloured Mungo.

'Left foot in the stirrup,' Fliss said, indicating with the toe of her own boot. 'Now give me your hand and – *up!*'

'What's happening?' I asked, instinctively tightening myself around her body like a koala clinging to a eucalyptus.

Fliss threw an evil smile back over her shoulder. 'Shut up and hold tight.'

With a crack of Mungo's reins (or so I like to imagine), we shot off across the stable yard at an alarming pace and galloped along beside the paddock fence towards the woods. Out of the corner of my eye I saw the dark blur of Bertie shimmering in the field. 'Next time we meet, Bertie Horse, you and I shall gallop like this, you see if we don't!'

Fliss rode a horse like she played piano, that same lightness of touch skilfully conducting Mungo's hooves through a series of complicated rhythms and time signatures as we thundered through the forest towards dusk. I'd never dreamed being on horseback could be so exhilarating or so rapid, and my giddy bob-bob-bobbing was clouded only by picturing what might happen if I were to let go of Fliss's middle and fly off into the trunk of a passing oak. I must have closed my eyes awhile at this point, because when I next opened one of them to peer over Fliss's shoulder we had turned off the main bridleway and were now weaving carefully between the trees towards a small clearing beside the Major Oak.

'You're not really supposed to bring them in this far,' Fliss said, tethering Mungo's reins to the fence overlooking the big tree. 'But the rangers don't mind, so long as we don't churn up the grass too much.'

I sat admiring the steaming Mungo from the wooden picnic table where we sat wishing we'd brought something to drink. 'He's a brilliant horse, Fliss. I'd no idea they could go that fast.'

'He was hardly even trying. I'm so glad you like him, though, Robin. He's a real beauty, isn't he?'

While Fliss was complimenting Mungo he'd been slowly unfurling between his hind legs two feet of brawny pendulum. It was like a ladder lowered from a zeppelin, and from which he now gushed ten fizzing gallons into the grass. Fliss laughed. 'He's not shy about weeing in front of strangers, either.'

'Well, you wouldn't be, would you?' I said, thinking I might wait until I got home.

By the time we got back to the stables and had made Mungo cosy for the night it was getting dark – though not so dark that as we turned into the lane at the back of Vern's house we didn't recognise it was Betty running towards us, her tongue flapping at the side of her mouth like a fat rasher of bacon.

'Who's this creeping about my back garden again?'

'All right, Vern,' I said, as he secured the rope loop over the gatepost. 'You coming in or going out?'

'We're just off for our walk before bedtime. What've you two been – now then,' Vern interrupted himself, chuckling as he nodded to where I'd started rubbing the inside of my thighs. 'You want to get that looked at, Robin, if it's causing you mischief.'

Fliss laughed. 'He had his first riding lesson tonight, Vern.'

'Did he? And how did he get on?'

'He was really good, actually. Once he stopped being a baby.'

I shook my head. 'Horrible. It's not much easier on the back of somebody else, either. Kills your legs.'

'Rather you than me,' Vern said. 'I think I'll stick to motors.'

'Thanks for warning my dad about those joyriders at the station, Vern,' Fliss said. 'He had the locks changed on the shutters and some improvement made to the alarm.'

Vern smiled shyly under his cap. 'Better safe than sorry. Robin said he'd had no bother. I'm glad to hear it.'

When we got back to Fliss's Lionel was out at one of his meetings and Ruth had just made two cups of milky coffee to take over to Grandma Dot's, where the two of them, she swooningly informed us, were getting ready for *Moonlighting*, starring Bruce Willis.

'Fancy going upstairs to listen to some records?' I said, Fliss smiling as we sipped ice cold cartons of orange against a twinkling granite surface. 'After you've played me *Head Over Heels* on the piano, I mean.'

'I learned *Solsbury Hill*, as well. It's quite late, though,' Fliss said. 'And I always have a shower after I've been riding.'

'Oh. Okay,' I said. 'I'll just finish this, then, and be off.'

Fliss slurped the last of her juice through her straw and wrinkled her forehead. 'Why?'

'You just said...'

Fliss slid her arms around my neck and pressed her nose against mine. 'I didn't say you had to go, did I? The steam might do wonders for those places where you're sore.'

'Ow,' I winced, though not wanting her to stop. Through the kitchen window, across the designer-stubble lawn, Grandma Dot's curtains were alight and flickering with television fireworks.

Fourteen

1

The cars hadn't left Midland Auctions until two hours after they were due to be delivered to Stonebridge Motor Company.

'Bloody administrative error,' Mr Honeywell tutted over the front counter, the first time I'd known him swear. 'Most infuriating, Robin, it's...' he sighed now. 'I can only apologise for the inconvenience, I'm sure you and Rocky will have made plans for this evening.'

'Ricky,' I corrected.

'Yes, sorry, *Ricky*.'

So, same as the first trip, Honeywell pulled up, on the stroke of eight o'clock, at the bus stop opposite the showroom. The nasty tweed cap was back but this time the boss was at the wheel of a dark blue Vauxhall Senator, in which Ricky and I were sped, along with whichever is the most excruciating of Vivaldi's four seasons, to The Half Moon Inn, near junction 29 of the M1, where we found gleaming at opposite ends of the car park a white Sierra Cosworth and a red Escort RS Turbo.

'Nice,' Ricky said, licking his lips as we got out of the Vauxhall. I'd no need to ask which he'd be taking.

'Two of the fastest production cars on the road, gentlemen,' Honeywell said, perhaps as a subtle warning, and along with the keys he slipped me a notelet headed with the Ford logo and name of a big, well-known dealership on the outskirts of Manchester. 'I bought them for our forecourt, actually – we seem to do well with sports models – but Wilmslow have taken deposits on both of these, unseen, so I, er, sold them on, and with quite a profitable margin.'

'That's very good, Mr Honeywell,' I said with a sense of relief. I don't know, something about that last trip, those two cars for British Steel at Sheffield, had struck me as being a bit odd. A moonlit bombsite overlooking the padlocked gates of a brewery straight from the pages of Dickens, it hardly seemed the place for a dealer principal like Mr Honeywell, a man who owned golf shoes and a picnic basket, to carry out his high-level business dealings. But this was more like it, a main dealer at Wilmslow.

'We'll follow you, then, Mr Honeywell,' Ricky said, itching to be away in the Sierra Cosworth.

'Oh, I thought I'd, er, – perhaps I didn't. Sorry, gentlemen,' Honeywell said, buzzing his window down all the way to poke his head out. 'There'll be a vehicle for you to bring back this time, er, yes, just an old trader. If you could lock it away in the yard on your return, I'd be much obliged. You've keys, Ricky, haven't you?'

Ricky patted the pocket of his jacket, across the denim shoulders of which he'd now foolishly added several more hideous patches proclaiming Rainbow, Rush, and Deep Purple, poor thing. 'I do, Mr Honeywell.'

Beneath the yellow interior light Honeywell gestured at the notelet, on the back of which I found neatly inked directions to Wilmslow. 'You may take this, Robin,' he said, flicking open a natty leather-bound map book. 'But you should have no trouble following those notes. Straight up the A6, then off here, do you see, just before the Stockport road?'

'I'm sure we'll find it, Mr Honeywell,' I said.

'I've no doubt about it. You two chaps know your way about.

I'd prefer to be going with you myself, of course, but what with the, er, quarter's finance penetration, business lease incentives and so on...'

Sensing the grin, I glanced across the bonnet at Ricky, wondering if these phrases made any more sense to Honeywell as he spouted them than they did to us.

'Well, safe journeys both.'

We swung onto the forecourt just before half past nine. It was huge, more like a well-manicured airport car park than a used Ford sales pitch, with two hundred saloons and hatchbacks spread in dazzling metallic rainbows beneath the floodlights. While behind the glass walls of the showroom a dozen more basked in a soft blue haze as if chasing an all-over tan for their perfect bodywork. The whole place, though, was deserted, the showroom locked and, outside, anything more valuable than a plant-pot hemmed in behind high-security steel bollards.

'I thought Honeywell said this bloke would be waiting for us?' Ricky said, sliding into the passenger seat of my RS Turbo after five minutes in his own company. 'What's his name again?'

I angled the paper towards the light. 'Jack.'

Ricky tapped the Sierra keys irritably against the dashboard. 'Well, Jack, where the bloody hell are you?'

The 1988 Escort RS Turbo isn't fitted with an ejector seat, but that didn't stop the pair of us from being launched almost through the sunroof when a few seconds later a set of unseen knuckles rapped hard against the misted window.

Once I'd steadied my hand enough to turn on the ignition, I buzzed down the window an inch.

'A-right, son? Yi find us nae bother?' an unexpectedly Scottish voice rasped from beneath an equally unexpected camel-coloured cowboy hat.

'Yes,' I said, hoping that would do for an answer. 'Are you Jack?'

'Aye, course I'm Jack. Who else would I be, Boy-fuckin-George?'

'In that hat, you might well be,' I didn't think to say, being momentarily thrown by his brusque manner. This was not the way I spoke to my customers in the showroom at Stonebridge Motor Company.

'These look nice.'

'They are.'

'That Cossie's a beast,' Ricky said.

I signalled to Ricky that I thought it was safe for us both to get out. 'Is there something for us to take back, Jack?'

'Aye. Dougie, where's the keys? It's yer wee thing over there.'

Cowering in the shadows on the far side of the forecourt was a goggle-eyed old Mini, finished in the same shabby blue as my MG, with one primer-grey wing and a full set of missing wheel-trims. I turned back just in time to catch the keys lobbed into my face by Jack's accomplice.

'Paperwork's on the seat,' said Dougie, who despite his aggressive tone seemed to be no more than a bobble hat attached to a child's pair of black-and-white Adidas.

'There's an envelope in this one,' I said, 'for both cars. Radio codes and all that, I expect.'

Jack nodded, scanning a swift expert eye over the Escort's gleaming red bodywork followed by the Sierra's white. 'Aye, nice. Yi got the keys?'

'Behind the sun-visors.'

At this, Dougie made a sudden break towards the Sierra.

'Get the fuck back, Dougie,' Jack growled. 'I'll be driving the Cossie, thank you. You take this here *Turbo*.'

I wanted to compliment Jack on the at least half-a-dozen Rs he rolled into the word *Turbo*, tell him I thought it was easily up there with DCI Taggart saying '*murder*', but I didn't feel this was quite the time for chitchatting about the Scots tongue.

'We best ha' these away to the valeters' place for cleaning in the morning,' Jack said, smiling as he touched the wide brim of his hat. 'Cheers now, boys. Drive safe, eh?'

'You too, pal,' I said.

One the way up, as we chased the glorious spring nightfall through the Peaks I'd been able to savour my cassette of Simple Minds *Live In The City of Light*, the band at their flat out stadium best, through the RS Turbo's quadrophonic sound system. Now, as we headed back in the Mini, we had no cassette player, not even a radio. Nor, for that matter, a second gear, a working fuel gauge or very much in the way of a floor beneath Ricky's feet.

To keep his mind off all this, I shouted above the screaming little engine something I'd been turning over in my mind since we left Wilmslow. 'Ricky, do you think they were really taking those cars to the valeters overnight?'

Ricky blew out his cheeks. 'Yeah, why? Probably take them for a thrash round the ring-road first, I bet. They seemed well dodgy, though, didn't they? But so do most blokes in the car trade. Look at you: well dodgy. Keith and Darren: well dodgy. All the salesmen, Honeywell, Vern...'

I laughed. 'How does Vern seem dodgy?'

Ricky stared out at the dark hills. At first, I wasn't sure if he'd gone silent or if the Mini's angry din, like a washing machine filled with marbles, had suddenly got louder. I think it was both. 'Probably shouldn't say anything,' he said eventually. 'Maybe not dodgy, but he has been getting a bit weird lately. Don't you think?'

'Not that I've noticed,' I said, wondering if Vern had started sharing his joyriding burglar theories with Ricky as well as me. I hoped not. 'Weird, how?'

'Don't say anything, bud, but... he's been going through old service records and asking me which customers I remember having the nicest cars, you know, nice, fast, pinchable stuff, like those we just dropped off.'

'What, and you think Vern's nicking them?'

'No, but... Oh, I dunno. He's probably just stalking a customer who reminds him of an old squeeze from his army days. Either that or he's going senile. He's nearly sixty.'

We hurtled into a blind hairpin bend, swerving hard, in the absence of any brakes, to avoid a flock of highly casual sheep.

'Jesus Christ, Robin!'

'I think we ran over something,' I said as the Mini bucked, tyres squealing, back into line.

Ricky peered out over the stubby bonnet. 'It's all right,' he said. 'It was only a headlamp.'

2

Ken was back on frontline duties, his exploding organ having been made safe by Tuxfield General's crack appendix disposal unit, and without the loss of a single life or comrade's scrotum. It was fortunate, because nobody else could have relayed the details of the accident with quite such gruesome relish.

'Blood all over the pavement,' he announced, his smacking lips sucking out what joy remained of morning break. 'Whatever car hit the lad must be hell of a mess – *hell of a mess*. Miracle he didn't go through the windscreen. They reckon,' Ken went on, tossing the *Evening Post* across the table, 'they reckon he'll never walk again, poor bastard – and only twenty-three.'

Between the crumpling of crisp packets, private murmurs and deep contemplative sighs rose around the table. With great force Ken spat twice into the dustbin before turning his furious squint on me and Ricky. 'Twenty-three and made a cripple. Eh? Now then, what about that? You'd like that, would you?'

'Course not, Ken,' I said wondering how come I was suddenly in the Old Bailey, standing accused, rather than in the canteen, munching a potted-meat sandwich. 'It's an awful thing to happen.'

Ricky shook his head, pushed the newspaper away across the table towards Vern. 'I don't think anybody would like that, Ken, would they?'

'No need for cheek,' Ken snapped. 'I seen a young lad hit by army lorry once. Place called Liz-yoo-er, in France. Canadian he was – about your age. Leapt out of a ditch without looking and... The mess it made of him, by God! You wouldn't laugh at that, pair of you. We had to scrape him off road with us shovels.'

Ricky's boot tap-tapping against mine under the table was the only sound during the tense silence that followed and I fought hard against meeting his eye. I couldn't have been more grateful when Vern, putting on his glasses, cleared his throat and shook open the paper.

'Still no name. Just says Stonebridge man, 23, hit by car which mounted pavement before driving off. Witness, also unnamed, says the white car, travelling at high speed, appeared to clip the opposite kerb before losing control.'

'It's that bad corner,' Darren said. 'Up by the fishing ponds, on the road to Oakerby. How many crashes has there been up there?'

'Too many,' Ken said, emptying his nostrils into the dustbin for emphasis.

'What sort of car was it?' Keith asked. 'Does it say, Vern?'

'No, nothing other than it was white and speeding.' As Vern folded the paper and tossed it onto the table he threw me a glance from under his cap. 'Right, then, I suppose it's time we got back to work.'

3

Such morbid, speed related tragedy would normally have provided talk enough for Wednesday's morning and afternoon tea breaks, and lunch hour as well, had it not been for the fact that on Monday night, the same night Ricky and I delivered those two cars to Wilmslow, a red Escort XR3i, registered only that afternoon, had been stolen off the forecourt of Stonebridge Motor Company.

'Like I said, we got back...' I turned from the policeman to where Ricky sat half swallowed up in the caramel leather sofa. 'Yeah, about quarter past?'

'A quarter past eleven?' Sergeant Pollard clarified.

Ricky nodded. 'Something like that. Then I – we – locked the Mini in the back yard, so it would have been five, ten minutes after that when we left.'

We'd been summoned to Mr Honeywell's office where, blending with the décor and lingering fug of cigars, the presence of this steely, moustachioed copper completed the illusion of being on the set of *The Sweeney*. As Ricky repeated what we'd both told him three times already, I decided that if in the next two minutes we were looking at a ten stretch in the Scrubs I'd lob the swivel chair I was sitting on through the frosted glass and make a run for it.

The copper's sixth sense perhaps alerting him to my violent potential, he now came and stood right over me.

'But neither of you,' he said, a hand on the wing of my swivel chair, 'recalls noticing whether or not the red Ford Escort XR3i was present on the front corner of the forecourt when you arrived at, and then shortly afterwards left, the garage premises between approximately 11.15 and 11.25 Monday evening?'

I furrowed my face in concentration as Ricky again gave the same answer to the same question. 'No, I don't think I even looked.'

'Me neither,' I said. 'But it must have been there, though, or we would have noticed the gap. Wouldn't we?'

Mr Honeywell, who during the interview had remained erect behind his desk, alternating between fingering his buttonhole and smoothing his tie, nodded me a smile of encouragement.

'Ricky, I saw you driving in past the forecourt as I arrived a short while ago,' Sergeant Pollard continued. 'Can I ask if you noticed what, if anything, is now in the place of the red XR3i?'

Ricky scraped an oily palm across his chin and gave a little laugh of surprise. 'No, Sergeant, sorry, I –'

'No need to apologise. It's remarkable the things that go unnoticed, even right under our noses. Thank you, Ricky, Robin.'

Sergeant Pollard scribbled in his little notebook then thanked us both again before turning to Mr Honeywell.

'Who was it you said, Mr Honeywell, had been responsible for locking the forecourt security barriers on Monday evening?'

'Er, it would have been Andrew,' Mr Honeywell said, getting up and coming round his desk with clasped hands. 'Terrific young salesman, Andrew, yes. Shall I, er, have him come through, Sergeant Pollard?'

'If you would, please, Mr Honeywell. Thank you.'

It being a lovely sunny evening, Ricky and I had a slightly more thorough wash than we normally would have done, and after clocking off went for a shandy in the garden of the pub next door.

'Cheers, bud,' Ricky said, clinking glasses. 'When Honeywell collared me and asked if either of us had noticed anything unusual, I just automatically said no. I should've said I'd brought the Mini back here on my own, after dropping you off, but – you know how he gabbles on, you can't get a bloody word in. Then when that copper turned up and Honeywell said we'd locked it away together, I thought, I can't suddenly change my tune now, how would that look?'

'Well dodgy.' I narrowed my eyes. 'You sure it wasn't you who nicked the XR3i? What about mounting a kerb and crippling a pedestrian – that you as well, was it?'

Ricky blew his bitter froth into my eye. 'That's rich from a bloke who spins his mates' vans sideways through hedges.'

'Will you never forget that?'

'Nope. Your round.'

When I returned with more drinks, Ricky downed half a pint in one gulp and said, 'What will happen about Andrew then? Reckon he'll get the sack?'

'For forgetting to lock a security barrier? I hope not. He's all right, Andrew. Brilliant salesman.'

'David must be raging.'

'He is,' I smiled. 'That red XR3i was going to be his new company car.'

4

Sheila had a dentist appointment Thursday morning, so of course the workshop was rammed with big jobs and the phones never stopped ringing. From opening up to Sheila getting back just after eleven, I must have answered a dozen calls and made nearly as many again, though only two are of any interest to this increasingly gripping tale.

The first, before 9.30, was David, asking if I'd have a minute at lunchtime to pop through to his office. There was something he needed to speak to me about. I could guess what that would be. I'd done well, I supposed, to have dodged it for as long as I had. The second, on the external line, and which I'd not been expecting, came about an hour later.

'Good morning, parts and service department, Robin speaking, how may I help?' I said, hating myself, as I did every time, knowing Jim Kerr would never have stooped to such arse-licking customer care bollocks, building site or anywhere else.

'Hello, *Robin speaking*,' mocked a young woman's voice, breathless as if she were running for a bus. 'Guess who?' I didn't need to. The teasing giggle gave her away and immediately I pictured her smile lighting up that rainy grey corner of Smiths video Manchester.

'Millie!' I said, my own little grey corner lighting up in beaming delight. 'How did you know where to...'

'I'm a TV researcher, Robin. My job is finding information and people.'

'Good work, Detective Smith.'

'Hardly. You said you worked at a car dealer in Stonebridge. Not exactly a sprawling metropolis, is it?'

'What do you mean? There's a Co-op and a Kwik Save. So, now you've tracked me down, am I in trouble? Only, I've been helping the police with their enquiries once already this week.'

Millie gasped.

'Oh god, Robin Manvers, what have you done? I'm going to regret tracking you down now, I can feel it.'

'I haven't done anything. A car was stolen off the forecourt the other night, and the police wanted to know if I'd seen anything. I was working late.'

'As a *Sales Executive*?' Millie said, her voice loaded with suspicious eyebrows.

'Sorry about that. I do really work in sales, but only at weekends. For now.'

'Oh *really*?'

'Really, Millie.'

'Anyway, the reason I called, apart from to say hello, was to give you my address. And to ask yours. I meant to get it before you left the studio the other week. Now, though, what with all your lies and being questioned by the police –'

'Shop!' shouted Vern, cueing a plastic thunder of oil jugs.

'*Robin!*' bawled Ricky.

'Coming!' I called back over my shoulder. 'Sorry, Millie, I'm wanted.'

'I can hear. Is it the police again?'

'Worse. Car mechanics. Millie, it's lovely to hear from you. Maybe I could –'

'Stores!'

'Service!'

The thunder grew louder.

'Robin!'

'I reckon he's gone home again.'

'Quick, what's your address?'

'You won't write, of course,' Millie said. 'Like last time.'

'Millie, I was seven!'

We said goodbye and I ran to the workshop counter stuffing Millie's address in my smock pocket. It only occurred to me seven hours later, as I leaned against the side of the MG, tanking it up with four star, that during our little phone conversation neither I nor Millie had once mentioned Fliss or her audition for *Show Me The Stars*.

Fifteen

1

David's jacket swung on a logoed hanger from the top handle of his filing cabinet. 'Suspended,' he said, and peeling back a lapel, showered the lining with Ralph Lauren's finest. 'On basic salary.'

'Bugger-all, in other words,' Graham sighed with bewildered Geordie sympathy.

We were seated in the cramped fish tank of David's office. Or rather, the sales manager and I were seated. Graham, as usual, filled the doorway, rocking on the balls of his feet, half engaged in recounting Andrew's suspension by Honeywell, while with the eyes of a Kalahari bushman he tracked a middle-aged couple as they wove between the rows of used cars with a young Labrador.

'As you know, pal,' David said with an adoring glance at his latest over-complicated watch, 'we've been ridiculously busy. I don't know how we'd have managed at weekends without you to help us. And with August coming up...'

'Some good money to be made this year, Robin,' Graham put in. 'I've sold two today already and signed another one up for Andrew. I'll have it for myself, if he's given the sack, mind.'

Settled on a burgundy Orion, the Labrador couple were now squinting towards the showroom window, a gesture which, Graham had once told me, was the car sales equivalent of a middle-aged divorcee inviting you upstairs at two in the morning for coffee.

'Here we go,' Graham winked. 'This pair aren't leaving till that Orion's been gift-wrapped and wearing a Sold sign.'

'I realise it's a bit sudden,' David said, slipping into his fragrant jacket and pushing the door to. 'Especially as I said there was no hurry. Only, with Andrew being off – temporarily, I hope – I need another really good, keen, salesman in here as soon as possible.'

'Yes, of course,' I agreed.

Graham pushed, grinning, through the door and grabbed a set of trade plates. 'Just taking these folks out on test-drive. Cash buyers. No part-ex. May as well chalk it up on the board now, boss.'

'That's what I like to hear, Graham.' David closed the door again. 'Andrew had nothing to do with that car being stolen, Robin. He's a dozy twat, forgetting to lock the barrier, but we've all done that. You come and join us in here, pal. We'll have a good time, you'll see.'

As I smiled my mind started to whirl, confronted suddenly and unavoidably by these two alternative and incompatible future Robins, the one up on the catwalk at Wembley Stadium, the other down in the showroom at Stonebridge Motor Company.

'Thanks, David,' I said. It was as though I were looking down on somebody else as I took the outstretched hand and gave it a less than firm shake. 'I'll speak to Sheila this afternoon.'

As I squeaked across the tiles back through to the parts department I overheard Graham busily working his magic. 'Does Henry the dog want to test-drive the new car, or is it just you two?'

2

Side two, track three of *Sister Feelings Call* – the, as you will know, initially free companion LP to 1981's exquisite *Sons and Fascination* – is the song *Careful in Career*. Drawing on Simple Minds' love of Neu! Can and Kraftwerk, and with evident sonic traces of Roxy, Magazine, and Bowie at his Berlin best, it's a clattering off-centre collage of niggling high-fretted guitars, drone-twang bass, and darkly swirled synths woven together with some coolly abstract ghost moaning from Jim Kerr about having come so far, although from where he's come exactly, he chooses to keep to himself.

'What are you listening to, Robin? It's bloody awful.'

'Go away, Cath, you don't know anything.'

To me, though, as I pored over the lyrics and listened to the track for the seventeenth time in a row, it was obvious Jim was singing about that Glasgow building site he'd worked on when he was about the same age as I was. Suddenly the song was no longer one of my lesser favourites on a highly treasured record, but a sign, a personal message, in fact, from Jim Kerr himself, one which had lain hidden for over six years waiting for this moment when I would need his guidance, when he would reach out and urge me to be careful in my own career, to remain strong and follow my one true destiny.

'*Mam!*' I heard Cath shout, clattering down the stairs seconds after I let her in on this discovery. 'Mam, I think our Robin's gone properly mental. He just told me Jim Kerr's been leaving him secret messages in his records.'

3

Electric gates humming in my wake, I rounded the side of the house to find Ruth seeing her scrubbed-up and black-tied husband into the driver's seat of her new Sierra.

'Good evening,' I accidently greeted them in my best showroom voice. 'Are you going somewhere exciting?'

My prospective Lionel-in-law rolled his eyes. 'I wouldn't say *exciting*, Robin,' he groaned, twisting to fasten his seatbelt.

'Hello, Robin,' Ruth said. 'It's his Local Traders' Association quarterly dinner.'

'Oh.'

'Many more of these dinners and I'll soon start to look like one,' said Lionel, scarring me with an image of him being rotisseried, naked, over an open fire, with an apple the same shade as his face bunged in his mouth. I let out a nervous splutter, which he, of course, took as applause for his joke.

I nodded towards the back of the car, only noticing now that attached to it was a large, twin-axled horsebox, the sort I'd seen on display at Markley Hall Equestrian.

'If Mungo's going to dinner, couldn't you just ride him there and save petrol?'

'Oh, Robin!' Ruth laughed as she settled her hand softly on my shoulder and left it there. 'You *are* funny.'

'I think my saddle days are behind me. No, Robin, it's booked into our workshop first thing,' Lionel said. 'Brakes keep sticking on the nearside. Both wheels, I think. I'm just going to run it up there now, on my way out.'

'Could do with some air in these tyres,' I said. 'They look a bit low this side.'

'Low, is it?' Lionel craned his fleshy round head through the car window. 'Well, thank you, Robin. I'll see that Iain gives it a thorough going over tomorrow.'

'Fliss is in her room,' Ruth said, patting me with a warm smile. 'Just go up. No point in shouting with her music blaring.'

I was met halfway up the deep carpeted stairs by *Sign O' The Times*, an epic double album crammed with enough funk, rock and soul jazzy sexiness to satisfy any young lovebirds wishing to soundtrack their locked bedroom fumblings with impeccable taste. Fliss, of course, had always known Prince was one seriously talented MF, and by now, her having played me his stuff relentlessly, I could hardly disagree.

'I mean, anybody who has a global hit riffing about crack habits, gun crime and poverty-driven infanticide, and yet still manages to make it sound horny as hell, has to be a friggin' genius.'

'Oh, Robin, do you really think that?' Fliss purred once Ruth was safely inside Grandma Dot's sitting room and we'd set about undoing the permitted zips and buttons prior to hitting the duvet. 'I'm so glad. I knew you would... though... he's just un... believe... able, one hundred percent... absolute... musical genius.'

That Fliss took such delight in my appraisal of one of her biggest idols thrilled me to the holes in the socks I'd no time to remove. Every word I used I'd wholeheartedly believed and had come from the heart, even if they were stolen from a half-remembered review in a year-old *Melody Maker*. They didn't mean any less for not being my own. I mean, Vern hadn't written the words to *Fly Me To The Moon* or *Mack The Knife* but Betty never questioned where his heart lay when he threw off his cap and got down to serenade her.

Aurally and carnally cheered on by Prince, there were some other words, also not of my own composition, that I had come very close to using during our under-duvet movements that evening. Three little ones, comprising of one, four, and three letters respectively. Only something came up, or rather out, of the drawer of Fliss's bedside table.

'I got this today,' she said, hovering flauntingly over me.

'What is it?'

Fliss sighed.

It was a letter, postmarked Manchester.

I remember we took our time about separating at the boot room door that night, and afterwards, in between leaping up onto the usual garden walls and once from the window of a glassless bus-shelter while singing *All The Things She Said*, I floated almost the entire way home. I say almost, because as I turned up the hill to the estate I ran straight into Billy Eyesore, our heads nearly butting as my dry ice-weaving arms folded against the zips and studs of his leather jacket. And yet my mood was so light, high on the helium of kisses and all that, my instinctive reaction, rather than to leap back and square-up for a rematch of the great rumble at the phonebox with him and Clay, the Glue Boy Wonder, was to greet Billy like a long-lost pal.

'Oops! Oh, hello, mate,' I said. 'How're you doing?'

Billy, who looked quite high himself, though probably not from mainlining kisses, seemed in a less friendly mood, and eyed me warily over a crooked roll-up as he scuttled sideways out of my path to half bury himself in a dusty privet like a crab evading a famished seagull. It was clear Billy was not looking for a fight, and yet, despite my joyous mood, my fists bunched at his damp odour of sweat and nicotine-burned leather as he scrubbed past.

'Where's your pal, tonight?' I said as Billy, his eyes locked on mine, sprang out of the hedge and, continuing his crab-like stylings, began to jog lazily sideways down the hill. He'd gone perhaps only a dozen feet when he stopped and, still watching me silently, rummaged in his pockets before relighting his roll-up and blowing a thick skyward cloud of grey.

Billy snapped shut his lighter and slipping it through a zip took a few inching steps backwards. It seemed he both wanted to get away and to stay put. But then, in a pathetic little voice, he spoke. 'Haven't you heard?'

'Heard what?' I said, with a reassuring nod to a slippered and dressing-gowned pensioner as she put out a single empty milk bottle.

Billy made a sound I can only describe as a huff. He shook his head, took a long drag on his fag. The old woman closed her door.

'Heard what?' I repeated.

Billy shook his head again and spat phlegmily on a gatepost before resuming his sideways jog. 'You'll find out,' he said, turning away.

I walked up the hill mildly baffled until, reaching the front gate, a thought occurred to me. I started to turn back with ideas of running down the hill after Billy. But after quickly checking the MG was locked, I decided against it. I was tired, and I'd better things to dream about.

4

I booked out the 48,000-mile service items, front and rear brake pads and an offside electric window motor for a police-spec Granada to Vern's job sheet, then, after ensuring Sheila was in deep at the front counter, returned to resume our twice-interrupted conversation.

'You've spoken to nobody else about it, have you?' Vern frowned, drumming two hands of dark fingers on the back counter.

'Nobody.'

'Well, I reckon between us we've got half a picture of what might be going on. Unless what we've got turns out to be a lot of different pieces belonging to a lot of different pictures, all unrelated, in which case, we've got bugger-all.'

I nodded thoughtfully. 'I rang Kevin at the body shop this morning to see if he'd got any smashed-up newish XR3is in the yard.'

'And?'

'Remember the afternoon we dropped off that corpse car? There were two down there, a red one and a white one.'

'Can't say I noticed. And both XR-whatsits, you say?'

'Yeah. Kevin says both have been collected in the last few weeks. Same wagon both times, a bloke who's been coming for years.'

Vern made slow patterns in the pools of spilt oil on the counter. 'These two motors, write-offs, were they, or damaged repairables?'

'Kevin reckons repairable - if you know what you're doing. He fancied buying one of them for himself.'

'Kevin'll never buy one. He's no time for fixing up sports cars with a missus and five kids to feed.'

'Five?' I said, my surprised tone a mixture that was roughly one part admiration to twelve parts sympathy. 'He'd never fit them in an Escort.'

'He'll need a minibus, the way he's going,' Vern laughed, removing his stained cap to shake some cool air through it. 'Why don't you have a run up later, then, when you've tucked your young woman up? I shouldn't mind having another nosey about.'

Vern gathered up his various filters, spark plugs and gaskets, cradling them in his overalled arms across the workshop to where the police Granada sat raised high on the ramp in his bay.

'A better idea, Robin,' Vern said, returning to collect his oil jug. 'More sensible, anyroad. I could just leave an anonymous note inside this copper's glovebox and save us both a lot of trouble. What do you reckon?'

'Saying what, though?'

Vern shrugged his shoulders. 'That's just it, lad, isn't it? Saying *what?*'

Later that afternoon, Graham took a breather from rearranging the technicolour fan of used cars overlooked by the front counter and waddled in sipping his mug of tea. 'Heard the news, Robin?' he said, the fleshy wattle of his twin chins jiggling as he turned to look back over each of his shoulders. I paused trying to camouflage an over-ordered delivery of radiator caps and reached for a biscuit to dunk in Graham's tea.

'You cheeky young bugger, get your own mug.'

'What news?'

'Red XR3i pinched Monday night. Police have found it, stuck in the bushes out by Carburton Lakes. David's away with Ken now to fetch it back on the wagon.'

'Is it smashed-up?' I said. 'Burnt out?'

'Police say it's not too bad. Door lock and ignition's been busted, I suppose. Not far from the fairground's where they found it. You never really know, do you, but it's funny how whenever travellers are about stuff goes missing.'

5

The thunder and squeal of a coal train braking, snaking, downhill with a dark rake of empties pursued us for a good quarter mile along the cinder path, and it was only as we turned to follow Betty's tail over the damp ballast towards the ruined signal box that the night air regained its still silence.

'Good girl,' Vern whispered as Betty, after circuiting the gloom, settled on a pile of rough sacks to watch for rats.

Unlike my last visit, when all there was to see were rats, we hadn't been in position for more than two or three minutes this time, five at most, when from the direction of the old station came the sound of a diesel engine shuddering into life. It wasn't another train, but something much less powerful, a bus or a lorry. From inside his coat Vern produced a small, ancient-looking pair of binoculars and, pushing back his cap, leaned against the splintered window-frame as he scanned along the platforms and the dark length of the building.

'What is it, Vern?'

'I can't see a bloody... Ah, now then...'

A trembling pool of yellowish light flooded the far side of the station. There immediately followed a heavy crunch of gears and then a sudden jerk as the pool swung in a wide rightward arc, briefly illuminating the near platform and lower steps of the footbridge and beyond to where the farthest reaches of the station yard ended abruptly in a wild and jagged wall of overgrown hedgerows.

'There's a wagon,' Vern said.

'I can see it.'

'Without glasses?'

From the window we watched as the vehicle, a long flat-backed transporter, emerged from the shadows on the far side of the station, made another wide scraping turn, left this time, before accelerating noisily away down the station approach road.

'What did you just see then, Robin?' Vern said as very slowly he swept from one side of the railway yard to the other with Phileas Fogg's binoculars.

'Car transporter. Yellow-and-white. Looked like an old AA wagon. Nothing on the back and kicking out a ton of black smoke.'

'Piston-rings gone,' Vern said matter-of-factly. 'Yes, that's what I saw. The driver could, mind you, have... He could've just come up to turn round in the yard, or nip for a jimmy riddle, have half-hour's kip.'

In the near distance a motorbike roared for attention and, drawing ours, was just as quickly gone again.

'He could have,' I agreed, though I didn't for a second believe that's where Vern's heavy silence was now leading him. 'Do you think there's any–'

'Sshh!' I felt Vern's tight grip on my upper arm. 'Wait...'

Repositioning myself at Vern's shoulder, I followed the sightline of his antique goggles. 'What?'

'You have a look. Can you see a light from that left side?'

I put my head through the strap and raised the binoculars to my eyes. They smelled like the old biscuit tin my grandad used for storing his shoe-polishing kit. I adjusted the focus while slowly, carefully, tracing along the platform side of the building as Vern had indicated, but there was only darkness and shadows cast by the moon, no light, not that I could see. I traced the other, the near side. Then I traced the roofline and the whole of the immediate station perimeter and back along the platform side once more. Other than for some new and unimaginatively explicit graffiti on the black steel panels that covered every door and window, the building was as dark and deserted again now as it had been on our previous visit.

'Can't see anything, Vern.'

'Must be my old eyes,' Vern said. 'And that moon is bright now I come to look at it.' He pulled up the collar of his donkey jacket and clicked twice into the darkness with his tongue. 'Come on, Betty, let's find them rats.'

We'd never had a dog and I didn't really see the point of them. But as we crunched hesitantly across the ballast I found myself wondering what Betty thought we were playing at, the three of us, creeping about a derelict railway yard hissing 'rats!' in the middle of the night. She seemed, as she zig-zagged, tail-wagging, between Vern and me, to be thoroughly enjoying herself, and it struck me, as I looked across at her keeper, that she wasn't the only one.

Suddenly, with a couple of short, high-pitched woofs, Betty

set off as if from a starting pistol, covering a swift twenty yards before Vern whistled her to heel. 'She's seen something.'

The dog's attention had been roused by a figure which had appeared on the station side platform and begun to walk slowly, casually, in our direction until Betty, in her bounding excitement, had frozen him (it appeared to be a man) to the spot in ghostly silhouette for the briefest of moments before he'd turned and scuffled back the way he had come.

'There's a bloke,' I said.

'Get shifting.'

I don't know if it was primal instinct, or the impressive survival skills learned from John Wayne (Vern) and Scooby Doo (me), but the two of us immediately dashed for cover behind a large pile of tarred wooden sleepers about a hundred yards from the end of the platform. Peering over the top of the black timber wall we waited expectantly for another vehicle to appear from behind the station and, like the transporter, make its way down the approach road. But instead, the next sound we heard was of more footsteps, running again, though now, it seemed, in the opposite direction. A dull clattering rumble followed, one we quickly recognised as the sound of those feet pounding up the steps and across the sealed-off footbridge, but by the time we'd crossed the yard and were close enough that we could see the bottom steps on the far platform, whoever it was that had been trying to get away had already done so and was now long gone, probably via the car park of Markley Hall Equestrian.

'There's nobody here now,' Vern all but whispered as Betty dipped to leave a puddle against the timber and barbed-wire barricade blocking the footbridge. 'That said, I'm inclined to get off home before I'm brained by some bugger with an iron bar.'

I took a moment waiting for my heart to roll back by about 160 bpm, while Betty sniffed along the length of the platform before disappearing down into the overgrown goods yard and towards the big pile of sleepers where we'd taken refuge. 'Come on, then, let's get going,' I said, feeling in no hurry to hang about.

But instead of turning to leave, Vern stood gazing up at the station chimneys, straightening his cap which had gone a bit skew-whiff in all the excitement. 'Actually, seeing as we're here,' he whispered. 'I wonder if we should perhaps have another quick look round, see what's what.'

'You're fearless, Vern.'

'I'm shaking, more like. Now, if anybody leaps out, Robin, I'm relying on you to sort them out. I can't, I'm an old man.'

Old or not, Vern seemed determined to get to the bottom of whatever had or had not been going on at Oakerby station. It was as if having got a whiff that something dodgy might possibly be taking place he had for reasons I couldn't fathom made it his number one priority in life to find out exactly what that something was. Quite how much time he'd already spent on his investigations before bringing me into his confidence, and then along on these late-night stakeouts, I was never really sure. Like I was never really sure if he'd even have involved me at all if Fliss hadn't been my girlfriend.

Aside from fresh tyre marks left by the transporter there was nothing to suggest there'd been any other recent activity at or around the station, dodgy or otherwise. While the thick steel panels welded, locked and bolted across the building's many windows and doorways showed no sign of disturbance or forced entry.

'Nobody's breaking in here, Vern,' I said as we stood before the largest of the steel panels, a split section heavy grade sheet about ten feet by eight, sealing what had been the main doorway leading to the platform from the station's booking hall. 'Like we said before, it's rock solid.'

Vern nodded. 'I think you're right, lad.' And then from somewhere else within his donkey jacket he drew out an iron crowbar, the sort I'd only ever seen used by cartoon burglars, and struck one, two, low ringing notes against the heavy steel. 'Nobody's been breaking in here... No, and that's because they don't need to.'

I must have given Vern a blank look.

'Whoever legged it across that bridge, and the chap driving that wagon, were up to no good, and I don't mean they're secret sweethearts. No, my feeling, Robin, is whatever's going on isn't about breaking-in, either here or your future father-in-law's concern across the way. I think whoever they are can get inside here no trouble at all, and that they can get in whenever they choose to.'

Vern rattled one of several large padlocks with the hook of his crowbar.

'It's what they're getting inside to do that concerns us, and I reckon between us we're more or less getting close to the bottom of it.'

'Are we?' I said, unconvinced.

Vern licked his lips. 'Think. What was on the back of that transporter?'

'Nothing.'

'What are these?' With the toe of his boot, Vern indicated a set of fresh tyre marks running along perhaps a third of the length of the platform and all the way up to the large steel panels.

'Tyre marks.'

'But not from a transporter.'

'Really?'

Vern shook his head. 'Nor do I think they belong to the car of a courting couple.'

I remembered Ricky's crack about the old goat going senile, but I could see all too clearly now what Vern seemed to be suggesting and it made perfect sense. 'You think there's a car inside the station?'

'Well, I don't think that transporter arrived here empty, same as it left. And why would anybody park a car, in the middle of the night, in a derelict railway station?'

'I thought for a minute you were going to crowbar that padlock off, you know, like break in,' I said as we made our way back through the woods.

'I thought about it. I was bloody tempted,' Vern said. 'But if we had done, they'd know we were on to them and likely as not they'd be gone tomorrow.'

'You love all this snooping about and detective stuff, don't you? I shall have to start calling you Poirot.'

'I prefer Maigret, myself.'

'What does he do?'

'Well, about now I expect he'd light his pipe and ruminate.'

In bed a short while later I did a bit of ruminating myself, once I'd looked up the word in the dictionary. Of the many explanations Vern and I had imagined for our latest discoveries, few made for comfortable viewing in my restless mind's eye. And it was only by turning on the light to closely study the pictures of Susanna and Belinda that I was able to get myself off.

Sixteen

1

'I know from David that your contribution to the sales team's recent success has been considerable,' Mr Honeywell shouted above the rumbling shriek of the key-cutting machine, 'so I just wanted to express how delighted I am that you're to join them on a more permanent basis.'

'Thank you, Mr Honeywell,' I shouted back. I didn't usually approve of holding these top-level business conversations with my back turned, but the dealer principal was, as ever, running late for somebody far more important.

'I'VE NO DOUBT YOU'LL BE A GREAT –' the silly old fart went on before realising I'd silenced the machine, '– er, a great asset, Robin.' I blew the key cool before buffing it to perfection on the front of my smock.

'I'm very grateful for the opportunity, Mr Honeywell,' I said. 'I'll miss working in here, though, with Sheila and the mechanics.'

Honeywell finished straightening his silk kipper, pinned it with a gold bar before re-buttoning it inside his suit of pinstriped grey. 'And they'll be sure to miss you, Robin,' he said, absently fingering his buttonhole. 'But it's not as though you'll be going very far.'

'No, I won't be going very far,' I said with an inward shiver. 'Shall I charge this to used car sales, Mr Honeywell?' I added, as he took the key and pressed his thumb against the sharp serrations before dropping it into his jacket pocket.

'Yes, if you would, Robin, thank you.'

Having turned to go, Honeywell made only one step across the rubber tiles before suddenly switching back to pause in an awkward midway twist so that, for a second, he resembled a twenties hoofer frozen mid jazz hands.

'Oh, er, Robin – Sheila's spoken to you regarding Gillian, has she? She spent some time with you a short while ago, of course, but I think perhaps another week under your supervision, before she steps into the breach, should have her more or less up to speed with everything?'

'Oh yes, a week should be plenty, Mr Honeywell.'

'I'm much obliged to you, Robin. Much obliged. She's a bright girl, Gillian, sharp, but I'm sure there's still much for her to learn.'

I doubted that last bit very much, but smiled anyway as Honeywell made a sharp toothache wince at his watch and strode away towards the showroom muttering about loss leaders and hefty depreciation on these fleet-sourced flipping something-or-others.

2

Friday night. What I remember is this...

Walking home from Fliss's with a half-eaten, slowly melting Topic for a microphone, I'd got as far as the Windmill chippy when I launched into the second verse of one of my all-time favourite Simple Minds songs, *Hunter and The Hunted*. And in anticipation of those lines about Kyoto in the snow and heaven being far away, I'd leapt onto the yellow bonnet of a Triumph Dolomite that hadn't shifted from the pavement in years and bobbed and skipped a few of my best signature Jim Kerr stage moves. Then, leaping again on to the car's torn vinyl roof, I pushed back my enviable fringe before, slinking lizard low, I cast an entrancing left-handed collage of sweeping arcs and karate-chop zigzags across a dry iced crowd of sixty thousand.

As the song built heavenwards to the second chorus, the swirling groove drawing my reverently gaping devotees ever closer with each tap of my size nine kung fu-slippered foot, I slid gracefully down the Dolomite's steep rear window and sprang a low scissor kick before, dropping to splayed knees, I arched myself lithely over backwards on the boot lid to gaze up, up, up into the clear night sky as I sang the words with all my young heart's passion to the most brightly winking of stars.

At least, that's how I like to remember it. Because after that arching lithely over backwards bit everything went black, and the next thing I knew, a couple of whiskery old boys were swaying concernedly over me, post-Legion, I imagine, asking all these daft bloody questions.

'Is he all right?'

'Are you all right, son?'

'Can he gerrup?'

'D'you think you can gerrup?'

'They've busted his nose good and proper,' one of them said, shaking out a pristine tartan handkerchief.

'Here y'are, son,' said the other, pressing it into my hand. 'They've busted your nose good and proper.'

The nose was not news, my tongue was thick with it, the salty blood-snot tang sticky on my inflatable dinghy lips. It's the strangest thing, but as I sat there fuzzy against the kerb, my first thought was what my customers might think, faced with The Elephant Salesman, all black and blue, in his borrowed Next suit. Fortunately, it so happened that it was a Friday ahead of my weekend off, and there'd be a good fortnight's healing time before I left the parts and service department for my smart new life in the showroom.

'Who's gone and hit him?' one of the old boys said.

'Who's gone and hit you?' asked the other.

I shrugged, saddened at spying my microphone lying beside the Dolomite, its chocolatey sweetness silenced forever with road dust.

'He wants to get himself home. Where does he live?'

'Where do you live, son?'

I lay back, my head against the cool pavement, and pointed a bloodied finger up towards the twinkling night sky.

'Up there,' I said. 'I live among the stars.'

3

'Wow, what happened to you, panda boy?' smirked Cath, who for some reason I found half-pyjamaed and brushing her teeth vigorously outside my bedroom door.

'I tripped over.'

'You better not have been wearing my tights.'

'Shut up. And if you must do that when I'm still waking up, put some clothes on, I feel seasick.'

An old Triumph and a bloodied shirt front being about as much as I could remember of the previous evening's incident, it's perhaps not surprising the first person I thought of as I met my fat lip and darkly rainbowed eye in the bathroom mirror that morning was my uncle Alastair. A few days after my second driving test I'd received a postcard saying, 'Your mother tells me you passed,' adding that if I ever fancied giving the MG a good run I'd be very welcome, any time, to visit him and his good lady at Snettisham.

A little hazy, I dialled Fliss first and then Alastair, the phonebox bouquet of piss and fags a reminder to keep a vigilant eye over my aching shoulder. It would be hours, I knew, before Gluey and Billy unstuck themselves from their rancid fleapits, but I was taking no chances. I mean, if it wasn't the two of them who'd jumped me last night, then who was it? They'd probably followed me after I left Fliss's, or, knowing the way I usually walked home, had hung about near the chippy, lying in wait. Daft as it sounds, for a second or two I wondered if perhaps I hadn't become more than usually carried away with my grand performance on the Dolomite roof, lost myself so completely in being Jim Kerr that I'd missed my footing, gone arse-over-tit and landed on my silly away-with-the-bloody-fairies face – but really, how likely was that?

After Mam had filled the back seat with sandwiches and inflicted agonies on my throbbing eye and lips with her unwanted kisses, I called for Fliss and shortly after eleven we were burbling along sugar beet roads, between spring-bright hedgerows, heading for this place in Norfolk.

'It's pronounced *Snet-cham*,' Fliss said, lazily flicking through the night before's *Evening Post* that Mam had sent, along with a railway magazine, for Alastair.

'Who says?'

'Mum. She and Dad used to do gymkhanas near there. How does your uncle Alastair pronounce it?'

'Norfolk. Are you looking forward to it even a little bit?' I said, prompted to change the subject by Kate Bush, who'd just clicked over on the stereo to splash into her ninth wave with dreams of sheep.

With a conclusive slurp Fliss crushed the carton of juice she'd been sipping and lifted her neat black eyebrows. 'I said we were not allowed to talk about it till nearer the time, remember?'

'Okay,' I said, sniffing at the potted-meat sandwich she was waving under my nose. 'I listened to your tape again this morning.' I took a bite. Swallowed. 'It really is brilliant, you know.'

Fliss smiled shyly. 'Well, I'm glad you like it. But I'm still not sure I want to go on that stupid programme. It's...'

'What?'

'Please, Robin, let's not talk about it.'

Fliss then cleverly switched to happier topics by stroking my thigh for a few miles before asking if I thought Alastair and his wife would like her.

'Charlotte isn't his wife,' I said. 'I told you, she's his good lady. And, yes, absolutely, I think they'll love you just as much as I do.'

Had I really just said that? I cursed my mouth, resented my thigh for its weakness in the presence of hot hands and hoped Fliss wouldn't ask me to repeat myself. She didn't. Instead, she held up the *Evening Post* where she'd folded it over at a page showing a bad photograph of a thin black-and-white face, which, even with only half an eye on the road, I wasn't properly able to make out.

'Isn't he that horrible yob who pushed you over and called you rude names?'

The road being quiet I risked a glance. 'Yes, that's him. Likes to call me 'wanker'.' There was more to it than that, of course, years more, truth be told, but as with my investigations with Vern, I hadn't wanted to bother Fliss with unnecessary details. 'Why, what's he done?'

'Well, I can tell you that it was definitely not him who beat you up last night.'

'Nobody beat me up last night,' I corrected. 'They jumped me, two of them. From behind. It was an ambush.'

Fliss leaned forward against the seatbelt to look at my face. 'It doesn't look too bad. You've got a black eye, though.'

'I'll batter the pair of them next time, if they try it,' I said, less than convincingly. 'And how do you know it wasn't him?'

'Because it says here he died in hospital on Thursday.'

'Died?' My lips felt suddenly very dry and began to hot throb all over again. I knew if I touched the bruise beneath my right eye it would sting like a bastard. 'How?'

'You know somebody was run over on the road near the fishing ponds? It looks like it was him – Clayton Clements, 23, of Abbey Street, Stonebridge.'

'The Glueboy Wonder's dead?' I said, remembering how his pal Billy Eyesore had slunk away from me into the privet a few nights before.

Where's your pal, tonight?

Haven't you heard?

'I hadn't heard. Bloody hell. Clay's dead...'

'He was really horrible to you,' Fliss said, tossing the paper into the back seat among the sandwiches. 'Sad for his poor mum, though.' I looked at Fliss mildly stunned. 'I never thought of him having a mum.'

We lost a mudflap overtaking a caravan near King's Lynn. This, for some reason, caused Fliss to need the toilet quite urgently. I went as well, while it was on offer, then nipped inside the petrol station to find a telephone.

'I saw it in the *Post* last night,' Vern said. 'I rang you first thing, at the showroom, but Andrew said it was your weekend off.'

'Andrew?'

'He's been reinstated, apparently. I thought he would be. Now look, even if he were a layabout, that young lad's dead. So if there is a connection with what you and I have been taking a close interest in lately, well, it puts a very different light on things.'

I nodded thoughtfully into the receiver. 'The *Post* mentioned a white hatchback again, speeding, possibly stolen.'

'Ah, and I think I've an idea whose it might have been.'

'Whose? Edwyn Matthews?'

'Too long ago now. No, Ben Evelyn, the barber. His XR-whatsit was taken from the car park opposite his shop, side of the bingo hall, same night that lad was run over.'

'Ben cuts my hair.'

'Ben cuts everybody's hair.'

'Not yours, Vern, surely?'

'Good job you're on the end of a telephone or you'd get what for.'

'I should give Ben a ring,' I said. 'See if we can sell him a new car.'

'The sales lot have corrupted you already. I expect Andrew's probably sold him one by now, it was him who told me about it when I rang this morning.'

'Oh - Vern,' I said before I hung up. 'Clay's got this mate. They always went about together. When I get back, I'll find out where he lives.'

'What're you talking about? Who's Clay?'

'The lad who got run over, the layabout. His name's Clay Clements.'

'Was, you mean. Right you are, then. I might have a ride down to the body shop. If Kevin's still there, I wouldn't mind picking his brains about a couple of things.'

4

It was only on finding the Cadbury's Buttons egg Mam had packed for our drive to Norfolk that I realised it was Easter weekend, key dates of the confectionery calendar having little impact now that my almost only focus was on counting the days until the Nelson Mandela 70th Birthday Tribute Concert.

Wembley Stadium
Saturday 11th June
Turnstile B
Gates 11 a.m.

Since their arrival, the two tickets had been caressed so often between my fingers I was convinced the ink had already begun to fade, and that by 11th June all I'd have for my fifty quid plus coach fare would be a pair of blank, useless, squares of paper.

The same went for the enclosed leaflet, with its references to Artists Against Apartheid, The Anti-Apartheid Movement and Amnesty International. Until recently such things had, as Midge Ure almost said, meant nothing to me, phrases like *prisoners of conscience* and *the universal declaration of human rights* seeming like the worthiest student guff that belonged to only the dullest corners of the music papers and Neil from *The Young Ones*. It sounded too much like politics, and I couldn't see how politics had anything to do with me or my music. I knew, of course, about Live Aid, the whole world knew about Live Aid, but I'd missed most of that while out on my BMX – though, disappointingly, I'd managed to get home in time to see Queen.

It was only when Simple Minds gave the proceeds of *Ghostdancing* to Amnesty International that I started to wonder if the music I loved might sometimes be about more than just the incredible noise made by five young men with cool hair and astonishing trousers. It was all there in the imagery, the blood on the sleeve and that classic Anton Corbijn shot of Jim Kerr and the white dove which, of course, I'd so lovingly recreated with Jack Kettley's incontinent homing pigeon. I suddenly now saw in that image a living thing being given its rightful freedom; I saw the deliberate use of monochrome, the harmony of black and white together and with all the many shades between; and I saw Jim Kerr, my idol, moody against a bare, cold stone wall; and I just knew there was something I had to do.

I had to find a T-shirt with Jim Kerr and that dove on it.

Seventeen

1

'Oh dear, have you had an accident?'

'Um, no, it's always looked like that,' I said, turning to look back at the MG.

'Your face, idiot,' Fliss said, before adding in a suspect tone, 'he tripped over a kerb, Charlotte, walking home last night.'

'Late, was it? Well, it happens to the best of us. In you go, loves. Oh, no need to take your shoes off, Felicity, just go straight through.'

I'd been unprepared to find Alastair's good lady in a wheelchair. But as was immediately apparent from the moment she greeted us at the front door of the cottage and shooed us in towards a big kitchen table set out with cake and a teapot, this was not something Charlotte allowed to hinder her, so I saw no reason why I should feel awkward about it either.

It was mid-afternoon when we arrived and Alastair was out, minding the bookshop. So after a cup of tea and a heavy slice of getting-to-know-you fruitcake, I left the ladies to it and turned, as per Charlotte's instructions, into the lane at the end of the drive and wound the picturesque half mile or so to the village.

'I hope you'll enjoy them,' Alastair was saying to a customer as the door tinkled behind me. 'It's a very nice set.' I lurked among the tightly crammed shelves and makeshift looking bookcases, listening, baffled but impressed, while he wrapped two heavy volumes in brown paper and spoke of *Orwell, a harrowing dystopia*, and *the later journalism* in a voice so articulate, so confidently unlike anybody from Stonebridge, I suspected Charlotte had bumped-off my uncle and brought on a substitute university professor who looked just like him.

The shop was old, tiny and cavernous, with every surface, nook and void crammed with books, pictures of books, and pictures of people to do with books. Books teetered in towers, wound along walls, and gathered to form soundless grottoes, while in several places more books doubled as shelves upon which were stored books and more books. Framing a tiny lopsided window were a few shelves marked FILM & MUSIC. I scanned the kaleidoscopic spines but found nothing about Simple Minds, the one I already had at home perhaps being the only one in print. But what I did see, when on hearing the goodbye tinkle of the door I turned towards the counter, propped on the counter beside the till, was a book about Nelson Mandela.

'Found anything you fancy?' Alastair said, coming over after quietly writing something in a big, heavy looking notebook. 'Crikey, what've you been doing?'

'Oh, I tripped over a kerb, messing about. I mostly read books about music, Alastair,' I said, not entirely truthfully. For although I'd long been a voracious reader of music papers and the small print of record sleeves, my non-fiction intake at that time consisted, apart from my Simple Minds book, almost solely of *Observer's Guides*. The novels I'd read through choice – not counting children's classics and twenty of the twenty-four adventures of *The Famous Five* – numbered perhaps three or four at most, *Moonraker* being the only one I can now remember. And yet there was something about the atmosphere of that little shop that really got into me, made me want to take part in its quiet purpose. It was a bit like the feeling you found in the best second-hand record shops (though they were rarely so peaceful), in that you sensed the place was heaving with hidden treasures, tens of thousands of magical things you never knew existed, but which would improve the quality of your life beyond all measure if only you knew where to look for them.

But this was not a second-hand record shop, and I knew neither where to look, nor what to look for. After turning about, though, I spotted a couple of shelves labelled MYSTERY AND CRIME.

'Have you got any books by George Cinnamon?' I said, pleased with myself at remembering. Alastair, smiling, reached for a couple of green-and-white paperbacks. Despite the name on both covers being Georges Simenon (misprints, I assumed), I knew it must be the right bloke when Alastair said, '*The Stain on The Snow* I think is one of his best. And the Maigrets are always very popular. He wrote about a hundred-and-eighty books, so plenty to keep you going, if you like them.'

'Do you like them, Alastair?' I asked.

'I do, very much. I read that Maigret myself only last week. Here, if you like a good rock and roll tale...' Alastair handed me a brick-thick paperback about The Beatles, another on the life and death of Jim Morrison. He must have sensed as I turned the selection of books in the dusty light my self-conscious struggle of desire versus funds.

'How much is this one?' I said, holding up the Morrison.

'Don't be daft,' Alastair said. 'Take them all if you want them.' The bell tinkled, in welcome this time, as a tall young woman with a face full of red curls strode casually in, throwing down a paper bag bearing the name of the village baker while she hung her heavy tweed Crombie on a stand beside the counter.

'Alastair, you sold the Orwells!' she said, turning excitedly to look for my uncle. 'Alastair, you are the best.' Then, flicking on a kettle guarded by a tabby cat, she settled in a shabby armchair with a magazine to eat her sandwich, which she managed to do while looking as pristinely provocative as I realised her mother must have done a quarter of a century before.

Belatedly sensing my presence, this lovely woman looked up.

'Oh, I'm sorry! How *rude*,' she said, long pale fingers half-covering her mouth. 'Hello, I'm Tina. Are you–'

'Robin,' I nodded, sucking in my by now not-quite-so-fat lip and favouring her with my best, unbruised, side. 'Very nice to meet you.'

'I'm Charlotte's daughter.'

'Yes,' I said, smiling stiffly. 'I thought so.'

As I spoke across the shop I was drawn again to the hopeful young face of Nelson Mandela. I felt foolishly uncomfortable asking for the book in front of Tina, like buying a packet of rubber johnnies or that Roxy Music LP with the two models wearing see-through knickers. But the feeling evaporated immediately when Tina, rising from her armchair, assured me that not only was the Mandela book an excellent choice, but I was on no account to pay for that one either.

'I wish I could join you all this evening,' Tina said as Alastair put on his coat, 'but I'm going to a concert in London, a band called The House of Love – do you know them, Robin?'

'No,' I said. 'I hope they're good.'

'Do you want running to the station later?'

'Ah bless you, Alastair,' Tina said. 'No, Richard doesn't finish till five, so we're going to drive down.'

We made our way back via the butcher, the baker and the florist, and with only a small detour via the Rose and Crown for a couple of pints, during which Alastair seemed to be greeted by everybody who came into the beer garden. A little while later, when we arrived at the cottage's pale-yellow gates, we were met by the light tinkling of a well-tuned piano and a duet of female voices escaping harmoniously from the open leaded windows.

Did-ul-um, did-ul-um, did-ul-um...

'Not Bruce Hornsby and The Range.'

Alastair laughed. 'She's forever playing this bloody tune, my good lady.'

'Mine too,' I said. 'It's her dad's favourite.'

'Dear me.'

We went inside, Alastair laden with a joint of beef, several species of vegetable and a large bunch of flowers, me with a bagful of books and a slightly fuzzy head. What I hadn't noticed was that somewhere along the way Alastair had also picked up a couple of dainty boxes of chocolates, expensive-looking and tied up with neat little bows of white ribbon. 'These are from Robin,' he said, flashing me a wink as he handed one each to Fliss and Charlotte. 'Happy Easter.'

'Happy Easter,' I said.

The evening flew by in an Aga-cosy haze of delicious food and wine and easy, friendly, conversation. Charlotte, having eased herself out her wheelchair in favour of a wooden walking stick, moved about slowly but surely, repeatedly refusing help, as she prepared dinner.

'Are you sure I can't do anything, Charlotte?' I asked.

'No, you sit down and relax, Robin, thank you. Everything's in hand. Fliss is in charge of the music, Alastair's going to finish peeling me those last few vegetables – that's if we haven't lost him to his railway magazine.'

'I'm good at peeling vegetables,' I lied.

After dinner there was background atmosphere courtesy of Joni Mitchell, Nick Drake, John Martyn, Carole King and Fleetwood Mac, punctuated at several intervals by Fliss and Charlotte, seated side by side at the piano, as they performed some of those same songs plus others, well-known and obscure – including *The Way It Is* by Bruce Hornsby and The Range – with, so it seemed to me, a brilliance to match anything that had come from the record player. It sounds like I'm romanticising, I know. But as I sat at Charlotte and Alastair's kitchen table with a glass that never seemed to empty, I felt as if I'd crossed over into another life, a life I liked the look of and didn't ever want to leave.

After an enormous late breakfast cooked by Alastair, Fliss and I left Snettisham around noon on Sunday with a promise to return at the earliest opportunity. In the honeysuckled porch of a hundred fairy tales there were kisses and much affectionate embracing, Alastair even allowing Fliss to gather him in her arms for a gentle squeeze. I felt suddenly very grown-up, like an adult, but in a good way.

As I opened the car door Alastair said, 'I bet she goes a bit, Robin, doesn't she?' I froze a moment before deciding he meant the MG – well, you know, I'd been squeezed by Fliss many times myself and it never failed to set my mind wandering. 'Oh yes,' I said. 'Yes, she goes all right.'

'They're both so lovely,' Fliss said later that evening as we lay beneath her duvet feeding each other shards of chocolate egg and listening to some records. 'They don't seem old, do they? Even though they are, obviously.'

'Alastair's never seemed like an uncle. He never talked to me like a kid, even when I was one. And Charlotte seems really nice, she's...'

'She's cool.'

I rolled over and lay between Fliss's legs, looking down into her dark, long-lashed eyes. She really did have the most gorgeous lips. I traced them gently with my fingertips, marvelling at the memory of the songs she had brought to life so wonderfully with them, with Charlotte, at the piano. I'd never seen her so confident in her voice, in her musical self; her behaviour the reverse in fact of what I should have expected, performing in a kitchen in front of two complete strangers.

'I just felt very relaxed with them,' Fliss said. 'I don't know... Charlotte's got such a beautiful voice, and she plays blues piano really well, a lot like Christine McVie.'

'But not as well as you. You played and sang so beautifully. I told you they'd love you, didn't I?'

I kissed her lips very gently. She kissed mine back. And again. They didn't seem to be throbbing anymore, which was handy.

I felt her wriggle out of something flimsy down below. 'Do *you*, Robin?' Fliss said, blinking up at me from the pillow. 'Do you love me?'

Over in the corner, on the turntable of Fliss's hi-fi, Prince was revolving at 33rpm into *Girls and Boys*. Two more songs and one of us was going to have to get up and turn the record over.

2

Neither of us having mentioned it in our brief, interrupted, phone conversation, Millie's letter, which arrived the Tuesday after Easter, began with her saying how glad she was that Fliss had been invited to appear on *Show Me The Stars* as Kate Bush.

I knew she would be, though. I threatened my producer that if he didn't get her on the show he was PROPERLY CRAZY and I'd burn down his office – Haha!

It was so lovely to speak to you on the phone, Millie continued, writing in that same breathlessly hurried voice as she spoke. *I hope the police haven't locked you up and you're reading this letter in prison!! Haha!! You know I felt a bit like a scary stalker person, tracking you down at the garage and ringing you – I promise I'm not, though, so please don't think that!*

> *Seriously – I hope you don't mind me writing to you. It seems funny, doesn't it, bumping into each other like that after all these years? Spooky coincidence. Woo-oo! You'd better write back, Robin Manvers, because if you don't, remember I know where you live!*
>
> *I'm only joking! Oh god, now you think I'M CRAZY! I wouldn't blame you if you didn't write back now – Haha! (But please do!)*
>
> *I loved your Simple Minds T-shirt, by the way. Such a cool band. You probably know this already, but they're playing at a big concert at Wembley stadium for Nelson Mandela in June. (He won't be there, of course, because he's in prison in South Africa.) I'd really love to go to see Stevie Wonder and Peter Gabriel (and Simple Minds!) but it's a long way from Manchester and probably sold out anyway.*

Millie signed off with love and a kiss above each letter 'i' of her name. I was flattered she remembered my T-shirt from all those weeks ago. I mean, I'd no idea what she'd been wearing, although that was difficult, her smile always commanding your full attention.

I can still see it now.

Eighteen

1

'Once you're turned on, you just slide this end in here...'

'How many girls have you said that to, Robin?'

'It's a little bit...

'Stiff?'

'So you might have to...'

'Wiggle it a bit until it goes all –'

I'd never been more grateful for the squeak of the office door and its accompanying whiff of pricey perfume.

'You'll soon get the hang of it,' I said, wiping my sweating hands on my smock. 'Sheila did. She cuts a fine key now, don't you, Sheila?'

'Oh, I wish I could, Gillian.' Sheila shook her head. 'I mucked up two on Saturday morning before I got it right. Maybe you'll have the knack of it, though, like Robin.'

'I don't know about that,' Gillian said, dipping her head, all doe-eyed and Princess Di-like. 'I'm not very good with my hands.' I somehow managed to keep a straight face, which was not easy, especially with one of those not-very-good hands cupping my right buttock.

Sheila, oblivious to my crisis, lifted the less grubby of the two telephones and prodded four times for internal. Key-cutting class temporarily halted, I observed how as she waited for somebody to answer Sheila's eyes wandered carefully over the nail-nibbling Gillian, taking her in from shaggy crimped streaks to sharply tipped toes before settling, with a pursed twist of the lips, on her plumply gaping neckline.

'I'll see if we can find you a roomier smock, Gillian,' Sheila said, with that kindly tone and giveaway smile of the glamorous older woman. 'That one looks a bit tight for you – Ah, hello, David love, it's Sheila. Those carpet mats for Mrs Stibson are in stock now. Yes, that's right. I'll get Robin to pop through with them. What was that? No, Gillian's busy.'

2

After leaving work on Tuesday I parked up opposite the phonebox for about half an hour, repeat listening to the 12-inch remix of *I Travel* while praying the stereo wouldn't gobble the tape or flatten the MG's battery. The evening before I'd dawdled home from Fliss's hoping I'd come across him, furtively shambling to or from wherever he went to do whatever he did other than shamble furtively, even leaning awhile against the yellow Dolomite – though this time resisting my natural performer's urge to take to the roof with my chocolate microphone and serenade the heavens – but of Billy Eyesore there was not a sign.

'You mean Jason Wakeling?' said Cath, an obscene bath-pink tangle of limbs as she sat painting her toenails on the hearthrug.

I dissected and savoured a four-square section of potato waffle, dipped in the oozings of a freezer-fresh chicken Kiev. 'About five-foot-six, spiky piss-coloured hair, and a face like flaky pastry.'

'Looks like Billy Idol?'

'But worse. Like a scone with raisins for eyes.'

'That's Jason Wakeling,' Cath said, wrapping a leg round the back of her damp head to blow dry the first five toes. 'He's best friends with Clay Clements who looks like Sid Vicious. Only he's dead now, he got run over by a bus in Tuxfield.'

'No, he didn't.'

'That's what Tracy's dad said.'

'Tracy's dad's an idiot.'

'Dare you to tell him that.'

I mopped my plate with the last section of waffle. 'Cath,' I said. 'Do you know where he lives, this Jason Wakeling?'

'Down on Fitzwilson Street, the end house, next door to Robbie Atkinson.'

'Thanks.'

Cath stretched out her shiny, now white again legs, tilting her head and wriggling ten glistening toes. 'Why do you want to know where Jason Wakeling lives?'

'Never you mind,' I said, getting up to carry my plate into the kitchen. 'Oh, and next time you do that,' I added, popping my head back round the door, 'please wear more than just a towel. You put me right off that Kiev.'

A bottle of Strawberry Fizz nail-varnish clattered against the kitchen door.

'Mam! Our Robin's being disgusting again!'

3

The jolly cheeked little woman took a step back and bawled up the narrow staircase. 'Jason? Jason! One of your friends is here.'

I smiled, having almost asked her if Billy was in. 'He won't be a minute, duck,' the woman said, the living room door brushing closed behind her.

As I waited on the doorstep I realised I wasn't exactly sure why I'd come looking for Jason Wakeling, nor, now that I was here, what I hoped to achieve by it. Friend. How did she know I hadn't come to smash her son's scabby little face in?

'What do you want?' Jason said, struggling sullenly into a ravaged pair of 10-hole Docs.

'Heard about your mate Clay.'

'And I bet you're sorry. *I'm going out,*' Jason shouted at the closed living room door as he snatched up his Tippex-spattered leather jacket.

I fell in with Jason's brisk lurch over the garden fence and into a sunken lane that ran behind a builder's yard and the tiny bakery which, during the winter of 1984-85, had given free hot loaves daily to the wives of striking miners and the occasional paperboy huddled at six a.m. outside the newsagent's opposite.

'Where're we going?' Jason called back over a shoulder smudged with Dead Kennedys.

'I'm following you, mate.'

'Nobody's making you.'

We marched towards the park in edgy, simmering silence, broken only by *fuck sakes* and *bollocks* each time Jason had to stop to relight his roll-up, which seemed to be about every two or three hundred yards.

'I wouldn't bother, mate,' I said, making conversation.

'Piss off.'

Turning onto the narrow riverside path I again fell in behind, ducking choking clouds and shoulder-height nettles and brambles for half a mile or so to the new wooden bridge, where on reaching its mid-point Jason swerved to a sudden halt and draped himself, like a Sex Pistol's washing, over the balustrade. I waited, anticipating that Jason, during our walk, would've worked up a heroic gobful of phlegm to hawk into the silvery spring current, or a gizzard-green oyster that he could dribble into the palm of his hand for some careful zoned-out study.

What I hadn't anticipated was:

'Do you fish?'

'Fish?'

'Fish,' said Jason as he gazed intently down at the shimmering slivers of life that darted across his reflection. 'With a rod and line.'

'No,' I said, our shoulders almost touching as I joined him to peer over the balustrade. He smelt like the morning carpet of a rough pub. 'I had a cousin once who was into it.' I mentioned a name.

'I know him. Big lad. Fished many a time with him at Oaky ponds. Some good carp at Oaky.'

'Did Clay fish?'

Jason nodded. After a thoughtful silence he buried his nose and mouth in his hands and made a sound like a Scottish express blowing off steam.

'If he'd have stayed fishing with me... he'd... he'd still be... ah, the bloody idiot.' Another roll-up was fumbled from a small tin, a match struck, clouds coughed. 'Clay, he... he wanted to go mushying... in the woods.'

Across the river a sandstorm rose from the BMX track, clouds of yellow fallout billowing towards the cricket pitch as a knot of riders kissed the dirt.

'Mushying?' I said, thinking their relationship had perhaps been much closer than I realised.

'Magic mushrooms. Woods's full of 'em.'

'Ah.'

'Clay had this spot in the middle of Sherwood Forest where he swore that if you necked enough mushies you could see knights in armour galloping through the trees on horses, chasing after Robin Hood, like. He properly fuckin' believed it an' all.'

'Cool.'

'It's bollocks. I've never seen anything like that and I've got well trashed up there, no end of times. He must've been on his way back to the ponds when...' Jason stopped and sniffed in my direction. 'Isn't your name Robin?'

'Yeah, why?'

'You don't look like a Robin.'

'You don't look like a fisherman.'

The smile that squeezed apart Jason's drawn face seemed to surprise him even more than it did me, though it wasn't to linger long.

'Jason, can I ask you something?' I said, turning away from the water. 'About... about the accident.'

'Why? What's it to you?'

'It's a long story,' I shrugged, 'and we've probably got it all wrong, but a lot of fast cars have been nicked round this area lately –'

Jason reeled back, shaking his head. 'No way, piss off! Neither of us can fuckin' drive, so don't even think –'

'I wasn't, it's... I work at Stonebridge Motor Company. About a dozen customers we know of have had their cars stolen, either off their drives or from where they work, mostly. One was nicked off the garage forecourt.'

'So? What's that got to do with me and Clay?'

'Well, we – me and one of the mechanics – we think it might be the same gang that's been nicking them all, and that car that hit Clay could've been another one that they'd just taken. One just like it was nicked that night in Stonebridge.'

Jason turned back to his fishes, reeking roll-up aglow between his lips.

'I stayed with him at the hospital two nights. They knew straight away he'd never walk again.' I tried not to see the tears that had begun to abseil down Jason's raw cheeks, the flutter in his cracked lower lip. 'But do you know what pissed him off most of all?'

I shook my head. 'What?'

A thick plume of smoke rose above Jason's head, a sudden breeze catching and curling it back through his hedgehogged yellow hair. 'The silly cow had ripped a great big hole in his new tartan bondage trousers.'

Tartan bondage trousers? Perhaps as well as Merrie Sherwood, Clay's magic mushrooms had also transported him back to the King's Road in the summer of '77. But out-of-date clown's trousers wasn't the detail of Jason's story that had just snagged my attention.

'Mate,' I interrupted. But this Jason wasn't for stopping.

'I know you think he was just some druggy waster, same as me, but he weren't. He was all right, Clay, if you got to know him. He was right set on getting off the gear and everything, sorting himself out, he really was. He'd been looking for a job.' Jason eyed me sideways through damp red slits. 'That's why he hated you so much.'

'What did I do? He's the one who started it all, nicking my dinner money when I was eleven.'

'He took against you. Reckoned you thought you were something, with your flash car and your pretty little girlfriend from *Oooh! Windmill Way*. She's not my type – no offence – but Clay fancied the pants off her.'

I could have argued the MG was hardly flash, and if there was one thing that I'd been made aware of all too often growing up it was that I was definitely not something; that what I was, and what I always would be, was nothing. But Clay was dead, and dead was even less than nothing, so what was the point?

'If he'd just stayed fishing with me...' Jason said again, scraping a ragged leather cuff across his eyes. 'Silly bastard.'

The pair of us looked upon our own fishes as his words sank in.

'Jason, you know when you mentioned Clay's trousers, you said he was pissed-off at the silly cow for ripping them. Why did you say that?'

'What?'

'Who did Clay mean?'

'Driving the car. It was a woman, driving like a fucking maniac, proper flying.'

'A woman? Driving the car that hit Clay?'

'That's what Clay said. He said if it weren't a woman then it were a bloke with a woman's hairdo.'

'Like Jon Bon Jovi?'

Jason properly laughed at this. I did too. He wiped his eyes again, on a Tippexed "God Save The Queen", and nodded. 'Yeah, she did sound a bit Bon Jovi. Silly cow.'

We crossed over the bridge and began to walk slowly along the edge of the cricket pitch back towards town. 'Clay were all right,' Jason said again. 'He weren't a bad lad, not really.'

'My sister said the same tonight,' I said. 'She reckoned you were all right as well.'

'Who's your sister?'

'An idiot, obviously.'

Jason smiled and held out a roll-up, nodding for me to take it.

'I'm fine, thanks, pal.'

'You going up Windmill Way?'

'Yes,' I said.

'I'll walk up with you.'

Nineteen

1

Far from the domineering, cobwebbed old crone my imagination had cast for Mrs Priestley, I found her in real life played by a friendly faced and sprightly woman, who with her tight-bunned hair and flared green corduroys could easily have passed for Vern's wife or sister. Younger sister, at a push.

'Whatever they made her out of, I don't think I inherited much of it,' Vern smiled after his mother had put away a squaddie-size portion of homemade steak and kidney pie, new potatoes and parsnips before, smiling apologies, excusing herself from the table.

'I'll leave you boys to talk about your motor cars. I want to finish varnishing that banister so I can get back to my crossword.'

'Swims fifty lengths every Thursday, 9 a.m. Have some more, Robin, if you want some,' Vern urged as he refilled his plate. 'She'll outlive me, I'm sure.'

'Thanks, this pie's absolutely delicious.'

'Mother doesn't run to a wide menu,' Vern said, getting up to swing the kettle whistling from flames to teapot, 'but what she does she does very well.'

After he'd washed up, Vern smoothed open a crisp new sketch pad and took a big gulp of tea. 'This woman driver... From what we've seen...' he mused, tapping the rubbered end of a freshly sharpened pencil against his lips. 'Perhaps there is no connection, then. Anyway, let's put that one aside for now and see what else we reckon we've got between us, shall we?'

As I scraped my chair round beside his, Vern took a handful of scrappy notes from his inside pocket and set them out on the table in careful rows like a game of Solitaire. 'I've been accumulating this lot for months, but whether I'll be able to make head or tail of it all now...'

I asked for a sheet of paper and quickly jotted down a few points of my own, hoping there was nothing I might have forgotten.

'I suppose we should start with the motors...' And turning his sketch pad side on, Vern, with me confirming the exact models, wrote down the following:

VEHICLES KNOWN STOLEN TO DATE:

Matthews – Escort RS Turbo
Parsons – Orion Ghia
Rowlett – Orion Ghia
Adcock – Escort XR3i
Cavendish – Fiesta XR2
Belshaw (Miners' Union) – Sierra Cosworth
Jarvis – Fiesta XR2
Sales Dept – Escort XR3i
Crawford – Sierra XR4x4
Dilks – Escort Cabriolet
Marsh – Granada Scorpio
Heald – Orion Ghia
Bartle – Capri 2.8i
Owen – Sierra Cosworth
Evelyn – Escort XR3i
Hopkinson – Escort Cabriolet
Paling – Escort RS Turbo
Mowbray – Fiesta XR2

'Is that your last one?'

'Yes,' I said. 'How many's that?'

Vern totted-up a figure and underlined it. 'Eighteen. More than I thought. And that's just those we know about through our place.'

I finished my tea as Vern, sitting back in his chair, took off his glasses to alternatively rub his eyes and blink for a bit. 'What have they all got in common, would you say, these cars?'

'They're all sporty or high spec Fords,' I said. 'And most are only a few months to about a year old – a couple a bit older, but not much.'

'What else?'

'A lot of them are local, taken from drives overnight.'

'A lot, but not all,' Vern said. 'Matthews's Escort went from the Village Hall, didn't it?'

'That's right. On a Saturday afternoon.'

'Belshaw's Sierra, that was the miners' HQ at Tuxfield. Your barber's Escort from the bingo car park. What about Dilks, cabriolet? Is he the tall chap, likes an embroidered waistcoat?'

'Yes. Sheffield University car park.'

'Any others away from Stonebridge?'

I scanned my notes. 'Miss Jarvis's went missing from Nottingham Vic Centre. Owen's outside Lloyds Bank at Derby. Vern, isn't Derby a bit far away for a local gang?'

'Ah but look what it is.'

'Sierra Cosworth.'

'Nowhere's too far away if it's a car you're really after – if you've got a buyer waiting for it.'

I looked at Vern. 'A buyer? What...' I held up the sketch pad, ran my eyes up and down the neatly printed columns. Instead of eighteen names written beside eighteen cars, what I now saw was a shopping-list. 'You mean like somebody stealing cars to order? Not just nicking them for joyriding?'

'Think about it,' Vern said, clanging open a shiny pedal-bin to resharpen his pencil. 'How many of these cars so far have been found? Joyriders take motors, have their tear-up, then either dump them or set them alight – that's if they don't manage to kill themselves or somebody else first – but they usually turn up, one way or the other. None of this lot has.'

'They found the red XR3i off the forecourt. According to Graham, Honeywell thinks it was travellers who took it, when the fair was here.'

Vern shook his head. 'Nah. Above all else, travellers are practical people. If they did want to pinch anything they'd pinch a lorry or a trailer, something useful to them, not some hairdresser's hatchback. Yes, it's a bit of an anomaly, that one, Robin.'

'A what?'

'Anomaly – doesn't fit the pattern, like your woman driver. Put a question mark beside that one as well then, for now.'

'Vern, you know those four cars Ricky and I drove to Sheffield and Wilmslow,' I said, double-checking my notes to be certain, 'there's at least one identical model on our list – same age, colour, spec.'

'But they weren't these same cars, though, were they? Don't suppose you wrote down the reg. numbers?' Vern grinned.

'I did on the second trip,' I said, taking a folded Post-it from my wallet. 'And I remembered the first two, here, look. I checked in the service department files and none of them was a Stonebridge customer's car.'

'And was there any paperwork when you handed them over?'

'Both times there was a sealed envelope left on the passenger seat, with the radio codes and warranty stuff for both cars. Honeywell said the rest had been faxed straight to British Steel and Wilmslow Ford.'

'It all sounds right enough.' Vern refilled the kettle and waved a match at the gas. 'Did you ever stop off anywhere on these trips, see anybody you recognised?'

'Didn't really see anything at Sheffield. We parked the Orion and Sierra and waited in Honeywell's car till two smartish blokes got out of a Granada and drove them away. And Wilmslow, there was a psycho Scotsman and an elf in a bobble hat. Ricky thought they looked well dodgy.'

'Not as dodgy as Ricky, I'll bet. Digestive? Plain or chocolate?'

'Chocolate, please. Ben Evelyn's XR3i, that was stolen the same night that–'

I paused, sipping my tea while Mrs Priestley, who'd appeared silently in the doorway, crossed to the cooker to fill her hot-water bottle from the just boiled kettle.

'I think Betty's itching for her walk, Vernon.'

'Yes, Mother. I'll just finish my tea and we'll get off.'

'Goodnight, Robin. It was very nice to meet you.'

'Goodnight, Mrs Priestley,' I said. 'Thank you again for the lovely dinner.'

'It wasn't much, but you're very welcome any time. Don't forget to lock up, Vernon. Goodnight, love.'

'Goodnight, Mother.' Vern lifted his eyebrows, the ghost of a bashful schoolboy smiling for a second in the dim light. 'Where were we?'

'Ben Evelyn's XR3i, stolen from the bingo car park the same night Clay Clements was run over near Oakerby ponds.'

As I spoke, Vern jotted: EVELYN – WHITE XR3i – OAKERBY PONDS – <u>CLAY CLEMENTS</u>?

'Poor sod,' Vern said, underlining the name. He put down his pencil and let out a long, deflating sigh that made him seem like a depressed relative of the kettle before picking up his pencil again and adding the word 'WOMAN', isolating her in a heavy lead box.

'Anything we've missed, Robin, any wild theories, or owt else that strikes you as suspect? We should probably think about calling it a night.'

'What about all the cars you saw up at the station?'

'Now, where are they?' Vern shuffled his pieces of paper. 'Ah. These were the two racing about the station the first time. Those I saw leaving under the railway bridge, what's that, five days later... that was one on its own, on the main road and... there's one or two more here I'm not very certain about.'

'They don't all match cars on the list,' I said. 'But they're the right sort.'

'No. It doesn't necessarily work against us, though. I might have put down the wrong model, anyroad, you know my eyes – and it were dark.'

As I shook my head I suddenly remembered. 'Vern, the transporter.'

'Fine pair of detectives we make. Only link we might've found and already forgotten it. Now, when I spoke to Kevin last Saturday he told me that yellow-and-white wagon is a chap named Parker, from Lincoln. Been taking accident-damaged motors from the body shop for years, although Kevin reckons he's been coming more regular this past year or so.'

'Where do they take them?'

'If the insurance writes them off, to breakers' yards, usually. They're stripped for parts and then scrapped. But some will get repaired, properly or otherwise, and end up back on the road. All depends how bad they are, you know.'

I flicked through the pages of notes and Vern's sketch pad. Between us we'd pulled together an impressive haul of information which, if the many dots could be joined together to reveal one or more of the several scenarios that now seemed to be suggesting themselves, we might very soon be sitting on some seriously incriminating, and possibly very dangerous, evidence. But while those dots remained unjoined, all we had in front of us, after more than two hours collating our investigations, was no more than a pile of scrap paper and a few shaky theories that still posed as many questions as when we started.

I now thought of another:

'If people are nicking cars from drives and car parks without much trouble, why would they need a transporter?'

'I wonder. And we have only seen that wagon up there once. But whoever was with him that night didn't want us catching them at whatever they were up to at the station, did he?'

'He didn't have anything on the back, either.'

'Not when he left, he didn't.'

'No. But do you really think the transporter and the cars being stolen are both part of the same thing?'

'Well, I think that's where you and I need to focus our attentions next, put it that way.' Vern reached for his donkey jacket and shook Betty's lead from a pocket. '*Come on, Betty.* Where is she? I told Kevin, the moment he hears this chap Parker is next due to pick up a motor, to let us know.'

'And then what do we do?'

A slow smile crept across Vern's face. He shook his head. 'We'll come up with something between us, I'm sure.'

As we followed Betty to the back door Vern took a slim green paperback down from the Welsh dresser. 'Thanks again for this, Robin.'

'You're welcome,' I said. 'Sorry you've already got the other one.'

'One Simenon is more than kind enough. I'll look forward to it. I recommend you give the other one a go, though. I reckon you'll enjoy it.'

'I will,' I said, patting my pocket. 'I might even start it tonight.'

Twenty

1

'Ah, look how pleased he is to see you,' Fliss said, shoving me in through the stable door. '*Hello, boy!* Are you pleased to see Robin? Yes, you are.'

Rubbish. Bertie the horse was no more pleased to see me than I was to see him, but I'd made a promise to Fliss, and so as the spring evenings grew longer I found myself ever more frequently clambering up into the saddle of the great withering-eyed beast.

'He's trying to eat my jacket again,' I said as Bertie took his turn to shove me, with his bony big nose, across the yard towards the paddock. 'No, Bertie! Stop it! Get off!'

His taste for Harrington collars aside, Bertie was a handsome and impressive animal. So handsome and impressive, in fact, that from a distance I occasionally even fantasised about being able to handle him like Clint Eastwood's Man With No Name, leaping from my beginners' mounting-step onto his broad shiny back where with a flick of the reins he'd twirl a tango between my rubbed raw thighs before rearing up on his hind legs and letting out a shrill whinny as we galloped away into a dusty desert sunset.

The reality, though, once I was seated, was that Bertie and I just clip-clopped along at not much above snail's pace beside Fliss and Mungo, like a sort of equestrian double date with Fliss and Mungo the going-steady couple of vast experience and me and Bertie the awkward, nervously sweating virgins. (Or rather, *virgin*. I know for Bertie there had been others.)

This particular Friday, I think it was, Fliss having decided I was now capable of being let loose on the public bridleway, we'd been riding along for nearly an hour in the shade of the forest before we reached the old sand quarry, a bleak, secluded spot, where Fliss suggested we stop to give the horses a rest and let them go to the toilet on the footpath.

'You're really coming on, you know,' Fliss said, smiling as she sat dangling her glossy boots over the edge of the craggy forty-foot chasm. 'Especially with the short time you've been riding.'

'Thanks,' I said, ungratefully. 'But Bertie and I don't want to just clip-clop up and down. We want to go Giddy up! Giddy up! and gallop flat-out through Sherwood Forest, like you and Mungo do.' I hadn't actually discussed this with Bertie, nor his part in my spaghetti western fantasy, but I knew instinctively we were both on the same page, progress-in-the-stirrups wise.

'And you will do, soon. You're doing a brisk walking pace now, that's very good. It won't be long until you can gallop, you just need more –'

'Magic mushrooms,' I said, a sudden and unexpected image forming aloud.

'I was going to say practice. I think the high altitude of horseback has made you a little bit light-headed.'

'Fliss, please come away from that edge,' I said, and as she came over to sit beside me I put my arm round her and drew her down among the dandelions and tall, rough grass. As she slipped out of one or two things I was hotly, blissfully aware why other lads might feel jealous of my being with Fliss, but it was not a thought that had ever crossed my mind before. Not once. Fliss was just Fliss, lovely Fliss, and she was just there, as I was just here, beside her... over her... under her... over her again, the sun on my back and her heat in my mouth and falling, falling a thousand feet as with a blink of her eyes she arches her back and...

I lay on my side in the flattened grass, looking on lazily entranced as Fliss lifted her bottom and carefully rearranged her jodhpurs. 'What are you thinking?' she asked, leaning over to kiss me so that for a few moments her dark curls made a sudden, ticklish nightfall. I slid my hand inside Fliss's half-unbuttoned shirt. Poor dead Clay, I was thinking. I probably would have hated me too.

'You should keep your big nose out,' I hissed into Bertie's ear as the animal glared at me in the same way Lionel had done, the first time I met him. 'I don't spy on you in your stable, do I, you dirty Bertie horse.'

When I turned to look across the shaded bridleway, all I could make out beneath the peak of Fliss's helmet was her smile. 'I'm pleased you two are getting on so well,' she said. Failing to steer myself and Bertie closer, I blew her a big kiss and she blew me an even bigger one back, from the palm of her hand. This was the moment where I flicked the reins, danced a horsey tango and galloped off into that dusty desert sunset. But Bertie, the dirty animal, was still giving me that funny look and seemed in no mood for games, so we just clip-clopped, at not much above snail's pace, back to the stables.

2

By Monday afternoon of her second week I gathered there were few Sheffield centre forwards – United and Wednesday – or 'hot' owners of nightclubs and sunbed centres to whose largesse Gillian had not been treated, although few, apparently, had measured-up sufficiently enough to deserve a second encounter.

'You know how sometimes you sleep with a fella just because it's easier than finding a taxi?'

'I can't say I do, Gillian,' I said. 'Chesterfield's always full of taxis whenever I've had a night out there.'

'Now and then I suppose you might be lucky and meet a really nice guy who'll drive you home without expecting to get into your knickers.'

I coughed.

'So where do you take your girlfriend out, then?'

'There you are, good,' said Ricky. 'Serve us quick, bud, Keith's coming and he's going to be ages.'

I helped Gillian sort Ricky out with some Orion service bits, pointing her towards the various bins as I filled his oil jug, and while Keith made a far more obscure request, the sort that demanded prolonged periods of frowning at the microfiche. 'Leave that one with me, Keith,' I said, moving across to the viewer. 'I'll give you a shout when I've found it.'

'You must take her out, Robin,' Gillian said, resuming her probing. 'It's Fliss, isn't it? What do you do together?'

I frowned at the microfiche viewer, sucked air noisily through my teeth and mumbled '*potentiometer*' and '*fuel-injection module*' knowingly.

'We don't go out much,' I said, not wanting to seem rude. 'We mostly stay in and listen to records. Go to the pictures, or for a walk.' Feeling this lacked glamour, I found myself adding, 'Horse-riding, sometimes.'

'Horse-riding? Shit, Robin, how old's your girlfriend, twelve? Bet that's why you don't take her out in town, she's too young to get served, you dirty cradle snatcher.'

'She's older than me, actually,' I said, proud of the fact, jotting down a part number before some more frowning at the fiche.

For a few minutes now I'd felt one of Gillian's softer upper portions moulding itself warmly around my elbow, sensed the lift of her dimpled chin against my ear. 'I forgot you like older women. What's she like, your girlfriend? Does she let you–'

I had the phone against my ear before the second ring, grateful of the generous cloaking properties of my dinner lady's smock. 'Hi, David,' I said. 'Yes, arrived on the van ten minutes ago. I'll bring it through if... Oh, all right.'

When, seconds later, David appeared at the front counter I gave him the Capri handbook he'd ordered for a customer and encouraged Gillian to make out the invoice, thinking it might keep her hands busy for a minute or two at least.

'Is that your new XR3i, David?' Gillian asked. 'The red one, out there?'

'It is, Gillian, yes. Well, mine until somebody wants to buy it. Or steal it.'

Gillian laughed very loudly at this and, rising to her full height, tossed her head back in a way that sent about eighty-five percent of her thick, highlighted curls tumbling onto her shoulder like a pile of wet washing.

'That would be just perfect for me. Town, Friday night, windows down, Level 42 blasting out the stereo...'

'I'll put a Sold sign in it now, shall I?' David smiled, his excellent teeth a glinting sun parting the copper-tanned clouds of his cheeks. 'For collection tomorrow afternoon?'

'Yes, please!' Gillian clapped. 'I'll take both of you out on my first spin.'

'Not if you're listening to Level 42,' I thought.

David calculated how many thousands Gillian would need to hand over, even with her generous family discount, to drive away her dream car. She sighed and then, changing tack, leant forward across the counter, squeezing herself towards his attention. 'I bet your wife loves being taken out in it, doesn't she? She's dead lucky.'

'I'm not married, actually, Gillian,' David said, sun glinting again. He swept back his sleeve, brushed a finger across his enormous watch, Submariner, Explorer, Fishmonger, one of those. 'Right, well, I've got a handover to do for Graham in about two minutes, it's his day off, so... ciao!'

Ciao?! In a single word I went right off David. Not so Gillian.

'Cor, he's right dishy, isn't he?' she said, remaining sprawled across the counter until the seat of David's trousers had squeaked fully through the swing doors.

'Stunning girlfriend, apparently,' I sighed comfortingly.

'Not stunning enough to marry.'

Hardly a minute had elapsed before Andrew, rapping his knuckles against the counter, waved a key under my nose while fixing Gillian with his cool, appraising beam. 'Can you cut me one of these, Robin, pal? No rush, customer's not due till four.'

'I'll do it for you,' Gillian said, stepping forward and taking the key from Andrew's hand. 'Hey, this is ever so warm, where's it been?'

'Gillian,' I said. 'This is Andrew from sales. Andrew, this is Gillian, Mr Honeywell's niece.'

'Yes, we've met,' said Andrew, his eyes granting me not so much as a flicker. 'So you'll be taking over, Gillian, will you, when Robin joins us in the showroom?'

'Only temporary,' Gillian said. 'I've got a job in London starting September, Modelling and Promotions.'

I winced in sympathy for the capital's first division football teams, wondering if I should at least warn their top strikers of her imminent arrival.

'I could've guessed you were a model. We're much friendlier here than down in London, though, if you change your mind.' Andrew winked at Gillian, then, smiling a nod my way, whistled off, clicking his fingers in time with his heels.

Having identified Keith's mysterious fuel-injection parts and found that we even had both of them in stock, like a dog with the master's slippers I carried them out to his ramp in the workshop before making a pot of tea to celebrate.

'Do you want to do that key for Andrew, Gillian?' I said afterwards, reaching under the counter for a blank.

'I don't want to muck it up. Will you show me again, Robin, one more time?' I looked on as Gillian, her smock gaping like no dinner lady's I could remember, leaned forward to set first the original key in the machine, followed by the blank to be cut to pattern. Gillian pressed the switch.

'I'm turned on, Robin,' she said.

'Good,' I said, refusing to rise to her innuendo, hard as she made it. 'Now, just take your time and ease it in slowly.'

It was, in some ways, as agonising to watch Gillian concentrating on her task as it was to have her squeezing your arse and pushing her breasts into your elbow. But she cut a fine key. Very fine indeed.

3

During school holidays Fliss would often help her parents in the Markley Hall Equestrian shop. She liked the money and enjoyed the company of her friends who worked there, most of whom she knew from school or the stables and were as horse mad as she was. The bus service to Oakerby, though, was at best occasional. So on Wednesday, knowing Ruth had to leave early to check on Grandma Dot before attending a charity fundraising cabaret with Lionel, I clocked-out on the tick of five-thirty and drove up to offer my services as chauffeur.

I'd picked her up several evenings after work, and usually by the time I got there the shutters were all down, and if not, very soon would be. So I was surprised, when I swung the MG into the car park, to find Lionel's Jaguar filling its allocated space and the workshop door peeled back to reveal a large, twin-axled horsebox being juddered high into the air on the hydraulic ramp.

'Robin! *Hello!*' Lionel called, striding out from the back of the workshop to greet me in his now familiar matey manner. 'Felicity didn't mention you were coming to meet her. In fact, I popped up on the off chance thinking she might like a lift. And, well, you know how it is, Iain and I got nattering, about one thing and another.'

I doubted whether Iain (with two Is) could natter, the wiry mechanic who leased the workshop from Lionel, and ran it as a separate though mutually beneficial entity, having remained stubbornly wordless on the few occasions I'd previously encountered him, just as he now remained waveless and nodless when I saluted him beneath his ramp.

'He's working late,' I said, pleased at being able to hand over in person the two sets of number plates I'd had made up for Lionel that afternoon. 'Plenty of work on?'

'Yes, it's been very busy all round, actually, Robin. Both the workshop and the riding side. Thank you kindly, by the way, for bringing these, I'll just... *Iain?*'

Lionel braved a fat man's jog to the workshop door, handing the plates to the mute mechanic before returning with a daft grin on his face and his cheeks glowing even pinker than before.

'Is that the horsebox you were –' I started to say, pointing to the ramp.

'That's right,' Lionel nodded, his meaty paw swivelling me round before it drew me into the quilting of his jacket and marched us towards the double doors of what I'd once heard him call his *equestri-heaven*. 'Bloody brakes still sticking. Iain thinks there might also be a wheel-bearing gone now. Highly dangerous any time, Robin, but with a prize animal onboard...' Lionel, eyes horror-stricken, shook his head. 'Doesn't bear thinking about. *Felicity!*'

'Hey!' Fliss waved, smiling from behind the counter as I trailed Lionel across the tiles. 'Till's all done, Dad, and the cash boxes are in the car.'

'Thank you, darling.'

With a staccato peal, white-hot rows of overhead spotlights clicked out, one after the other, casting into shadow the neat displays of Happy Horsewear and Premium Pony Products. In the far corner, where a cardboard Range Rover had been added to the gymkhana tableau of headscarf-and-wax-jacketed mannequins staring blankly at a horsebox, a narrow shaft of daylight penetrated through the open door to glint a sharp new moon off the buttock of a plastic thoroughbred.

'Home time.' Ducking beneath the counter, Fliss came skipping towards me with a delighted smile on her sensational lips, sensational lips that she now puckered and pressed lovingly against the plump rosy cheek of her father. My consolation prize a gentle squeeze of the hand, I seethed a moment wondering who the hell Lionel thought he was, before conceding, grudgingly, that he was her father.

Alarm set a-beeping, I hurried outside between daughter and father. By now the workshop was all locked-up, too. Lionel, twisting a stubby key, brought down the electric shutters over the big shop windows, and nodding across the yard (perhaps to avoid the itchy silence that descends upon all fathers confronted with the young oik he suspects of filthy doings with his daughter), he smacked his lips and said, 'You know, Robin, I think those brakes might have got the better of Iain.'

'Well, if he's stuck, my friend Ricky's magic with brakes,' I said. 'The other mechanics all hate brakes, but Ricky loves them, cars, vans, anything.'

'Thank you, Robin, I shall bear that in mind. I know Iain, he won't give up without a fight, but that's useful to know, very useful.' Lionel turned to Fliss. 'Must dash, darling. Meeting about the farmers' summer gala, then this blasted cabaret your mother's got me into, so I shall love you and leave you. Bye, darling. Bye, Robin.'

As Lionel's Jaguar purred away and Fliss and I strolled hand-in-hand across the car park, I glanced across the railway line. Since collating our notes in his kitchen, I'd accompanied Vern and Betty on two more late-night expeditions to the old station, and on both occasions observed nothing even vaguely suspect, at either the station, station yard or on any of the nearby roads. There had also been no new reports, for a week or two, of similar cars being stolen in the area, nor any word from Kevin about Parker, the driver of the yellow-and-white transporter. It was looking like whoever spotted us snooping about that night, before making his swift exit over the footbridge, had been well and truly scared off.

'I'm not ready to go home yet,' Fliss said, twisting in the front seat to face me. We kissed until we both felt hungry, and then, just as I was turning the key in the ignition, I saw, beyond the high mesh fence, the dark shape of a car emerging from the top of the approach road before it turned slowly towards the station.

'Just a sec,' I called to Fliss, and leaving the MG's door swinging, I ran round the back of Markley Hall Equestrian. The car must have come to a halt behind the station. I waited for it to reappear, listening for the sound of its engine, but all I heard was distant thunder, a deep throbbing rumble followed by the tiss-tiss tingle of the railway line. 'Please, not a train, not now,' I said as a stubby black snout edged out from the left side of the building and swung sharply round as if to drive up on to the platform. It was still early and the rays of the evening sun bounced blood orange against the car's windscreen, making it impossible to see the driver, even before the loaded coal train smashed through the picture.

'What is it?' Fliss said as I slammed the door shut. I turned the key, crammed the gearstick into reverse and spun the MG backwards through a ninety-degree nose turn, like a proper flared-trousered TV detective.

'Belt up.'

'Robin!'

'Seat belt,' I snapped. 'We need to be on the other side, fast.'

'The other side of where?' Fliss said, buckling up excitedly as if she thought this was a game we were playing.

'The railway line. Hold tight.'

Barely dabbing the brakes at the bottom of the hill, I screeched hard right into the thankfully quiet main road, echoed under the railway bridge and, screeching immediately hard right again, accelerated for all the MG was worth up the station approach. I drifted a wide corner, tracing the route of the dark car I'd seen, behind and then around the side of the station before swinging to a grit-shower halt perilously close to the edge of the platform. I climbed out, leaving the engine running and a bemused Fliss in the passenger seat as, leaping rusting barrels and shattered rooftiles, I sprinted a breathless circuit of the building.

'Gone,' I said, panting against the front wing of the MG. Beneath my fingers I felt an ominous crunchy bubbling of the paintwork, an eyebrow of perforations brewing above the headlight.

'*What's* gone?' Fliss said, throwing me the car keys over the bonnet. 'And why are we playing cops and robbers?'

'I don't really know,' I said, turning to look across the ragged wilderness of the railway yard. 'There was a car. It's a long story.'

'Is it, now?'

I leaned cautiously against the wing as Fliss positioned herself between my legs and slid her hands inside the old jumper I wore beneath my smock. My hands low on her jodhpurs, I felt, not for the first time, self-loathingly aware of how sensational Fliss always looked in her work clothes and how grubby and dead-end a loser I must seem to her in mine. But the cloud passed as quickly as it had appeared, knowing I'd soon be wearing a suit and tie to work every day, not to mention the delicious strawberry taste of her lips that were nibbling softly at mine. 'Want to tell me your long, weird story back at ours?' Fliss said, nuzzling.

'I should probably go home first, for some dinner. And a shower.'

'I'll make us dinner. I might even run you a shower if you're good. It's the Round Table cabaret, Mum and Dad will be very drunk and very late.'

'Clean clothes?'

'We can call at yours, if you want something nice for... afterwards.'

Afterwards, Fliss sat up in bed and sang me Fleetwood Mac's *Beautiful Child*, the whole song, unaccompanied. I don't know if it was the way she'd sung it, so soon after what had gone before, or that I drove home to *Shake off The Ghosts*, the closing instrumental track from Simple Minds' stadium-walloping LP *Sparkle In The Rain*, at irresponsibly high volume, but even before I drew up at Mam's gate hot tears had begun to stream down my cheeks, soaking the front of my jacket.

But that's a funny thing about happiness. If you're unaccustomed, sometimes even the promise of it can be terrifying.

Twenty-one

1

Monday, two evenings before.

I'm not blaming David Sylvian, but it was as we lay listening to him that Fliss decided she'd made a terrible mistake. I don't mean going out with me, or doing what we'd just done, but by agreeing to appear on *Show Me The Stars*. *Nightporter* is a brilliant and beautiful song, if you like that sort of thing, but it's hardly one to set the loins ablaze, not like *When Doves Cry*, and as soon as old Sylv got the fear in his heart Fliss suddenly sat up against the pillows and started buttoning herself back inside her shirt.

'I don't even want to be on television. And why am I dressing up and pretending to be Kate Bush? It's all just so... *stupid*.' Although Fliss laughed when she said this, it wasn't the way she laughed when she found something funny. There was a lightness to it, but which at the same time seemed filled with frustration and insecurity.

'You love Kate Bush,' I said, trying to be reassuring, though I knew this wasn't really her point. 'She's your idol. Everything you do – your music, your own songs – you measure by asking *'But is it the sort of thing Kate Bush might do? Can you hear Kate Bush singing that? Would Kate Bush say keep going with this, or Jesus, Fliss, what a pile of whiny old horse shit?'*

'Wow, is that really what I sound like?'

I flashed her a cheeky smile. '*Some*times. But that's good.'

She seemed to relax at this and, giving me a peck on the nose, bedded down against my shoulder. 'You know I love Kate Bush. But that doesn't mean I want to go and make a fool of myself in front of the whole country. What if she was watching?'

As you know, apart from a few fleeting moments, when the tape of her performing *Running Up That Hill* landed her an audition, and when she was then invited to appear on the programme, Fliss had never been exactly enthusiastic about going on *Show Me The Stars*. She'd been unsure from the moment Ruth posted her application. And whenever I'd since tried to talk to her about it her reaction had usually been to say, please, not now, or that it was still ages away and she didn't want to think about it before she had to, putting it off again and again, like I used to my school homework. She always said, of course, that she wasn't interested in performing for other people. It was playing piano Fliss loved, playing, composing and singing to herself – and me, if I was lucky – all those catchy and deceptively complex 'little tunes', slowly piecing them together with her 'embarrassing nonsense' lyrics, as she'd been doing since she was sixteen, to create these songs you felt you already knew so well despite them sounding like nothing or nobody else. I understood why she didn't want to go on the stupid television show. But having watched and heard her play in front of Charlotte and Alastair, I'd no doubt that if she did, she'd be phenomenal.

'But that was different. Charlotte is different.'

'She is,' I agreed, blowing a knot of fragrant curls out of my nose. 'You two really hit it off, didn't you?'

'We never stopped talking while you were at the bookshop. About music and books and our favourite singers, all sorts of things. It was like I'd known her all my life and she knew everything about me. Charlotte's properly cool. She gets it. Did you know she used to be a quite famous folk singer?'

'Really?'

'She knew Bert Jansch and Sandy Denny and went on tour and everything.'

'I know Alastair was in bands. In the sixties he played with the bloke who became Alvin Stardust.'

'Shane Fenton. Charlotte told me. She said they got together – her and Alastair – when they were our age, but then she moved away and married somebody else.'

'Mam remembers her. Did you tell her about the TV show?' I said, getting up to put *The Kick Inside* on the turntable. As the needle lowered I wondered if I'd done the right thing, if Fliss would ask me to take it off, like she'd done on the way to Manchester, but at the first taste of whale song she grinned and threw back the duvet.

'Yes. She gave me some really good advice, only now I'm not sure what to do with it. Are you coming back to bed?'

'Fliss?' I said once we were warm again.

'Hmm?'

'Do you think Kate Bush does watch *Show Me The Stars*?'

'Don't be silly, Robin.'

'What do you mean?'

'Course she doesn't. Why would she?'

'She might like to laugh at the terrible singers,' I said.

'Kate Bush wouldn't do that.'

'Why not?'

'Because she's nice.'

'How do you know? She might be a terrible cow in real life.'

'No way is Kate Bush a terrible cow. Impossible.'

'Why?'

'Her lyrics, her songs, the way she plays them and sings them, that's why. Listen... hear that? It's not possible that someone who makes music like this could ever be a terrible cow. So if you think that, Robin Manvers, you're an absolute moron and you can get your skinny arse out of my bed right now.'

'I was only teasing,' I said.

'So am I.' Fliss sprang up and flung a leg across my chest. I sympathised, thinking I must make a poor saddle after Mungo. 'Oh, I don't know,' she said, looking down into my eyes. 'What do you think? Should I go on stupid, idiotic *Show Me The Stars*?'

'It's up to you, Fliss,' I said, my hands on her hips. 'But there's no way you'd make a fool of yourself. I think your *Running Up That Hill* is just as good as Kate Bush. Better, because it's you. But you should only do it if you really want to. Don't feel like you have to, for your mum and dad, or anybody else.'

She leaned forward and we kissed. I started unbuttoning her shirt but hadn't got very far when Fliss sat back and took both my hands in hers. 'If I give you the number of the studio, would you ring and tell them I can't do it? Say I'm really ill or something? You could ring that nice girl, Millie.'

'Yes, of course,' I said, not mentioning that I already had Millie's work number as well as the address of her flat in Manchester. 'I can ring her in the morning, if you're absolutely sure?'

Fliss frowned for a moment, then slowly unbuttoning her shirt she slid herself down my body until our underwear met. 'I don't want to talk about it anymore, Robin,' she said, pulling the duvet over our heads. 'Kiss me, will you?'

Twenty-two

1

At half past ten a small crowd gathered in the corner of the workshop to see the kettle boil for morning tea break. For most the ritual would pass unremarkably as always, the first stop on the daily trudge towards five-thirty. Vern, however, had woken up that morning with other ideas, ideas he now quietly began to put into action.

'Oh lovey, I do hope she's feeling better soon,' said Sheila, butterfly fingertips settling on the arm of Vern's overalls. 'Not like your mother to be unwell now, is it? She's fitter than women half her age.'

'She's eighty-four next,' I heard myself chip in automatically. 'Sorry, Vern, none of my business.'

'You keep your nose out, young Robin,' Ken said, jabbing me with such a good left to the kidneys I dropped my sandwich box in a stagnant pool of anti-freeze. I wondered how wrong it would be for me to floor Ken – seventy-one, decorated war veteran, recent appendectomy – with a dead leg, but it was hardly the right moment, so I let it go, for now.

'You tell your mother, Vern, to ring through to my phone any time,' Sheila said, crinkling her eyes. 'You've no need to ask.'

'It'll only be if she feels she wants the doctor,' Vern nodded gratefully. 'I expect she'll be right as rain again by now.'

'Sorry about that, Vern,' I said as soon as we were alone and dipping our teabags. 'I feel a bit on edge.'

'Me an' all, lad. I've been thinking about that car you said you saw last night,' Vern mused, drizzling milk with conspiratorial gravity. 'It has to be the same one, has to be.'

'I nearly called in to tell you, but it was late by the time I left Fliss's and...'

'I'd probably have still been up there. I wandered up a bit earlier than I reckon to do and, as I say, it turned up just after nine o'clock. It has to be the same car.'

'He must have come back, then,' I said, nodding yes to sugar. 'It was about half six, quarter to seven, when I saw it. Three spoons, thanks.'

'It was getting dark, but I saw it clear enough and it matches your description exactly.' Vern stirred his tea, raised it not quite to his lips before putting it back down on the workbench. 'I thought those notes of ours were explosive enough as they were, Robin. But with this new, er, element thrown into the mix, it's turning into a right bloody stew we're cooking. Car-thieving aside, if this all turns out to be what we think it might be – and *who* it might be – somebody's looking at a charge of manslaughter.'

'Shit,' I said. 'I'm starting to wish we hadn't got involved now, Vern, are you?'

Vern lifted his tea and blew before taking a long, contemplative sip. 'Well,' he said turning to me with a sly grin. 'I wouldn't go so far as to say that.'

We carried our mugs across the workshop to the door of the canteen. 'So if Kevin hears from our friend...' I said, meaning Parker, the driver of the yellow transporter.

'If he hears from him today or tomorrow, as he expects he will do, and he lets us know in good time, then it looks like we're on.'

'And you're sure he definitely went inside the station, the bloke in the black car?'

Vern nodded, pausing at the canteen door. 'We were hidden behind them sleepers – you know, me and Betty – but I heard all right. Those big steel panels over that main entrance must be hinged on the inside. You'd think they'd have oiled them. It was a good half-hour or more before he came out again.'

'And you didn't see any other cars or the transporter?'

'No. But when he came out of the station, the chap who'd been driving the black car, and was locking up, there were somebody else with him. I could hear them talking. Not what they were saying, mind. They must have driven away together, because after they'd gone I didn't see another soul.'

In the canteen talk had turned to the FA Cup semi-final and Forest's chances against Liverpool on Saturday, so I was glad when the Ford parts lorry rolled into the yard, forcing me to cut short my break and help the driver unload. It had always baffled me how so many blokes wasted their adulation on footballers when there were rock stars around, actual living gods truly deserving of worship. I mean, apart from Debbie Harry, how could you seriously admire anybody who made their living skipping about in shorts?

I signed for the delivery and was just putting my back against a tall pallet of oil and batteries when Mr Honeywell clipped up on his loafers, overgroomed as ever and beaming like the host of a quiz show.

'Where will you manage to stow it all, that's what I wonder.'

'Oh, we'll squeeze it in somewhere, Mr Honeywell,' I said. 'Actually, I think a lot of this will be going straight back out to the council.'

Honeywell took in the further three pallets beside the one we stood by awkwardly and shook his head. 'You and Sheila have that department running like a well-oiled machine. Yes, I do hope you've passed on all your great wisdom to my niece, young Gillian.'

'Oh, I think she'll be all right, Mr Honeywell. Gillian picks things up very easily.'

'She does indeed. Well now, what I wanted to ask you, Robin, if I may, was if perhaps you and Rocky –'

'Ricky.'

'Ricky, yes, erm, if perhaps you and Ricky might be free tomorrow evening to assist with another used vehicle transfer?'

'Well, I'm free, Mr Honeywell,' I said. 'And I'm sure – oh, he's here now, look.'

Ricky, returned from a road-test with Keith, leapt from the passenger seat of a driving-school Fiesta to rattle open the workshop door. I waited while he pulled it shut again then whistled him over. 'Tomorrow?' nodded Ricky, balling a polythene seat-cover between his filthy hands. 'Can do. Where to this time, Mr Honeywell?'

'Doncaster,' Honeywell said. 'Ford main dealership, as per last time. Bob Hague's old place, yes, he must've been there twenty years, Bob, er... Well, I'll furnish you both with full details, directions and so forth, later this afternoon, but, say, departing 8 p.m. again?'

'Great,' I said.

'Anything to come back, Mr Honeywell?'

'There will be a return vehicle, Ricky, yes,' Honeywell said, brushing a thread from his lapel and reminding me of something Vern had said that night at his kitchen table. 'One, I'm assured, somewhat more comfortable than the Mini you were forced to endure over the Pennines a few weeks ago. There's a Sierra and an Escort to be delivered, convertible, possibly, I can't quite remember now. Well, very good. I'm much obliged to you, gentlemen.'

'Thanks, Mr Honeywell,' Ricky said as the dealer principal pivoted on his heel and strode away towards the showroom straightening his cuffs.

'Yes, thanks, Mr Honeywell.'

I abandoned the pallet in the middle of the yard and, following Ricky into the workshop, went to find Vern.

'He's out on a breakdown, lovey,' Sheila said. 'Only to Mrs Pollard, down the back lane. Sounds like a flat battery.'

'Mrs Pollard?'

'Wife of Tony – Sergeant Pollard. Vern serviced his police car the other week. Good you reminded me, Robin – Vern's taken a battery from the display. Pop a note on the job sheet, would you, in case we need to invoice. I did tell Gillian to do it, but that handsome driving-instructor was at the front counter and I'm not sure she was listening.'

2

It was an especially busy afternoon in the workshop and at the front counter. By the time Gillian and I had finished emptying and putting away those four pallets of stock, and she'd made one of her lukewarm, sparrow's-piss cups of tea, it was four o'clock.

'What did Uncle Giles collar you for this morning?'

'When?' I said, cupping my hands to warm the mug.

'Just after tea break. I saw him waffling at you and Ricky in the yard. He seemed very serious.'

I couldn't see any harm in telling Gillian about the driving we'd done for Honeywell, but now that we had a plan in place (or Vern had), one that might be actioned at any moment, I thought the fewer people who knew anything at all about any of it the better. Even Ricky, my best friend who'd been with me on both trips, knew nothing about what Vern and I had been up to these past months, and, now especially, I thought it best that it should remain that way.

'Oh no, nothing serious,' I said. 'It was about me moving into the showroom next week as a sales trainee.'

'Ricky as well?' she said, arching a heavy brow.

'He could hardly take me off the YTS and leave Ricky on it, could he? He's promised to set Ricky on as apprentice to Vern, on proper money.'

'Nice. I bet Ricky's pleased.'

'Over the moon.'

'Maybe now he'll be able to take Mandy out again. Has he said anything to you about her?'

'Me? No. To be honest, Gillian, I think the only thing Ricky thinks about right now is his van and his spanners.'

'What about you, Robin?' Gillian said, taking my hand and gently easing me into an aisle of gaskets. 'What are you thinking about... right now?'

My usual reaction to these encounters with Gillian was to laugh them off, to coolly step beyond her reach knowing I'd be saved any second by the bawl of a mechanic or the squeak of Sheila's office door. But this time there came neither. Nor did I attempt to move away. And as I gazed into her eyes I was back in the MG the night I gave her a lift home from Chesterfield, my heart racing as Gillian popped open my dinner lady's smock and sent her ticklish fingers curling around my sides, climbing the ladders of my ribs. She moved in to kiss me. I moved in to kiss her. Her own smock was open now, and as I closed my eyes I anticipated the soft, warm places my grubby hands were about to soil.

And then the telephone rang.

'Oh hello, Kevin,' I said to the click of receding heels. 'Today? Before half past five?' I shook my Casio from my sleeve. 'Yes, I'll sort that out for you straight away, Kevin. Thanks a lot.'

This was it. Action stations.

A smirker had hovered up to the front counter waving an accessories brochure, so I left him to Gillian while I frowned at the microfiche for a minute or two before dialling the number of the cleaner of the two telephones from the filthy one beside it. After two rings I picked up the clean phone and hung up the filthy one. Gillian, who was busy costing up every available Cortina spoiler, saw nothing.

'Good afternoon, parts and service department, Robin speaking, how may I help?' I said, hating myself only slightly less knowing there was nobody at the other end. Still, this was a performance, and I threw myself into it. 'Hello, Mrs Priestley, how nice to...' I said, brilliantly convincing. 'Have you? Oh dear, I *am* sorry to hear that. Yes, *yes*, of course, I'll just go and get him for you now – one moment please.'

Oscar in the bag (handy if the music career didn't work out), I put down the receiver, made a grim face at Gillian and charged through Sheila's office like a bull on roller-skates. 'Vern's mum on the phone,' I gasped, not stopping.

Vern's acting, while obviously lacking my panache, was in its way just as credible. With a simple, anxious 'Hello, Mother?' and 'Yes, all right, I'll be there shortly,' he tight-smiled his thanks to Sheila and was tearing up the road in his Escort Harrier before you could say *bloody hell, he must've been touching thirty*.

That morning, Mrs Priestley had polished off her usual fifty lengths at the pool, where, setting a new personal best, she had then swum another five lengths to pass the remaining few minutes of her early bird session. At the precise moment Vern drove off the forecourt to rush to her rescue, she'd in fact just taken a large axe from the shed and was setting about chopping a storm-felled oak into logs for the kitchen fire.

Twenty-three

1

Ahead of the transporter's arrival, Kevin had cleared a space around a metallic blue Escort XR3i Cabriolet. Barely eight months old, the car at first sight still appeared immaculate but for where the front wing had been peeled all the way back, over the wheel, like the lid of a sardine tin, and the passenger-side door gouged along its length with a deep, council-green scar. The headlamp on this side was also smashed and the indicator lens missing, while the front bumper hung lopsided from a single retaining bolt. But otherwise, immaculate.

'Hit a kerb, has it?' Vern said, walking round to wave the mug of tea Kevin had made him at the shattered front wheel. 'Gone into a lamp post?'

'No. Wasn't even moving, Vern. Parked on the street outside the owner's house. Got hit by a dustbin wagon.'

'Chuff me.'

'Or so Craig was saying, anyway.'

'Craig?'

'What's-her-name's lad, in your office – Sheila. He's an assessor for one of the big insurance firms, I forget which one now, Royal Falcon, is it?'

Vern glimpsed at the speedometer. 'Only three thousand miles – and they've written it off?'

'Doesn't look too bad,' Kevin agreed. 'Thought it'd be a nice easy job, a wing and a door skin, front bumper and what-have-you. But it's taken a right heavy knock on that front corner. Whole bodyshell's twisted.'

'You can see where the bulkhead's moved, dashboard's come away. Quick, gimme a bit of that sandpaper, Kevin,' Vern said with a nod towards the main road. 'Wagon's here now, look. I'll make out I'm busy.'

The yellow-and-white transporter swung into the yard and hissed to a shuddering halt. Vern, kneeling in the open doorway of the spray booth, rubbed haphazardly away at a convenient boot lid, watching from under his cap as the driver winched the mangled cabriolet up the ramps and onto the back of the lorry. Whether the man joking with Kevin, as the two of them secured the tarpaulin shroud over the open top Escort, was this chap Parker, Vern couldn't be sure, having never seen him clearly before, but it was the same transporter, all right, of that he was certain.

'Right, then...' Vern said under his breath. Twenty minutes earlier he'd parked his own car on the main road, a short distance from the body shop. A smart move, he congratulated himself, as with a discreet nod to Kevin he now slipped through the gates and walked calmly towards it.

The Harrier's engine humming along to Sinatra's Greatest, Vern waited, his fingers curled around the gear-knob, his foot hovering over the clutch. He didn't have to wait long. Those strangers in the night had got only as far as their first hello when the transporter's nose edged through the gates and swung across the main road. Because rather than turning left, towards the town centre and Oakerby, as we'd both anticipated, the driver had turned right, and was now accelerating away, in a cloud of black diesel, towards Sheffield. Smart as his parking had been, the main road at half past five was very busy, and Vern's car was facing in the wrong direction.

2

'Goodnight, Robin love. See you tomorrow.'

'Goodnight, Sheila,' I called as I hurriedly locked the front counter shutters and turned out the lights.

'See you in the morning, Robin.'

'Bye, Gillian.'

I'd just that minute put down the phone to Kevin, who'd called to say the transporter had left with Vern in hot pursuit – well, in pursuit, anyway. That was one thing we'd failed to account for as we formulated our clever plan, the famously funereal Priestley pace. It was a small thing, but one that could easily put an end to this whole operation before it had even started.

Fliss had an essay to write up that afternoon, on *Pride and Prejudice*, but knowing she never dawdled over these things, and that I wasn't expected at Windmill Way before seven, I drove straight to the obvious place. Leaving the keys in the MG, I dashed to the stable yard, where I found her mounted at the centre of half a dozen riders about to set off on one of their early evening jaunts into Sherwood Forest.

'Fliss!' I said, panting and blinking up Mungo's nose to where she sat high and lovely in the saddle. 'Emergency! I've got to get to Oakerby station, fast. I'm meeting Vern. There's something going on... I need to get there now!'

Fliss, excusing herself, manoeuvred Mungo away from the group. 'What do you mean, there's something going on?' she said, looking very confused and, I have to say, not especially pleased to see me. 'Aren't you in your car?'

'Yes, but they'd see it!' I said, frustrated at having to state the obvious. 'Please, Fliss, will you?'

'Who'll see it? Robin, what's going on? Are you all right?'

She slid a shiny boot out of a shinier stirrup and started to get down from Mungo.

'Don't get down! It's to do with all these stolen cars. Fliss, please, will you?'

'Will I what?'

'Take me to the station. You and Mungo. Or just to the end of the embankment will do, the other side of the woods. But quickly! Now! *Please*?'

Fliss twirled Mungo so that his big brown head faced her friends. 'I'll catch up with you guys at the white gates, okay? I've just got to drop Robin somewhere. He says it's an emergency.'

I ignored the doubtful tone in which she said this and, positioning the beginner's mounting-step beside Mungo, leapt up into the saddle behind her. With a sharp crack of the reins, the sort I'd be doing myself very soon, we trotted, or possibly cantered, out of the yard and along the lane towards the bridleway. We picked up speed gradually until, after about fifty yards, Fliss, lifting her bottom against my chest, leaned forward and appeared to whisper something in Mungo's ear, at which point the animal's throttle suddenly opened all the way and the three of us rocketed off with me clinging on for dear life, thankful I'd missed my dinner.

'Robin, are you sure this is a good idea?' Fliss said, her eyes oozing second thoughts as I dismounted a few minutes later onto a stile beside the embankment. 'What are you hoping to do? Vern's an old man and you're...'

'What?' I said, gazing up the steep slope of her beigely-jodhpured thigh. 'The plan is to...' I shrugged. 'I've got to hurry.'

Fliss reached down for my hand and squeezed it tightly in her glove. 'Please be careful, Robin,' she said. 'And come straight to ours as soon as you can – promise?'

I scrambled back up the stile and gave her a long kiss (too long, really, considering it was an emergency). The smash of her helmet peak against the bridge of my nose hardly registered after the softness of her lips.

'I promise,' I said, climbing down with a pat for Mungo's side. 'Now go and catch up with your friends and be careful. I'll see you later.'

I joined the cinder path and began to run towards the railway yard, turning back only once in time to see Fliss and Mungo peel off from the bridleway and vanish, at full gallop, into the trees.

3

Although, as Ken liked to point out, it wasn't the 'proper army', Vern had travelled wide and exotically during his National Service, so he was not as surprised as some might have been when the Metro drew up in the shadow of the transporter and the short-skirted woman climbed, carrying her heels, up into its sleeper-cab.

'Now then...' was all he said, unfastening his seatbelt.

After turning in the main road outside the body shop, Vern, thanks to a blinking level crossing, had managed to catch up with the yellow-and-white wagon and its tarpaulined hump, keeping a safe distance while the driver took a leisurely circuit through the lanes of Whaley, Welbeck and Creswell Crags before doubling back to the Doncaster road and the sheltered lay-by on the edge of Clumber Park where Vern now patiently sat, watched and waited.

And waited.

'Well, Vern, you're all right here,' he said to himself, sighing as he uncapped his flask of over-brewed tea.

While Vern was busy fogging his windows, I'd taken up position seven miles away, just inside the doorway of the ruined signal box. In the warm evening sunshine the reek of rats and slack-bladdered car mechanics seemed stronger than ever, but

I had a perfectly clear view of the old station and approach road, as well as most of the derelict goods yard and sections of the closest platform and footbridge.

I looked at my calculator watch and calculated. If the transporter had left the body shop shortly before five-thirty, it should, even allowing for teatime traffic, have arrived at Oakerby station by six o'clock at the latest. But as a further twenty minutes passed, then thirty, and forty, it began to look like we'd been mistaken; if not altogether, about everything, then at least about tonight's anticipated manoeuvres, and I pictured Vern trailing Parker's lorry to some distant breaker's yard that had neither connection to crime nor to what was again starting to feel like an increasingly tenuous bunch of theories and coincidences which we'd cobbled together and labelled solid, explosive evidence.

After another half hour, when all I'd seen were two coal trains, one empty, one loaded, and an old bloke being walked by a Jack Russell, I stepped outside the signal box to stretch my legs. Cautiously at first, I took a few short strides into the long grass between the sleepers and lengths of rusting rail. Then, seeing it was quiet, I took several more strides, longer ones this time. Then I took several more. Before I knew it, I was leaping stubborn clusters of old bricks, iron and other murderously lurking hazards dotted like landmines, humming the guitar riff from Simple Minds' early classic *Wasteland* and thinking what a starkly atmospheric location this would make for my first album cover.

I was suddenly a long way out from the signal box and some distance from the pile of tarred sleepers where Vern and I had taken refuge, that time before, a hundred yards along from the slope of the platform. It had been dark then, though, whereas now it was still birdsong bright, and there I was, out and exposed in the middle of no-man's land, still riffing, still leaping, when the car appeared at the top of the approach road.

I dived down among the ballast as the driver crawled to a halt, exactly as he'd done the previous evening, at the head of the goods yard, before then turning towards the station and creeping briefly behind it to emerge onto the near platform.

'It has to be,' I said. The car, a Saab 900 Turbo, though overdue a wash, was instantly recognisable. I could think of only two people in the world who drove or had driven one of these quirky Swedish motors, one of them being Jim Kerr of Simple Minds, who would obviously have better things to do with his Thursday evenings than sneak about old railway yards, like rehearsing for Nelson Mandela's 70th Birthday Tribute concert in June, for a start. Also, Jim's car I was certain would be blue, for Scotland. The Saab that now crawled along the perimeter of Oakerby station was black.

'Bloody hell, Vern, where are you?' I hissed as I lay across the tracks like some kohl-eyed dame from a silent picture. During my plunge to the ground, I'd taken a nasty splinter in my hand, which was obviously Vern's fault. 'You'd better not be at home, tucking into one of your mother's dinners.'

But all thoughts of splinters and Mrs Priestley's cooking evaporated in a blink at what sounded like something heavy and metallic scraping or being dragged over concrete. From my position among the thistles all I could see was a looming gable end and the back of the station; nothing at all on the platform side. But whatever it was, it moved with a low, slow squeal, like a great weight on rusty hinges. I heard the Saab being revved softly and then its engine echoed loudly for a moment before all fell silent. Then the scraping again. The steel panels, presumably, like Vern had said.

Thinking I'd have a better view, and less chance of being spotted, I made a hunchbacked dash across the yard, weaving between buckled oil drums and dead bonfires to the wall of sleepers, where I sat for a moment to gather my breath and tie my bootlaces, which had come undone with all that leaping. When I edged round the sleepers and looked along the railway line towards the station, the platform was deserted, with no sign of either Saab or driver. However, at about the midway point of the front of the building, beneath where the words BOOKING HALL had been carved into the stone, a tall rectangular steel panel, one half of a pair of brutal black gates, I could see was partially open. This seemed like a golden opportunity. Golden, but also very stupid and highly dangerous. But if I wanted to see what was going on inside the station – and I did – I'd have to get closer. A lot closer.

4

The track having been lifted years ago, concealing myself under the platform edge was not as suicidal this side of the line as it might have been on the other, Markley Hall side, but it still left only a few draughty feet between my baby-skin back and the thousand tonnes of coal train that now thundered deafeningly past on a hundred-and-forty hot, bacon-slicer wheels.

'Christ, that was close,' I muttered, blinking black diamond shards from both eyes. When eventually silence returned and I'd tired of crouching, heart thumping, among the nettles, I popped my nose over the mossy edge hoping to catch a glimpse of who or what might be inside the station. The Saab and driver had to be in there, they couldn't be anywhere else, but I could neither see nor hear any signs of activity. Nothing at all.

The sun still shimmering above the wooded horizon, I'd tied my jumper round my middle and was wondering what to do next when I heard the echo of a lorry crunching its gears and slowing under the bridge in the high street, followed by the tired growl as it accelerated hard again and appeared to struggle uphill with a heavy load. The approach road. As the noise drew nearer,

I got down and pressed my back against the cool bricks, the sound of heavy tyres cutting through gravel like the tide going out as the vehicle swung round and clanged into reverse. The platform shook as it inched noisily along and hissed to a belching standstill two feet above my head. A big spider dropped onto my arm and it was all I could do to not scream and tear off across the railway line. But I didn't, and when he'd gone I looked across towards the sleepers, a hundred yards away, wishing I'd remained behind them. There were no spiders on the sleepers, and I couldn't see a bloody thing from here. But this had to be the transporter. It had to be.

If the choking diesel hadn't contaminated the evening air enough already, as the driver leapt down onto the platform a near fatal dose of Spandau Ballet leaked from his cab at shameful volume. There followed much crunching and scuffling of boots and then a loud clap of tarpaulin thunder before, with a ratcheting whirr, something – a vehicle, I felt safe to assume – was winched, creaking, down the ramps, off the back of the transporter. While this was going on, there came again the squeal and scrape of the black steel panels being opened onto the platform. Then I heard the voice of a man I didn't recognise.

'Where's Smiler?'

Followed by another that I did.

'Yes, he – ahh, here he comes now. Iain! *Good evening.* Much obliged to you for, er, coming out.'

A third pair of feet scuffled to a halt above my head, though there remained only two voices.

'Simple switch job, this one, Iain,' the familiar voice said. 'All glass present and unmarked. The vehicle inside has been etched all round. Most inconvenient, but a habit I fear will be sure to catch on, unfortunately.'

A glowing fag-end landed in the ballast an inch from my boot and with a chesty cough a heavy-duty trolley jack clattered across the platform. As feared, Vern had clearly failed to keep up with the transporter, but where the hell was he? He knew that if things went to plan, Parker, if that's who this was, would lead him to the station. What was I supposed to do now, here on my own with this lot?

'*Heave!*'

'Steady... Mind that wall...'

'Bloody jack.'

'Watch it doesn't... Right you are... Now keep her coming straight.'

The voices receded as the three men pushed the vehicle inside the station, only rising again when a wheel of the trolley jack ran aground on loose masonry. Just as I was rising to sneak a look over the edge of the platform there was another squeal and scrape as the steel panels were pulled closed and locked from the inside.

I took this opportunity to make a sharp retreat to the sleepers, where I leaned awhile watching and weighing up the situation. If the transporter were to leave now, I thought, along with the black Saab, as surely it would do, then what was to say the gang would ever need to return to the station? From the conversation I'd just overheard there was at least one other car inside the building besides the one that had just been unloaded, and presumably these would be removed by somebody at some point. But the chances of ever catching all three culprits together again like this, in the act, red-handed, or whatever you liked to call it, seemed highly unlikely.

We'd been keeping tabs on Mr Honeywell for some time, of course, ridiculous as the idea often seemed, but our suspicions had been confirmed when first I and then later Vern had seen the Saab up at the station the night before. Exactly what Honeywell's involvement was in all this we didn't yet know, but it was clearly very shady and almost certainly illegal. What we hadn't properly discussed, perhaps not really believing it would be a situation we'd ever find ourselves in, was if we were to blow the lid on all this, as they said in *Miami Vice*, and went to the police, where that would leave the staff of Stonebridge Motor Company. It wouldn't affect me so much, of course, being bound for far greater things. But Vern had worked at the garage for nearly thirty years and surely wouldn't want the aggro of starting again at his time of life. He was practically a pensioner.

So not for the first time I felt that it might be better for all concerned if we were to just forget about the whole damn thing; that Ricky and I should pocket our tenners for delivering those two cars to Doncaster tomorrow night, as planned, while Vern put away his notebooks and went back to reading detective novels rather than trying to be the hero of one.

With a piercing scrape of steel I was jolted from gazing into the woodwork in time to see Parker, the transporter driver, holding out a huge hand as Mr Honeywell stuffed it with banknotes, while the third man, Iain-with-two-Is, looked silently, sullenly, on. For a moment I really did wish all three of them would just hurry up and sod off, so that I could do the same. And perhaps I would have done, had it not been for a sudden and unexpected new arrival on the scene.

Twenty-four

1

It was the bounding footsteps which alerted me. Gripped by the dealings beside the transporter, I'd neglected to keep a watchful eye on the other side of the railway line. But at the heavy trip-trap-trip of a fourth figure rattling across the footbridge, I remembered the peeled-back section of fence behind Markley Hall Equestrian, through which Iain-with-two-Is must also have made his earlier, silent entrance (in tread as in voice, it seemed), while I was cowering beneath the platform.

As I spied round the rotten bulwark of my hiding place, manfully taking another splinter, I could see Mr Honeywell wearing the tripwire smile of a fasting crocodile as he waited by the steps of the footbridge, arm ready with a fraternal squeeze for the newcomer's shoulder. I didn't want this to be happening. I didn't want to be there. But there I was, watching it happen. And, frozen to my boots, all I could do now was look on numbly as this surprise new guest at the party spoke in a voice which, like his face, was big, angry and all too distressingly familiar.

'Giles, I thought we'd agreed, *not before dark*?'

'Li –'

'No, no, I distinctly said, and Giles, you assured me that it would –'

'Lionel, *Lionel*,' Honeywell broke in smoothly. 'Lionel, please.

Listen. There is none more cautious than I, as you well know, when –'

'But Giles –'

'The coast was clear, we were in and out in a matter of minutes, and, as you can see, we are now leaving. I would suggest, Lionel, that you do the same.'

I couldn't have agreed more. It was already bad enough that Honeywell, my boss, was balls-deep in all this, but Lionel, Fliss's father, as well? In an instant the situation had become a million times worse and even more ridiculous. Dangerous, too. Well, we couldn't go to the police now, that was for sure. If we did, that would mean not only...

As I took in the enormity of what I was witnessing, of what it could very well lead to, my first thought was, naturally, for Fliss's bottom. I pictured it bouncing in the saddle as she raced through Sherwood Forest with her friends, a scarf of black curls streaming behind her as she coaxed Mungo with a laughing smile. All I wanted to do was to run as fast as I could back to the stables, to take Fliss in my arms and kiss her and kiss her and to go upstairs and listen to some records.

But that wasn't going to happen, at least not now. Because inside the station a car started up, and a few seconds later the black Saab with Honeywell at the wheel was driven out and parked at the far end of the platform, while Parker and Iain-with-two-Is swiftly closed and padlocked the steel panels behind him.

'Once those two are gone tomorrow night,' Honeywell said, wiping his hands on a silk handkerchief as Parker climbed up into the transporter's cab, 'our business here is concluded.'

'It had better be,' Lionel nodded significantly. 'Grateful as I am to you, Giles, I've had enough. Now I can't speak for Iain,' (*Somebody ought to!* I thought), 'but I mean to get on with developing this site. Nursing homes. That's where the future lies – old people. I want it all gone, Giles. All of it.'

'Now, Lionel,' Honeywell said, gracious as ever as he smoothed his tie and winced at his watch. 'We've all done very well from this little arrangement, and I will of course see that you are suitably compensated for your invaluable assistance and, er, extended patience. I know I said it would be only for a few weeks, but –'

But Mr Honeywell never got to finish that sentence. Because just as Parker crunched into gear and was pulling away, the station yard suddenly erupted with police cars, a jam sandwich blur of flashing lights and whooping sirens as first a Ford Granada then one of those big wedge-shaped Rovers screamed up the approach road like a pair of Christmas trees fired from a cannon. The Rover, without slowing, screeched sideways towards the station, where with a sharp tug of the handbrake its driver managed to both block the transporter and shower Honeywell with a gravel tsunami as he sprang for the open door of the Saab.

As one policeman leapt to help Parker from his cab by the ankles, the voice of Tony Hadley leaked embarrassingly out, bellowing *Instinction* like he believed it was a real word. Meanwhile, another bobby went sprinting after Honeywell who, after being gritted from loaf to loafer, had about turned and was now scurrying back along the platform and down the slope into the overgrown goods yard.

'Go!' I shouted encouragingly, not entirely sure who it was I should be encouraging.

You wouldn't have thought it to look at him, but Mr Honeywell moved like a young whippet, a grey and impeccably dressed young whippet, and for a moment it seemed he might easily outrun the copper and be away towards the embankment. Very impressive for a motor trade dealer principal, he'd soon covered a huge amount of ground across the derelict wasteland of my future album cover, before, perhaps inevitably, he was brought down when, slipping on a damp, half-buried section of rail, one of his John Lewis premium leather loafers shot off into the air at a wild and spinning angle and he plunged nose-first among the nettles, 'Damn'-ing and 'Christ'-ing and clutching a badly twisted ankle.

Having remained all this time dug in behind the sleepers, now seemed like a good time for me to shift to somewhere slightly less in the front row of all this blue-lights-and-handcuffs stuff. And I was about to make a dash for the approach road when another police car, a tiny Vauxhall this time, nee-nah-ed onto the scene and began to bump like a toy pulled on a string across the yard towards the old signal box, where the Granada had raced a few seconds before. I decided I was probably in the safest place after all, and, leaning back against the sleepers, got another splinter in my finger.

Four police officers – three male, one female – were now in uniformed pursuit of Iain-with-two-Is, who I have to say looked a more than worthy challenger to Honeywell as he leapt and zigzagged between the treacherous industrial debris like he was on a freshly mowed croquet lawn. Two of the coppers made a sudden dive for him and missed, while another had returned to the Vauxhall and was now chasing him back towards the station. As I moved to the other end of the sleepers to follow the action, I heard a familiar noisy exhaust note as first Vern's car and then Ricky's van appeared at the top of the approach road, Vern carefully parking the Harrier beside the fence, while Ricky skidded his postman's pride and joy to a ninety-degree halt before abandoning it with the driver's door wide open.

Looking left and right for dashing coppers, I ran waving across the station yard, giddy with the relief of a freed kidnapee, or a Cold War spy exchanged by the Russians for one of their lads at Checkpoint Charlie.

2

'Where the hell have you been?' I said to Vern, sounding nowhere near as glad as I was to see the old sod.

'I got held up. Wagon driver stopped for refreshments in a lay-by. And about an hour's kip afterwards.'

'A kip? I've been here hours. Jeez, Vern, you won't believe what's been going on.'

'I can see. Looks like they got here just in time.' Vern nodded to the police Rover. 'Is that Giles Honeywell they've got in there?'

'And Parker,' I said, 'the transporter driver.'

Vern smiled and a damp twinkle came into his eye that I'm sure wasn't just your regular seniors' seepage. 'So who's that, then,' he asked, as five coppers scrabbled across the rails towards the signal box, 'the chap they're chasing now?'

'Iain.'

'Ian?'

'With two Is.'

'What?'

'He's the bloke who runs the workshop next to Markley Hall.'

Vern adjusted his cap, gave me a long look. 'Horse place, over the railway?'

'Your lass's dad's shop?' said Ricky. I nodded affirmation on both counts.

'That blue soft-top's gone off the back of the wagon, I see. Did they take it inside the station?'

'Yes. Just like you said, Vern, those big steel panels in the middle are on hinges. Three of them pushed it in on a trolley jack. Sounds like there are more cars inside, what I could make out. I hid under the platform.'

'Good lad.' Vern looked across to the station. 'Did you see anything else?'

'Only the Saab. Honeywell drove that straight in when he arrived.'

'Same as last night.'

'What have you two been up to?' Ricky said, a questioning sideways grin as he elbowed my shoulder. 'Playing detectives?'

I turned to Vern, pointing at Ricky. 'Have you…?'

Vern shook his head, gave one of his bashful smiles.

'He wouldn't tell me anything,' Ricky said. 'Rang when I was in the bath and said I was to get up here straight away. I thought it were a wind-up.'

Vern scrunched his nose and resettled his cap. 'I reckoned if Ricky turned up we could rule him out of our enquiries.'

'Rule me out? What do you mean?'

'How did you ring him?' I said.

'Same way I rang Tony Pollard,' Vern said, indicating the sergeant's Granada which now winked like a blue-capped lighthouse on the farthest shores of the yard. 'Tony's an old pal of mine. Soon as that transporter turned in here, I nipped and used the phone at the hotel over the road. I bought a cob and then parked across the bottom entrance till I saw Tony's lights approaching. Then I shifted out the way, sharpish.'

'What was on your cob, Vern?' asked Ricky.

'Ham salad. It was a bit dry.' Vern stepped forward, shielding his eyes against the setting sun. 'Looks like they've got him.'

About fifty yards along from the end of the platform dusty dark clouds rose from a burst coalbunker where Sergeant Pollard and a fellow officer had at last felled Iain-with-two-Is and were now trying to wrestle him into handcuffs. Flailing like a netted trout – a silent one – he somehow managed to scramble to his feet and, with a nifty push-twist-and-duck manoeuvre, to dodge between the strong arms and legs of the law and make another desperate but impressive run for it. It looked more like a rugby match than the scene of a crime, with Iain-with-two-Is easily outpacing the five scurrying officers as he once more hared back towards the platform, hurdling a toppled telegraph-pole and a tin bath before he disappeared behind the station.

'Footbridge!' I called helpfully to the police officers.

But if the footbridge had been Iain-with-two-Is' intended escape route, then something changed his mind. Perhaps at the last moment spotting the policeman who stood guard beside the Rover holding Honeywell and Parker, or, desperate for the fastest possible way out of his increasingly sticky situation, Iain-with-two-Is made a sudden sharp swerve away from the platform and jumped into the driver's seat of the black Saab Turbo.

When, earlier, Ricky had leapt out of his beloved, souped-up van, leaving the keys in the ignition and the door wide open, I thought at the time that it was a silly thing to do. Very silly. And I was right. Because in less time than it took for Iain-with-two-Is to remember that the ignition in those Saabs is located beside the handbrake, I was tearing across the yard with a faint '*Sorry, pal!*' and turning the key in Ricky's reason for living. If I moved very quickly, so went my thinking, I could park my best friend's van lengthways across the approach road, preventing Iain-with-two-Is escaping the station yard and deliver him into the grateful hands of the Nottinghamshire Constabulary, who clearly weren't up to the task.

'Robin, no!' I heard Ricky cry too late.

Of course, it's only after you've floored the accelerator and are already hurtling backwards faster than a jumbo down a runway that you realise rear visibility in small vans isn't very good. I'd totally forgotten about this. Just like I'd totally forgotten about Lionel. Ever since the first shriek of a police siren Fliss's father had been cowering deep among the hedgerows at the farthest edge of the station yard, in a wild corner between the end of the platform and the bridge that carried the railway over the main road. The six officers chasing about Oakerby station were not aware that Lionel even existed at this point, and probably thought that once they caught Iain-with-two-Is they'd have bagged the whole gang.

With the footbridge no longer an option for Lionel – it would've been impossible now to cross it without being seen or (more likely in his case) heard – and with police attention focused elsewhere, he instead decided to make a dash for freedom by way of the approach road. It wasn't the stupidest idea. He might even have got away. But like I said, rear visibility in small vans isn't very good. And as the van smoked blindly backwards in a haze of shredding rubber, all I heard, pinned to the steering-wheel, was the roar of the race-tuned engine and then an almighty bang as Lionel bounced off the back doors and landed ten feet away, gurgling like a punctured radiator.

I came round to find Sergeant Pollard's Granada glaring at me through the windscreen, flashing a disco as it blocked the approach road. Embedded in its jam-sandwich side was the black Saab, clouds fizzing from all angles of its crumpled nose. I couldn't see Ricky, rear visibility in small vans not being very good. But I could hear him. Everybody could hear him.

Twenty-five

1

'There's one blessing about severe concussion, Robin,' Vern said as Lionel was driven away in the ambulance. 'You've a few weeks at least before your father-in-law finds out it were you who ran over and nearly killed him.'

'Oh, thanks, Vern. And what's the blessing about fractured elbows, dislocated shoulders and legs broken in three places?'

'Well, it'll be even longer before he can come after you, won't it.'

'Bloody hell.'

Ricky sniggered. 'I think he lost a couple of teeth, as well.'

'Mr Priestley... Mr Manvers...' a young officer called, waving us over to join the small, handcuffed party led by Sergeant Pollard.

'I'll go and see if I can straighten out my van,' Ricky said, narrowing his eyes. 'Second time he's crashed it, you wait till I see your MG.'

'Vern, Robin, I'd like you to join us for a tour of this lovely old building,' Sergeant Pollard said with that drawled sarcasm unique to coppers. 'During the course of which these gentlemen,' he sniffed, pursing his foxy 'tached lips at Honeywell, Parker and Iain-with-two-Is, 'will be telling us all about its fascinating history, and in particular the use it's been put to these past, what is it, ten, twelve months?' Naturally, Iain-with-two-Is was silent. But the other two who previously had been capable of speech now seemed to have lost that ability as well.

'We've all suffered a bump on the head and had our memories erased, have we?' Sergeant Pollard smiled. 'Very well.'

'This should be interesting,' Vern said against my ear as we followed the beam of Sergeant Pollard's torch into the woolly darkness of the building. Inside, the station had been gutted and apart from the odd wall or small-windowed partition there remained nothing of the old offices, waiting rooms or anything of that sort. It had that unsettling air of being both enormous and claustrophobic at the same time, like you got in some Peak District caverns, where all of a sudden you felt trapped by sheer blank space. One good thing about darkness, though, it made it a lot easier to avoid catching Mr Honeywell's eye, wondering what he thought Vern and I had to do with all this.

'*Hmm*,' Vern said when Sergeant Pollard brought us to a halt. '*Hmm*.'

I'm not sure what Vern had been expecting, but I knew from the way he said, '*Hmm*', and then said it again for twice as long, that it wasn't what we found. I was disappointed, too, and said, '*Hmm*', to prove it. Because far from uncovering the centre of operations for some vast criminal enterprise, endless gleaming rows of hot hatchbacks and high-powered saloons waiting to be delivered to the kind of buyers who asked no questions and gave no receipts, all that met our eyes when Sergeant Pollard flicked on a convenient floodlight was the blue Escort Cabriolet that had been rammed by a dustbin-lorry, slumped, lopsided and leaking, beside the jack on which it had been wheeled not two hours before. And alongside it, barely a copper's stride away, a pristine example of exactly the same car, its identical, undamaged, twin.

'Is that a light over there, Cameron?'

The young officer who'd invited us to join the tour stumbled over what sounded like a toolbox before flicking a switch and then, a few seconds later, another.

'Ah, well done, Cameron.'

'Sarge.'

About thirty feet away, half visible at the edge of the gloom, was parked an equally immaculate Sierra XR4x4, its shining black bodywork in such condition it would pass in any showroom for new. Encouraged by this, Sergeant Pollard strode off, scything his torch beam through the shadows, only to return almost immediately having found nothing but more shadows and a shaft of young moonlight that had pierced a hole through the roof. As the sergeant marched back to the cabriolets I decided to stop breathing, remembering that the ton of dust motes kicked up by his size tens would all be throbbing with deadly asbestos.

With the lights on, we could see now that neither of the undamaged cars wore number plates. Also, that the pristine cabriolet was in fact missing all its windows (hard to tell on a cabriolet, if they're wound down). Sergeant Pollard flicked his torch beam across an adjacent wall until it was reflected back through the hollow station from two dozen or more different angles. He then stepped across to the wrecked cabriolet and tapped the windscreen three times with his wedding ring. 'Nice glass,' he said, twisting his lips at Honeywell, Parker and Iain-with-two-Is. 'Good as new. Unmarked.'

From a workbench positioned between the two cabriolets Constable Cameron picked up a Ford chassis plate, two small holes shining through the grime where the rivets had been drilled out. Sergeant Pollard lifted his chin and inhaled slowly, as if breathing in all he saw for later consideration. He obviously hadn't heard about the asbestos.

'And are those registration plates, Cameron?' he said, moving towards the young officer.

'Yes, Sarge.' The constable held up a pair of brand-new number plates. Plain. No garage logos. Same as always.

'Our place?' Vern said quietly from under the peak of his cap.

'I brought them up last night,' I said, feeling sure Honeywell must be looking at me. I shuffled to the other side of Vern, but then Sergeant Pollard was looking at me.

'Do you recognise these number plates, son,' he said sternly. 'It's Robin, isn't it?'

I found myself turning to look at Honeywell, Parker and Iain-with-two-Is. I couldn't help it. But thankfully, rather than glaring hatred in my direction, they were all busily staring at their shoes – or *shoe*, in Honeywell's case, his left one having last been seen spinning across the goods yard into the thistles.

'Tell him, then,' Vern nudged.

'Yes,' I said. 'I had them made up yesterday, at work. Stonebridge Motor Company. Then I dropped them off last night.'

'Dropped them off?'

'With Lionel,' I said, indicating a vague direction with my thumb. Sergeant Pollard twitched his moustache and looked to Vern to translate.

'Chap he ran over,' Vern said helpfully.

'Is that something you do often, Robin? I don't mean run chaps over – have number plates made for Lionel?'

'Fairly often,' I said. 'He orders a lot for the horseboxes. And trailers.'

'Of course,' Sergeant Pollard agreed. 'And just the one set was it, yesterday? One set of number plates, one front, one rear?'

'No. He had two sets, yesterday.'

The interior light came on in the black Sierra, illuminating Constable Cameron as he leaned in to take something off the passenger seat. 'Is this the other set by any chance?'

'Yes,' I nodded. 'That's them.'

Putting the new plates back inside the Sierra, Constable Cameron slammed the door before crouching in the darkness to pick up another plate, yellow and grubby, from off the floor. 'I'll radio this one through to DVLC, Sarge. A fiver it's the original.'

'Don't bother, Cameron. I know that number,' Sergeant Pollard said, turning to Honeywell and shaking his head. 'I know it very well. Your friends at the golf club and the Rotary and the rest must've thought you were doing them all a jolly good turn when you personally supplied their cars, didn't they, Mr Honeywell? Super deals for the favoured few? What will your friends say tomorrow, I wonder?'

By the time we re-emerged onto the platform it was almost dark and the hedgerows at the far end of the station yard, where Lionel had hidden, glowed orange, like wild lampshades for the streetlights below.

'Cameron, if you'd secure the premises till the wagons get here,' said Sergeant Pollard, 'I'll get these gentlemen on their way. Perhaps a bit of police station hospitality will help the flow of conversation.'

'Officer,' I heard Vern say, stepping towards Constable Cameron as the steel panels began to make their familiar squeal and scrape across the concrete. 'Before you lock up, can I just borrow your torch for two seconds?'

It was more like two minutes, and the rest of us waited on the platform hearing Vern's scampering footsteps echo from one ghostly quarter of the station to the next before he reappeared, rubbing his chin with irritable fingers. 'It was a long shot,' he said. 'But I thought...'

'Yes...' Sergeant Pollard sighed, sucking his gingerbread moustache. 'I hoped it might have been here as well, Vern.'

As a coal train throbbed past, Honeywell, Parker and Iain-with-two-Is were being divided between the three police cars, a further indignity for Honeywell as he was forced to squeeze into the back of the tiny Vauxhall.

'I know for a fact one of those cars is stolen,' Sergeant Pollard went on, 'and I've little doubt about the other. If there are more, and I'm sure there are, we'll find them. Faced with a night in the cells, one of them will talk.'

I thought of another quip about Iain-with-two-Is but let it pass when Vern suddenly skipped towards a big stone at the edge of the platform and with a frustrated boot sent it clattering against the footbridge. My eyes hadn't climbed halfway up the steps before it hit me.

'Holy shit!'

'Pardon?' coughed Sergeant Pollard.

I don't know why I hadn't thought of it before. 'The car that hit Clay Clements near the fishing ponds,' I said, feeling my hands begin to shake. As Sergeant Pollard, Vern, Ricky and the three young coppers present turned expectantly towards me I thought I might be sick on my boots. And theirs. 'The white car...'

'Yes?' encouraged Sergeant Pollard. 'What about it, Robin?'

'I know where it is,' I said, looking at Vern and swallowing hard. 'I think I know where it is.'

2

Instead of attaching heavy chains to the back of the patrol cars and tearing the green shutters from their moorings, like I'd hoped, Sergeant Pollard, taking the keys from Iain-with-two-Is, let himself in through the side door, deactivated the alarm and just pressed a button. Then the shutters ratcheted slowly up. Very slowly. I looked at Vern and thought I might be sick again. The overhead lights flickered on. What if I was wrong? What if it wasn't there?

But it was there. The big twin-axled horsebox with the sticking brakes, raised high on the hydraulic ramp, its roof still brushing the fluorescent tubes as it had been the night before when I came to fetch Fliss. My mouth was too dry to swallow.

Sergeant Pollard ducked beneath the ramp, made for the control-box at its far post. 'Vern, would you mind?' he said, flapping a baffled hand. With a solid KER-THUNK the ramp began to drone its agonising descent. From where we gathered in the doorway I could see Iain-with-two-Is slouched, handcuffed, between two big coppers. He looked across with what seemed like a very uncharacteristic smirk before returning to his boots. It's empty, I said to myself, it's bloody empty.

'John, you take the towing-bracket with me,' Sergeant Pollard ordered. 'Cameron, Robbie, Jenny, Vern, the rest of you, if you wouldn't mind, grab hold wherever you can.'

With Vern and me at the rear, flanking the WPC, and the two young coppers along the side-ribs, we very slowly heaved the horsebox off the ramp and into the pool of pale light that spilled out from the workshop.

'Some weight to these things, Sarge,' the older policeman, John, said, pushing his hands into the small of his back.

'The brakes are catching.' I turned, stunned, to the source of this unfamiliar voice.

'So, you can speak, then?' Sergeant Pollard said, beating me to it. 'Anything you'd like to say now, Iain, before we go any further? No? What about your good friends?' But Parker and the uni-loafered Honeywell, cuffed either side the biggest policeman, looked anywhere but at the focus of all our attentions.

Very calmly now, Sergeant Pollard and Constable Cameron, as if in rehearsed synchronisation, unfastened the latches securing the horsebox's tailgate and carefully lowered the ramp to the ground. A hushed chorus of sighs and murmurs started up as they fixed the little wooden gates in place before stepping back to join in the pats and nods of satisfaction, serious and solemn coppers' expressions of a good day's work from a bad situation and all that.

I put my hand on Vern's shoulder and leaned against him, numb with relief more than surprise. It was a snug fit inside the horsebox, but it was in there, all right, a white Ford Escort XR3i.

'Well,' Vern said.

'Yes,' I replied.

Though clearly a new car, it was in far from new condition. Its nearside headlamp was smashed and the orange indicator lens missing altogether. A deep crease buckled the front wing and there was a much bigger depression near the centre of the bonnet where something had obviously smashed into it with great force before hitting the top corner of the windscreen, from where a storm of forked lightning flashed across the tinted glass. A spotlight and part of the front number plate were also missing, but from the section that remained hanging from its screw, beginning **E761**, it was almost certainly Ben Evelyn the barber's car, stolen from the bingo car park opposite his shop.

'It must have been going hell of a speed,' Vern said once the coppers had seen enough. After kneeling to look under the car he blew out his cheeks and scratched the bristles on the back of his head. 'Poor sod.'

I agreed, picturing for some reason neither Clay, nor the accident, but Jason Wakeling – Billy Eyesore – praying for a fish and wondering where his pal had got to. 'I hope he was so off his nut he didn't feel anything.'

'*Hmm*. He was right about the car, though, Robin – being white.'

Close up, one of the Escort's front tyres was flat and the wheel damaged where it had struck the kerb. There was also a strong smell of anti-freeze from the dark continents which formed on the wooden floorboards beneath its front bumper. A corpse car then, although, lacking the visceral gore he'd predicted, one unlikely to arouse Ken to narrative fruition.

'Looks like Robin's been driving,' Ricky said, misjudging the mood rather as he pushed between our shoulders. 'What's that on the windscreen wiper?'

The tailgate shook beneath Sergeant Pollard. 'Well spotted, son,' he said, bracing himself against the horsebox roof as he leaned over the crumpled bonnet. A small piece of patterned fabric, red with black, white and blue stripes, roughly diamond-shaped and about the size of a matchbox. 'I'll have Forensics take a look. It might be –'

'Bondage trousers,' I interrupted as the sergeant studied the scrap in his hand.

'*Bondage* trousers?'

'The night he was run over, Clay was wearing his new ones – they were tartan.'

Sergeant Pollard turned to Vern with a raised eyebrow. 'Can't say I'm very up on modern fashions.'

'Neither was Clay,' I said.

3

'She's at the hospital, Robin,' Grandma Dot said, looking very flustered as she ushered me in through her french windows. 'She went with Ruth, about an hour ago. Lionel's had a terrible accident. He's been run over by a car.'

'It was a van, actually,' I almost corrected her. I didn't, of course. I didn't know what to say. I just nodded and sighed, 'Oh dear, poor Lionel.'

'Will you be going through to see them, duck, or have you time for a cup of tea?'

Pleasantly Disturbed • 239

I nodded again. 'I'll make it, Dot,' I said. 'You sit down.'

After Vern had dropped me beside the MG, I'd raced from the stables straight to Windmill Way, declining the invitation to join him and Ricky for a cold meat supper, saying I had to see Fliss. Vern understood, naturally. But so wrapped up in the chaos of events since that phone call from Kevin late afternoon, the thought that Fliss might not be here waiting for me now that it was all over had never once occurred to me. And now as I smiled through Dot's diverting granny talk, about bunions, *Bergerac* and bird feeders, I felt suddenly very cold, the idea of Fliss all gorgeous and loving and tearful at Lionel's bedside doing nothing at all to warm me. I know I'd nearly killed him, but still, for the second time in as many days I couldn't help wondering just who the hell her father thought he was, muscling in on her affections.

'Drive carefully, Robin, won't you?' Grandma Dot said, quite innocently, giving my hand a squeeze before I cut across the bowling-green lawn and onto the path that ran round the back of the house. There were a lot of stars in the sky again, and a bright moon lit up the dining room window like a big television screen on which the picture had frozen. After making sure Grandma Dot had gone back inside I stood awhile, gazing in through the glass at the silent piano.

Epilogue

I Wish You Were Here

1

It has long been my ritual on Saturday mornings, while the rest of the house is still sleeping, to wander along the narrow lane into the village, accompanied only by church bells and birdsong, to gather the necessaries for a cooked breakfast. I feel like John Betjeman. Or a burglar. And apart from when I've had to go away for work, or we've been on holiday, I honestly can't remember the last time I didn't do this. I look forward to my little excursion all week.

Partly this is because I've never been one for sleeping-in, even before the kids arrived. But mainly it's that I still find it a huge thrill each time to walk away from the cottage, just so I'll then be able to walk back a little while later and admire it, in quiet solitude, as if I were seeing it again for the very first time.

You see, slowly crumbling around us though it is, I've never quite been able to believe that it's my home - or rather, I should say, *our* home. And often when I've been away, I've woken up in strange beds and cold sweats convinced that when I returned it would no longer be here. I don't mean demolished, or annexed by welly wearing Londoners, I mean gone completely, that it never actually existed at all. I have photographs, of course, and a phone that lets me see the pale-yellow gates and wonky, paint-flaking front door from the other side of the world, but I don't trust them. As with my wife and my children, I can only ever feel truly safe, and that they are truly safe, when I am here and able to touch them.

The cottage has changed little since Fliss and I first came to visit Alastair and Charlotte at Easter, thirty years ago. In the years that followed I returned many times, nearly always to find Charlotte painting in the conservatory and Alastair at the bookshop, the walk back from where usually involving a pocketful of paperbacks and a detour via the Rose and Crown. Charlotte was ill for only a few weeks before she died towards the end of 2009. Alastair, who'd always worshipped her, never quite recovered and followed a year later, shortly after having arranged with Tina for a successful exhibition of Charlotte's paintings to be put on at a smart gallery in Norwich. They were neither of them very old, still in their sixties, but as Alastair said the last time I saw him, in hospital, they had both seen plenty of life, much of it good, so could hardly complain.

I drove Mam down from Stonebridge. She brought grapes and a copy of *Steam World* magazine. We'd not been there long, and conversation was hardly flowing when, just as he'd done when he gave me his old runabout MG, Alastair reached into his bedside locker and tossed me the keys to the cottage.

'You can't, Alastair,' I said, staring at the mismatch bunch in my hand. 'No, no. It's too much.'

'We wanted you to have it, Robin,' Alastair said, his eyes drifting to a steaming centrefold express. 'I'll see your mother right and your sister. My good lady had a bob or two put away. Anyway, you won't be thanking me when you see the state of the garden, I've let it go a bit lately.'

Alastair and Charlotte both adored Fliss as much as she adored them, and after that first weekend I knew that if she were ever to visit them alone I should hardly be missed, unlike if it were the other way round. Charlotte of course had made a particularly deep impression on Fliss. And the night after the big showdown at Oakerby station, among all the chaos and confusion with Giles Honeywell, of finding the car that killed Clay Clements and me reversing over her father so that for weeks afterwards half his body was cocooned in plaster, the thing she seemed genuinely most worried about was that if she pulled out of appearing on *Show Me The Stars* she'd be letting down Charlotte.

'How would you be letting down Charlotte?' I asked as we sat pillow-propped against my headboard, gloriously soundtracked by Simple Minds' *New Gold Dream* LP. Having telephoned several times that morning and afternoon from work and got no answer, I'd been surprised to find her waiting in our front room, sipping tea with Mam and talking about *Jewel in The Crown* and life at the paper shop.

'When we went to stay, Charlotte said that it didn't matter what kind of music you play or where you play it, just so long as you know why you're playing it, and who you're playing it for. Most of all, she said you have to love the place where your music comes from.'

I narrowed my eyes. 'She didn't mean the record shop?'

'You know she didn't, idiot.' Fliss took my hand and held it to her breast. 'Where it comes from in here.'

'*Mmm*. And, er, do you love where your music comes from?' I said, in no hurry to remove my hand from this warm, magical place.

'I think so,' she nodded. 'Yes, I think I do, now.'

'That's great, Fliss,' I said. 'That's really great. But does that mean, then, that you are, or you aren't going to appear on *Show Me The Stars*?'

Fliss moved my hand up to her lips and kissed its back. Then she very slowly shook her head. 'Oh, Robin, I don't know. How can I, now, after what's happened?'

2

Perhaps not surprisingly, her uncle, the garage's owner, having been arrested the night before, Gillian didn't come in that Friday morning. My first reaction was one of relief, because it meant I'd get to spend my last day in the parts department with Sheila, just the two of us, and be able to fill her in about Honeywell's criminal shenanigans with far more spectacular detail than if Gillian had been there to hear me. But as it turned out, I'd barely stirred the first teapot of the day when Vern's oil jug thundered restlessly at the workshop counter.

'Robin! Robin, where are you?'

'What happened to '*Shop*!'?' I said, wondering why the urgency.

'She's been arrested, your young woman.'

'What?'

'Young woman who's been helping you in here, his niece – Gillian. They picked her up this morning.'

Later, about an hour after lunch, Sergeant Pollard invited Vern and me through to Honeywell's office where, perhaps hoping to appear a bit less copper-like and failing, he sat astride a corner of the desk, rolling a tyre-shaped paperweight between his hands and occasionally tossing it, for emphasis, into the air before catching it.

'Quite a talent, has Miss Delaney,' the sergeant said, before going on to explain, unlikely as it seemed, that Gillian, in her spare time, was a highly accomplished car thief who along with Iain-with-two-Is was believed responsible for stealing upwards of sixty cars, mostly high-powered Fords and many, though not all, having been either sold or serviced by Stonebridge Motor Company. I sat – half-swallowed by the horrible sofa – utterly stunned, more utterly than I should have been, knowing from experience what untrustworthy hands she had.

'I wouldn't have had Gillian down as the sort to pinch anything,' Vern said naively. 'Would you, Robin?'

'Well, not cars,' I replied, wondering how she'd manage in prison.

Sergeant Pollard gave a solemn nod.

'Many of these stolen vehicles having been either supplied or serviced by Stonebridge Motor Company,' he continued, 'Mr Honeywell had unrestricted access to files containing the home and sometimes workplace addresses of the owners, as well as every detail regarding their vehicle's age, mileage and specification. So once an 'order' for a particular model had been placed by one of his numerous shady clients, it had then been a simple job for him to match those requirements to any identical models on the garage's customer database. Then, after covertly establishing where and when a suitable vehicle was most often left unattended – and this is the clever part, I have to say,' Sergeant Pollard said, licking his moustache, 'using the vehicle's unique key number – also kept on file – Mr Honeywell would have a duplicate key made, which the thieves were then able to use to unlock and drive away the vehicles, often in broad daylight, in lightning-quick time and without causing any damage likely to impact the vehicle's onward value.'

'Well, well,' said Vern as the paperweight went up. 'So that's how they did it.'

'Very simple, really, Vern,' Sergeant Pollard said. 'Though only possible, of course, if you have both access to the key codes and the facilities to produce the duplicate keys.'

I had already explained how I'd personally cut several keys for Honeywell, for his own car, his wife's, and his daughter-in-law's, as well as others for his many friends and neighbours. Yet I still found myself sweating against the caramel leather when the topic came up again. 'I wish I'd never shown her how to use that key machine.'

'You didn't, Robin.'

'I *did*.'

'When questioned this morning, Miss Delaney said her uncle had taught her how to operate the key-cutting machine, and some while before she first came to work here at the garage. Mr Honeywell often worked beyond normal business hours, I gather, and apparently it was while waiting for her lift home that Miss Delaney would practise her key cutting technique.'

'I thought she learned quickly,' I said, blotting out visions of her straining smock. 'And it explains how we got through so many blanks.'

'What about the red car, Tony, that went off the forecourt?' Vern said. 'Honeywell reckoned it was travellers, but –'

'A convenient distraction. The car was, you'll remember, found close to the fairground site, but it had been placed there purposely by Miss Delaney, on the instructions of Mr Honeywell, after Mr Carpenter – Iain – had noticed two figures taking a sudden keen interest in the area around the station at Oakerby.' Vern gave me a sly wink, though this was hardly a recommendation of our skills in covert investigation.

'I knew there was something funny about that one. None of the other cars turned up, and when that one did, with no damage to the locks or ignition...'

'Mr Honeywell rather tripped over his own ingenuity there, Vern,' said Sergeant Pollard. 'Presumably why he then pointed us towards the young salesman, er...'

'Andrew,' I said helpfully.

'Thank you. Andrew had access to the keys and was that evening responsible for securing the forecourt barriers. Another convenient distraction, and an effective one, if only temporary. As for the accident-damaged vehicles...'

I'd been wondering about these.

'As far as we've been able to establish, only a handful of these were ever transported to Oakerby station. And as Robin overheard in an exchange between the arrested parties, this was in a rare few instances where a stolen vehicle's windows were found to be etched with either its registration or chassis number – Mr Honeywell, with typical propriety, ensuring that any stolen vehicle passing through his hands should do so with no trace of his fingerprints.

'In most cases, though, it was not the damaged vehicles he wanted, only their identities. Dozens of these donor cars it seems were bought for near scrap value and before they'd been declared written-off, so that their identities could then be transferred to the immaculate examples stolen to order by the gang. To all intents and purposes these "damaged" vehicles would then appear to have been repaired to such high standard any subsequent owner would be unlikely to have even the slightest cause for suspicion. Why would they? It is, after all, a pristine vehicle that's never been involved in an accident. Meanwhile the accident-damaged donor is scrapped, the stolen car's identity lost and the vehicle itself never found.'

'Vanished,' said Vern.

'Yet still driving about,' I added, my mind knotting with the puzzle.

'Once delivered, they were no longer Mr Honeywell's concern. His clients knew what they were getting. The motivation for the thefts, it seems, was simply good business. A stolen vehicle is untraced, after a period the insurance pays out, and your loyal Stonebridge Motor Company customer...'

'Comes to buy another car,' said Vern, shaking his head. 'The crafty bugger.'

Sergeant Pollard paused and put down his paperweight to take the first steaming mug from the tray. 'Thank you, Sheila, that's very kind, you really shouldn't have gone to the trouble.'

'Don't be silly now, Tony. I was getting thirsty. Robin and I always have one about this time, don't we lovey?'

I smiled. 'Thanks, Sheila.'

'The stolen vehicles,' the sergeant went on when the door had closed, 'as you both suspected, were, immediately after being taken, usually stored overnight at the station, where they were fitted with new number and chassis plates by Mr Carpenter before delivery to clients, many miles distant, by Mr Carpenter and Miss Delaney and, on occasion, most fortunately for us, by yourself, Robin, and your colleague Ricky.'

'The Sierra and Escort Cabriolet were going to Doncaster tonight.'

'They still are,' Sergeant Pollard said slyly over the top of his mug. 'Along with two of my officers.'

'Seems like a complicated operation,' Vern said. 'You say Honeywell had dozens more of these, er, identities?'

'There was a file full of logbooks in this drawer. Mr Honeywell hasn't been especially cooperative so far, but from what the others have said it appears there may also be a connection within the motor insurance business, who informed them of garages where potential donor vehicles lay awaiting assessment, and perhaps also assisted in their purchase. There is the question, you see, of how these vehicles, bought so cheaply – as write-offs, effectively – were then somehow kept off the insurance claims register in order to maximise their resale value – but as I say, we've no solid evidence regarding this at present, though we'll of course keep digging.'

Sergeant Pollard's mention of insurance had set a discomforting thought fluttering about the back of my mind, but for the moment I didn't feel that it was one I wanted to catch hold of.

'Which brings us to your late friend Clayton Clements.'

'He wasn't really –' I shook my head. 'Sorry, Sergeant.'

'As Clayton told Jason Wakeling at the hospital shortly before he, er, died, the driver of the car which struck him on the Oakerby road – a white Ford Escort XR3i, reported stolen by Ben Evelyn – was indeed a woman. The woman in question being, as we now know, Gillian Delaney.'

There was a cold silence as Sergeant Pollard turned pointedly to put his mug down, beside the paperweight, on Honeywell's desk.

'Stealing dozens of vehicles is a very serious crime,' he resumed, standing up. 'But causing the death of a pedestrian through reckless and uninsured driving in one of those stolen vehicles...' The sergeant seemed to regret not having his paperweight for this bit, so instead had a good suck on his moustache. 'Whether Miss Delaney and her uncle get what they deserve, I suppose we shall see in due course. Has many friends in high places, does Giles Honeywell. At least he did until he started pinching their cars.'

'One thing I meant to ask, Tony,' Vern said as I helped him out of the horrible sofa. 'Inside the station, you said you recognised that black Sierra.'

'Yes. That car belongs to our Chief Inspector. Only had it three weeks. He and Giles are old golfing pals. The smart club out near Worksop, not that place up the road with fifteen holes.'

'How did he take having his car pinched, your Chief Inspector?'

'As you'd expect, he was bloody furious.'

'Good,' said Vern clapping me on the shoulder. 'Good.'

As the two of us walked Sergeant Pollard across the yard to his police car, he turned slowly to Vern and said, 'So what was it that first gave you the idea Giles Honeywell might be involved in all this?'

Vern drew in his chin, and after a second or two foraging in the breast pocket of his overalls held out an oily hand. In his palm lay a very small round silver badge decorated with a blue-and-green insignia.

'Betty found this one night, on the station platform. I knew I'd seen it somewhere before, but until Robin and I sat down together to go through our notes I couldn't for the life of me think where.'

'Oh yes. I certainly know what that is. Must have fallen out of the buttonhole of somebody's suit jacket,' Sergeant Pollard said, pursing his lips in foxy satisfaction. 'Mind if I borrow it, Vern?'

'It's no good to me.'

Exactly a week later, at three o'clock on Friday afternoon, the staff gathered in the showroom to be informed by a beaming Sheila that the garage was, with immediate effect, under new management. As she announced this, and half expecting her to add that she and her husband had bought the place, I finally caught hold of that fluttering thought about insiders in the insurance business. I swallowed hard and quickly let it go again as Sheila turned and began to move towards where I was standing.

'But not only do we have a new owner,' she said, sounding beautifully Welsh, 'we also have a new name. From now on we shall all be the very proud employees – I know I will – of Priestley Motors (Stonebridge) Limited. Proprietor, mister Vernon Priestley.'

There were cheers and a round of applause as I turned to where Vern, until Sheila had pointed him out, had been hovering shyly behind me. I took my turn with Ricky, Keith and Darren to gather him in my arms and squeeze him tight, forgetting that while as usual Vern was filthy, caked in oil and antifreeze, I was wearing my brand-new suit.

3

As I crunch to the back door of the cottage the sound of Fliss at the piano comes tinkling through the open window to meet me, just like it did in 1988 when I returned, tipsy, from the bookshop with Alastair. It is one of her very earliest compositions, one I only discovered she'd recorded at the end of the tape of her performing that haunting version of *Running Up That Hill* five months after the events at Oakerby station that were to change both our lives. It's a beautiful piece of music, sparse and delicate, and seemed on that first hearing all those years ago to float out of the speakers and hover above my bed, teasing my heart up into its aching melody. I remember feeling that if I were to even blink my eyes I might scare it away. Fragile. A tune on butterfly wings. And then comes that voice...

You'll know the song I'm talking about, or rather the song it became, the version that burbles from the kitchen radio as I set the table for breakfast. *'Just hold on tight and drive us safely through the rain'*. There was a period in the late nineties when for about eighteen months you could hardly escape it, radio, television, the soundtracks of several of-the-moment films, though very few had seemed to want to. Same with its only slightly less successful follow-up. Fliss's music suddenly was everywhere. But not Fliss. Just as she'd always done since the start of her career, as she continues to do to this day, Fliss herself managed to maintain a similar enigmatic privacy to that of her life-long idol.

Fliss has been far more prolific than Kate Bush, of course. But – as she reminded readers in a rare interview in *Mojo* magazine last year – her other great inspiration is Prince, so she still has a very long way to go before she overtakes him. Though now approaching fifty, I could still hear her girlish laughter rising from the page, as I could her follow-up comment that she would gladly die tomorrow to have but half the talent her two heroes had in their little toes. In anyone else this might seem like false modesty.

Although her last-but-one album (she's released fourteen to date, including live and compilations) was the first to peak outside the UK Top Twenty, Fliss and her work have been enjoying something of a critical rebirth, due in part to her being regularly cited as a major influence by the sort of exciting young artist who breeds alpacas and gets nominated for the Mercury Prize. As for performing on television, a quick internet search will show she's done almost nothing in twenty years, apart from *Later... with Jools Holland*, from whom she received much praise and encouragement on the release of her debut record in 1994, and who remains to this day one of Fliss's few close friends in showbusiness.

4

On Sunday, ten days after I almost fatally reversed over her father, Fliss invited me up to the stables. I was hardly out of the MG before she threw herself into my arms, burying her face in my shoulder and holding me very tightly for what seemed a blissful if ominous age. On doctor's orders, she told me, the police had still not been able to question Lionel, who, though heavily sedated, remained in a stable condition.

Considering our location, it took a lot for me to resist that opportunity, believe me.

'Robin, I want you,' Fliss snuffled against my freshly washed *Tour Du Monde* '84 T-shirt.

'You've got me,' I said. 'I'm all yours.'

'No, I mean I *want* you.'

And pressing her lips softly against mine, she kissed me. And kissed me. And kissed me.

Then we fetched the horses.

Earlier in the week I'd telephoned Millie at the TV studios to say that Fliss's father was in hospital following a terrible car accident.

'Oh my god, Robin, I hope he's okay,' Millie said. 'That's awful. Please send Fliss my love, won't you? There are so many idiots on the road these days.'

I agreed and said that, regrettably, in the circumstances, Fliss wouldn't feel up to taking part in the upcoming series of *Show Me The Stars*, but perhaps next time. Straight away I saw what a huge relief it was for Fliss to be free from it, this thing which for months had been torture for her, that she felt she should do yet wished could also be made to just disappear. Well now it had. Though I doubt this was the way she ideally would have chosen.

There were other things, too, that Fliss had been putting off. Namely my lusty quest to make the unthinkable not only thinkable but actually do-able. Yet the closer we'd grown, frustrating as it sometimes was, the more I'd been prepared to wait. We would know when the time was right, Fliss said. Still, whenever I thought about it, which was often, I expected my virginity would almost certainly be lost in Fliss's bed, to Prince, who'd already done so much to encourage our under-duvet activities. (I mean, of course, that I'd lose my virginity in Fliss's bed while listening to Prince's music, not that I'd be deflowered by the great man himself, although that would certainly have added a memorable and most unexpected twist to this story.)

The reality, though, was quite different. And when that Sunday afternoon we did finally go all the way, it was beneath a big fat-bellied oak deep in Sherwood Forest, accompanied by no more than a whispering breeze and the occasional (thankfully distant) snorts of Mungo and Bertie. It was every bit as tender and beautiful as I knew it would be, and a rare moment in my life up to that point when I stopped wishing I was someone or somewhere else. I didn't even want to be Jim Kerr. It felt wonderful to be me. It felt wonderful to be with Fliss.

'I love you, Robin,' she said.

'I love you too, Fliss.'

'I know,' she smiled with tears in her eyes.

Afterwards we lay awhile saying nothing while knowing nothing said everything before we galloped – or as close as I was able – back through the forest and along the sun-striped bridleways to the stables. In the yard, after we'd put the horses away, Fliss suddenly became very upset, and holding me tighter even than she'd done beneath the oaks told me that as soon as her father was discharged from hospital the family, including Grandma Dot, would be spending the summer at the villa of one of Lionel's friends, in Spain, and then in September she would, if offered a place, be going away to university to study music. She said her mum, Ruth, thought they would probably have to sell Markley Hall Equestrian and that Lionel would be lucky not to go to prison.

Upset her, just once, and I shall take hold of you and hammer you into the ground.

These were the words Lionel had used the first time he ever set eyes on me. And now here we were, barely eight months later, with his daughter upset and crying inconsolably into my shoulder because of the greedy, selfish things he had done. Admittedly, my running over him hadn't exactly improved the situation, but that would never have happened if Lionel had kept better company.

5

I stuck around for nearly eighteen months at Vern's new and improved Priestley Motors, selling enough new and used cars to buy a Fender Precision bass that scraped me into a band with three achingly unkempt but well-to-do Smiths and REM nuts who were studying either English or Philosophy at Birmingham University. They were all pretty good musicians, leagues ahead of me, and we gelled from the start, but it very quickly became clear that if we were ever to perform anywhere beyond their Brixton squat-themed kitchen we would need to practise far more frequently than the once a week our present geographies allowed. I took the hint, and before they had chance to replace me moved to the bright lights of Digbeth.

Within a year all three of them had dropped out, much to their parents' shame, and in just a little over two more we were sharing a small flat in South Kensington, splashing out on gear of the playable, wearable and ingestible sorts and charging it all to our record company's expense account. It all seemed too easy then, and even more so looking back, and for as long as it lasted it was, for me at least, mostly nothing but fun and adventure all the cliched rock and roll way. What I remember of it.

For five-and-a-bit years we seemed to be on a continuous tour of Britain and Europe, opening for one pouting /grinning/scowling guitar band after another, many you'll certainly have heard of – some are still going – others that were forgotten before the Britpop bubble had even been blown, let alone burst. We played all the big festivals, two-thirds down the bill, and headlined many of the cooler, smaller, emptier venues in our own right. We got played on the radio. We sold some records. We were good. Good when what we wanted to be was the best. We wanted to be The Smiths. We wanted to be REM. *I* wanted to be Simple Minds.

It came to a natural end, as most bands do, unravelling gradually, invisibly, over time, until that one rehearsal where you all suddenly realise that whatever it was that first bound you together has gone. And while the band fulfilled many of my long-held fantasies about being on stage, performing loud music to vast and sometimes adoring crowds, I won't pretend that it didn't hit me like a dead pet when the time came to face the fact that I might never actually become the god-like charisma fountain of a frontman, heir to Jim Kerr, that I'd always known I was born to be.

I took some comfort in that one of the things I loved most about Simple Minds' music, apart from Jim Kerr's voice and leaping, sweeping stage prowess, was Derek Forbes's pounding, melodic basslines. Having mastered a pale imitation of his genius proficiently enough to just about get away with it, I was able, when it was all over, to set up a small studio with Steve, the band's far more talented guitarist and songwriter, creating incidental music for low-budget films and the occasional soundscape for the theatre productions and gallery openings of our sophisticated new friends.

We scored a couple of half decent romantic comedies and the theme for a cartoon that was too rude to air, but these days it's mostly adverts and music for TV shows. Not always the most inspiring, and not at all rock and roll, but, you know, I've done all that, and as long as somebody wants to pay me silly amounts of money for making music, which I still love to do, I'll be very happy to keep on making it. It is, as they say, better than working for a living.

6

A month after Fliss started university I was given my first company car, and unbeknownst to Lionel and Ruth, who'd decided it would be best for all concerned if Fliss put every aspect of her old life, especially me, firmly behind her, I would drive up and spend my days and weekends off with her in Durham.

It wasn't quite like old times again, but it was still us, just hanging out, enjoying her piano, or spending time under her duvet listening to some records. I loved her and I was no longer afraid to say so. But when I moved to Birmingham a year later, and then to London with the band, her own career was slowly beginning to take shape, and with her debut album four years in the making, Fliss soon had little time for anything else, not even her beloved horse, Mungo, who'd been relocated, along with Ruth and Grandma Dot, to North Yorkshire by the time Lionel was able to move again without the aid of a wheelchair or crutches – the extent of his injuries, incidentally, having spared him a jail sentence.

And then... well you know how it is with young love. You change, you grow up, you no longer want the same things or to be in the same place and suddenly, before you know it, it's the band all over again and whatever it was that first bound you together is no more.

But we stayed in touch, and wherever in the world we'd happen to find ourselves one would always be reminded of the other enough to write or pick up the phone.

I once called Fliss from a phonebooth outside Prince's Paisley Park studios in Minneapolis. On my 25th birthday I received a restaurant napkin signed by Bruce Hornsby and every member of The Range. We sent each other postcards from Berlin a day apart, only discovering our visits to the city had coincided after we'd both returned home. Even after Fliss married the producer of her third album I'd still be sent tickets to her concerts and invited backstage after the show. If you've ever seen her perform you will find it hard, perhaps impossible, to believe that this could be the same shy, reluctant performer that I remember her being at eighteen. On stage Fliss is every bit as wild and captivating as the voice you hear on her records. There is no doubt about who she is playing her music for or that she loves the place where it comes from.

Fliss's marriage failed when she was at the peak of her commercial success, following those two huge international hits and her epic take on Tears For Fears' *Start Of The Breakdown* which featured, two years later, on the soundtrack to the latest Hollywood vampire movie and went to number one in thirteen countries. Typically, Fliss even managed to divorce quietly, and I only heard about it through a friend who'd worked with her now ex-husband and ex-producer. She rang me a month later from some raw Scottish Isle – Jura, I think it was – where she'd gone to 'breathe, write and, you know, think good thoughts.' She sounded small and alone, which is perhaps what she needed to be just then, but as I held the phone tight against my ear all I wanted to do was... Anyway, by then I was living with Millie, in Nottingham, where after quitting Manchester and television she'd decided, after all, to follow her father and big brother Winston into Medicine.

Although Fliss hadn't yet left for Spain at that point, things being the way they were she could hardly sneak away to London with me for the Nelson Mandela 70th Birthday concert. I went instead with Ricky, and at Wembley Stadium on 11th June 1988 I met up again with Millie. (Simple Minds were mind-blowing, by the way, though I could have done with them playing an hour longer.) It was all very casual at first. We remained just good friends for several years before the occasional gig or afternoon at the cinema led to restaurant meals and weekends spent in country hotels or at each other's places. And it wasn't until much later, early '93, that we moved in together. We had a lot of fun, as we knew we would. Millie enjoyed me being in a band because she loved the music and knew it was what kept me alive. And also, being so intensely focused on her studies (Psychiatry) was probably glad when it took me away for weeks and months at a time, either on tour or in the studio. Millie liked her space as much as I did.

We lived near Millie's parents, Laura and Samuel, who I loved very much and who always treated me, in a good way, like a stray the family had taken in rather than as a serious prospect for their daughter. We were happy together. But I think we both knew the arrangement was always going to be temporary. It was if we were each doing the other a favour by being there, and for as long as that was what we both needed, were glad to do so.

I moved out after four years, but Millie and I remain the closest of friends. It's no coincidence our eldest daughter was born with the same name.

7

At the end of the nineties, when the studio was just about breaking even, Steve and I landed a commission to do the music for a couple of mental budget cinema ads, one for a Swedish car maker and another for a Middle Eastern airline. We thought it must be a mistake and expected, even as we banked the cheques, that the agency would see we were a couple of chancers and demand their money back. But they didn't.

The director on both projects was one of those swaggering thin-necked post-Blair geezer-blokes, a genuine aristocrat with a fake cockney accent who'd recently won a wheelbarrowful of awards for a pop video that sent an ex-boyband singer's solo career rocketing. Though an arrogant arsehole the guy was undeniably talented, and for whatever reason he'd taken a shine to us, so in early December we received via his office matching stiff card invitations to an exclusive New Year's Eve party organised by one of the major record labels. It was the sort of bash where guests got designer goody bags on the way in and German limos on the way out and was to be held in an east London hotel famous for its overpriced cocktails and undernourished clientele.

To celebrate not only the last night of the year, but of the millennium the theme of the party, the silver-starred script announced, was to be 1999; though, hilariously, this didn't mean the focus of frivolities would be the outgoing twelve months, but pop legends of the decade in which the Prince hit *1999* was first released – the eighties. I didn't particularly want to go, and not just because the invitation stated fancy dress was compulsory. But Steve had recently become a first-time father and his wife, very generously, I thought, had insisted he make the most of a rare boys' night out.

He said it'd be a surprise, but I knew before he turned up on 31st December with lemon-yellow hair and carrying those loose cream slacks, snooker ref gloves and white side-laced shoes that Steve would, of course, be going as *Let's Dance* David Bowie. Once out of the Smiths and REM phase of our band he'd most of the time dressed like that, anyway, somewhere between amphetamine City boy and charity shop Chicago mobster. As for me, eighties pop legends-themed fancy dress party? Do you really need to ask?

The week before, in the dank, patchouli-oiled emporia of Covent Garden, I'd picked up a voluminous white shirt with billowing loose-cuffed sleeves that would go nicely with the fitted black-sequined waistcoat, wide plastic belt and rumpled suede pixie boots the shop assistant had forced upon me for two quid, saying although they were in lovely condition they'd been stinking the shop out since they were last fashionable. Being now almost thirty and a single man living in corrupting London, I thought my sister Cath might not react too well to me asking her to stick a pair of her best tights in the post, so to complete the outfit I swung by Top Shop and chose some heavy denier black schoolgirl leggings, thinking these would also offer better protection on a chill December evening than anything my sister kept in her drawers.

8

Having discovered at the bottom of my wardrobe, after twelve years and god knows how many house moves, a thistle-brooched Tam o' Shanter, I shimmied into the ballroom behind Steve's Bowie Down Under resplendent in my full Jim Kerr late-'85 Rotterdam ensemble. Greeted by a Marie Antoinette-frocked Elton John and cheekily G-stringed Pete Burns, we recognised more faces than we'd expected, which isn't easy in a room where there are a lot of famous pop stars dressed as a lot of other famous pop stars, and soon we were drifting in and out of conversational groups, separating for a while before coming back together like partners in a dance, though for a New Year's Eve party there was, so far, little actual dancing going on. What there was, however, and which I hadn't realised until four drinks in, was karaoke.

I've always hated karaoke, and for a moment as I scanned the crowd unsuccessfully for Steve's yellow plumage I contemplated having one more glass, two at most, and slipping away. But then suddenly there he was, up on the stage, white-gloved and brandishing a shiny Fender Stratocaster, his old school tie skewed loose between red braces as he gave it the full bronzed and perspiring Outback Bowie performance.

Always an irritatingly good singer and mover, Steve's

performance surpassed even his costume, and I was only wondering who I might be able to share this penetrating observation with when a soft voice at my shoulder said those exact words for me.

'Yes,' I agreed, 'Steve's amazing, a real superstar. And I –'

And I didn't finish that sentence, because as I turned with a big proud smile, tipsily thrilled at my friend's triumph, there, standing right beside me, in a black silky nightdress, was Susanna Hoffs of The Bangles. Not the real one, I shouldn't think, dressed as herself, but for a single bloke on New Year's Eve she was more than Susanna enough for it to count. A big step up from the *Smash Hits* picture I had stuck up on my bedroom wall at seventeen, put it that way.

'Are you having a good time, Jim?' Susanna asked, her fingers lightly roving across the front of my Rotterdam ensemble.

'Jim? I think you've...' I blinked at the reflection of the sequins on my waistcoat and, remembering who I was, made a comic grimace as I waved the empty glass in my hand. 'Yes thanks, Susanna, I'm having a wonderful time. I love your outfit,' I said, flirtatiously. 'Are all The Bangles here, or just the prettiest?'

It was corny, I know, but I meant it; she really was almost as pretty as the real Susanna Hoffs, and when she replied, she said... well, I didn't hear what she said, because as I lowered my ear to her lips, over her bare and delicious-smelling shoulder I saw a figure who had apparently been coming directly towards us now suddenly stop, turn, and quickly begin to walk away again. I snatched two glasses of champagne from a hovering tray, shoving one into each of the girl's beautiful hands. 'Please excuse me,' I said. And, just like that, I did the unthinkable to Susanna Hoffs – I walked away and left her standing beside the stage on her own.

I squeezed past a convoy of canapes and through what seemed like every face and figure from a whole decade of *Top of*

The Pops until I was within touching distance of a wincingly corseted wedding dress. 'Kate?' I called after the slender, half-veiled back. 'Kate Bush? Is that really you?'

'Oh my goodness...'

Kate Bush shook a headful of crimped black curls as she slowly turned round, hugging herself tight, like a Brontë sister gone on honeymoon without pyjamas.

'Of all the legends I should meet tonight.'

'I was about to say the same thing.' I swallowed, brushing aside a waiter as rudely as I had Susanna Hoffs. 'You look fantastic.'

'I think I went a bit heavy on the eyeliner. But hey, gotta hide the wrinkles.'

As I shook my head my thistle-brooched Tam o' Shanter flew off, but very coolly I managed to catch it before it hit the carpet.

'Hello, Fliss,' I said.

'Hello, Robin.'

It was three years since I'd last seen or spoken to Fliss in person, and even then it had been another of those fleeting and awkward backstage meetings where it's hard enough to know what to say to an adrenaline-high performer at any time, but especially so when you are both also being clung onto by someone else and desperately wishing that you weren't.

Fliss took a step back and looked me up and down appraisingly.

'Nice tights, Jim,' she said, arching her neat black eyebrows. '*Snug*.'

'Thanks,' I agreed, adjusting the hem of my voluminous white shirt with billowing loose-cuffed sleeves. 'They're very warm.'

'So, you finally got to be Jim Kerr.'

'Well,' I smiled, 'to dress like him, anyway.'

'You used to love him so much.'

I nodded, looking into her eyes for words. 'I still do.'

'I love Jim Kerr, too,' Fliss said.

'Do you?' I swallowed, the dry ice, I think, causing my eyes to twitch a little at the corners.

'Yes.' Fliss reached out and took both my hands in hers. Holding them in the space between us, she gently stroked their palms with her thumbs. 'I've loved Jim Kerr since I was seventeen.'

'Funny. I've loved Kate Bush since I was about that age, too. A girl I used to know was completely mad about her.'

'She still is.'

We smiled at each other for a long moment, saying nothing while knowing nothing said everything until we both laughed almost silently beneath the applause for Whitney Houston.

'I didn't want to come tonight,' Fliss said. 'I hate karaoke. But I promised I would show my face for an hour, for the label. Wasn't Steve's David Bowie brilliant, by the way? He's so good.'

I nodded. 'I'm very glad you came, Fliss,' I said. 'I heard you interviewed on the radio the other week. I loved the new song you played.'

'Oh no, you weren't listening? I was awful. Hey, do you want a drink?' Fliss held up a finger as a tray fizzed past.

'Not really.'

'I'm so sorry, we're fine, thank you,' Fliss said, her magazine smile blushing the young waiter away into a happier new year. Freddie Mercury now strode like a white-vested peacock through the crowd and up the steps onto the stage where, after camply abusing a few fond hecklers and resecuring his wilting moustache, launched heroically into *We Will Rock You*.

'Oh Christ,' I said.

'*Hey!*' Fliss protested. 'I like a bit of Queen.'

'I remember.'

Perhaps feeling thirsty after all, Fliss smiled for a glass of water, took a slow slip before putting it down on a ledge. Looking shyly, teasingly, at me, she gathered up my hands again and said, 'Do you remember very often, Robin?'

'How do you mean?'

'About you... and me... when we were seventeen, eighteen, listening to Prince in my bedroom in Stonebridge?'

'I'm afraid I do,' I said, wondering how we came to be standing so close. 'I seem to remember it quite a lot. And I've tried very hard not to, sometimes, believe me.'

'Why?'

'*Why?*'

'Why do you try not to remember?'

'Because...' I saw Steve out of the corner of my eye. He struck an approving Bowie-like gesture and then went back to laughing with Robert Smith, Toyah and Alison Moyet. 'Because...' I said, 'I don't like that that's all it is. That that's all it ever will be – just something I remember. I –' I stopped.

Fliss turned and looked about the room. 'If there weren't so many people looking at us right now, I'd kiss you.'

'They aren't looking at us,' I said. But, as I now realised, they were looking at us. A lot of people were looking at us. Almost everybody in the room it seemed.

'We could always go somewhere else.'

'That would be nice,' I said, spreading my arms wide and twirling my Tam o' Shanter. 'Dressed like this?'

'Dressed like this?' Fliss echoed, wafting the flowers in her veil. She laughed, took my hand again and squeezed it gently. 'You could come back to mine, if you'd like to.'

I stood looking at her, blinking, like she was a painting on a gallery wall that I felt suddenly compelled to steal.

'Yours?' I said, feeling her warm, thin fingers twining between mine.

'I've still got my little flat, not very far from here. We could go there and... maybe listen to some records?'

I'd been longing to gather her in my arms since the moment I saw her. 'I'll just let Steve know,' I said, falling into her embrace and finding it as familiar as if that Sunday afternoon beneath the trees in Sherwood Forest had been only yesterday.

'It's all right,' Fliss said, gently patting my back. 'I'll tell him – while you're doing your thing on stage.'

I stepped back, baffled, unable to find the joke.

'I've waited a very long time to see Jim Kerr,' Fliss smiled. 'And I'm not leaving before he's had his moment in the spotlight.'

I turned to look across the dry ice smudged crowd. A few dozen legends who'd been smiling and waving our way now began to chant for Jim Kerr. Run DMC, Cher, and two-thirds of Fun Boy Three started the clapping. I noticed that David Bowie was now hiding, laughing behind a wall of Mark Knopfler, Tracy Chapman and two True Blue Madonnas.

The chanting grew louder and was a little out of tune, thanks mainly, I think, to Simon Le Bon.

'*Jim – Kerr! Jim – Kerr! Jim – Kerr!*'

Then a rousing goodtime DJ voice boomed from the shadows and called for Jim Kerr, too, inviting him to kindly make his way to the stage. I swore and wished Jim Kerr had buggered-off home hours ago, like he'd planned to do, and that he'd taken me with him. The spotlights flickered and roved, strobing through the thick clouds that now spewed across the stage from an engorged plastic snake.

Fliss lifted her chin and made careful, smiling adjustments to my Tam o' Shanter and voluminous white shirt with billowing loose-cuffed sleeves where it had become bunched in the elastic of my schoolgirl leggings.

'Go get 'em, Jim!' Fliss winked, and then she kissed me, softly but deeply, on the lips. I felt elated, blissed out, and at the same time like a man on the scaffold, feeling the chafe of the rope he'd foolishly tied for himself.

'You know I've never been able to sing,' I said pathetically.

'Then you'd better hope you've still got the moves, hadn't you? Because tonight, Robin Manvers, *you are* Jim Kerr!'

I took a deep breath and, ducking a barrage of drunken encouragement, slid centre stage without so much as a glance out into the hot and heaving ballroom. I eased the microphone from its stand and made a neat coil of the cable between my fingers, just as Jim Kerr always did. Then I assumed the position. Jim's position. Crouching low in the drifting smoke, I stretched out one suede pixie-booted heel as far as my not-quite-so-elastic, not-quite-so-young anatomy could bear, and with one billowing arm spread wide as if to halt oncoming traffic, I held the mic just beneath my chin. As I waited, poised, still as an owl, I half opened my eyes to look out into the steaming, flashing crowd. I was at Wembley Stadium. The Universal Amphitheatre, Los Angeles. The Ahoy, Rotterdam. I was up on the catwalk, a hundred thousand faces staring back at me, waiting, swaying, anticipating.

'You all OK?' I heard a faintly Scottish voice say, a little breathless as Charlie Burchill's opening guitar riff ricocheted from the speakers. 'From our album *Once Upon A Time*... this is called... *Ghostdancing*.'

The riff rang out for perhaps twenty speeded-up seconds and then I heard Jim Kerr's unmistakable voice belting out the opening lines about cities, buildings falling down, those satellites come crashing down. It sounded so incredible I turned to look back over my now dipping, diving shoulder, wondering if Jim Kerr himself were standing behind me, perhaps in on some sort of Hogmanay prank where I was the victim. But there was nobody on the stage but me. And the voice I could hear singing was not Jim Kerr at all, that was me too.

I was some way into the first chorus, bobbing buoyantly and sweeping graceful arcs, before I glanced to the side of the stage where Fliss was smiling, punching the air as she sang along with Steve, Howard Jones and Marilyn. With a shuffle and skip to stage right I tore off my Tam o' Shanter and sent it skimming above the heads of my adoring fans, dropping to my knees as I swept back my enviable fringe and held it there, an effortless idol, spotlight blind as I stared out into the auditorium. The second verse was coming up fast with that rousing line about the dawn in Eden. I knew if I was ever going to do this, it had to be now, and I sang the words like a god truly worthy of worship. I sang like Jim Kerr. And as the bass and drums came crashing in I launched myself into a high and mighty leopard pounce, landing textbook legs akimbo on the stage, one pixie-booted toe stretching out towards my adoring fans, one billowing arm carving through plumes of dry ice.

Acknowledgements

Thanks are due to several nice people: all at Scratching Shed for their faith and enthusiasm, in particular Phil and Ros Caplan, and my brilliant editor Tony Hannan, whose always 'bob-on' advice has been invaluable. My fab agents Charlene McManus and Emily Harris at Curtis Brown. Rock art geniuses Mark Rubenstein and Steve Wacksman for the fantastic cover.

I'm especially indebted to Paul Willetts for his wise counsel, generosity, and inexhaustible knowledge of the world of books and much else besides, and to legends Cathi Unsworth, Pete Paphides, John King, Harry Hill, Patrick Kielty and Andy Miller, and also Sara Bragadina and Simon Stewart, and Cath and Mike Harney, all of whom were exceedingly generous with their time, suggestions and encouragement.

Thanks to my old motor trade pals for answering daft questions about garage life in the eighties; a finer bunch you'll struggle to meet.

Finally, eternal thanks to all the brilliant artists whose music soundtracked my teenage years so inspiringly, especially Kate Bush, Prince, and, of course, Simple Minds, without whose magnificence I'd still be lying on my schoolboy bed staring up at the ceiling.

✠

Lyrics from the following songs are reproduced by kind permission.

Alive and Kicking – Words and Music by James Kerr, Charles Burchill and Michael McNeil
Copyright © 1985 JIM KERR MANAGEMENT CONSULTANCY LTD., UNIVERSAL MUSIC PUBLISHING LTD. and EMI MUSIC PUBLISHING LTD. All Rights for JIM KERR MANAGEMENT CONSULTANCY LTD. and UNIVERSAL MUSIC PUBLISHING LTD. Administered by UNIVERSAL – POLYGRAM INTERNATIONAL PUBLISHING, INC. All Rights for EMI MUSIC PUBLISHING LTD. Administered by SONY MUSIC PUBLISHING (US) LLC, 424 Church Street, Suite 1200, Nashville, TN37219
    All Rights Reserved. Used by Permission. Reproduced by Permission of Hal Leonard Europe Ltd.

Ghost Dancing – Words and Music by James Kerr, Charles Burchill and Michael McNeil
    Copyright © 1985 JIM KERR MANAGEMENT CONSULTANCY LTD., UNIVERSAL MUSIC PUBLISHING LTD. and EMI MUSIC PUBLISHING LTD. All Rights for JIM KERR MANAGEMENT CONSULTANCY LTD. and UNIVERSAL MUSIC PUBLISHING LTD. Administered by UNIVERSAL – POLYGRAM INTERNATIONAL PUBLISHING, INC. All Rights for EMI MUSIC PUBLISHING LTD. Administered by SONY MUSIC PUBLISHING (US) LLC, 424 Church Street, Suite 1200, Nashville, TN 37219
    All Rights Reserved Used by Permission. Reproduced by Permission of Hal Leonard Europe Ltd.

Running Up That Hill – Words and Music by Kate Bush © 1985, Reproduced by permission of Noble & Brite, EMI, London N1C 4DJ

Investigate our other titles and
stay up to date with all our latest releases at
www.scratchingshedpublishing.co.uk